"DANCE WITH ME, PRINCESS."

I feel that one word like a punch to the face and it's impossible to hide the wince. I deserve the hurt. I deserve the pain of his words and the smirk on his face while he stands here in front of me, watching me wrestle with my decision. He knows I won't storm off in a huff in front of all these people. He knows I won't tell him to go to hell. Not because I'm worried someone will hear me, because I know he's already been there. The scars that mar his beautiful face and the hardness in his eyes are proof that he's lived through torment I'll never understand, so I let him have this moment. I let him call me *Princess* even though it breaks off one more piece of my heart. I let him tug me roughly to him and I let him dig his fingers into my lower back as he holds me close and we begin swaying to the music.

"Was it worth it, Princess?"

My eyes move away from the other couples dancing around us and I tip my head back and look up at his face. He's scowling at me, his eyebrows clenched together and a curl in his lip indicating his disgust at what I'm doing, how I'm dressed, and what I've become.

"Was what worth it?" I ask, hating the quiver in my voice that lets him know I am not comfortable with this situation or with his question.

"Giving up. I just want to know if it was worth it, letting go of everything you'd ever wanted."

You're here, you're breathing, and you're alive. It will always be worth it.

Praise for *The Story of Us*

"The best book I have read all year. Heartbreaking and hopeful. Highly recommend."

-A.L. Jackson, *New York Times* and *USA Today* bestselling author

"Emotional and real! I couldn't read *The Story of Us* fast enough and know it will stay with me forever. Five heart pounding stars!"

-Aleatha Romig, *New York Times* bestselling author

"This is a story of an undying, unending love that was strong enough to heal even the deepest of scars. I highly recommend it to anyone looking for beautifully written, heart-wrenching and healing romance to fall in love with."

-Aestas Book Blog

"I fell hard for these characters, I felt their every emotion, their every up and down, and coupled with Tara Sivec's knack for storytelling, I would wholeheartedly recommend this book to anyone in a heartbeat."

-Natasha is a Book Junkie

Also by Tara Sivec

Wish You Were Mine

The story *of* us

TARA SIVEC

FOREVER
NEW YORK BOSTON

This book is a work of fiction. Names, characters, places, and incidents are the product of the author's imagination or are used fictitiously. Any resemblance to actual events, locales, or persons, living or dead, is coincidental.

Forever
Hachette Book Group
1290 Avenue of the Americas, New York, NY 10104
forever-romance.com
twitter.com/foreverromance

First published as an ebook and as a print on demand: June 2017
First mass market edition: November 2018

Forever is an imprint of Grand Central Publishing. The Forever Yours name and logo are trademarks of Hachette Book Group, Inc.

The publisher is not responsible for websites (or their content) that are not owned by the publisher.

ISBNs: 978-1-5387-4748-3 (mass market)

To the men and women
who have fought for our country:

We see you, we thank you, we
remember you, and we will never let
you go.

Acknowledgments

Thank you to my agent, Kimberly Brower, for believing in this story, and for helping me through all the hundreds of rewrites and different versions of *The Story of Us* until everything clicked and it became something I'm so incredibly proud of.

Thank you to my absolutely amazing editor, Michele Bidelspach, for falling in love with Shelby and Eli and seeing their potential when their story was only a few chapters long. Thank you for helping me bring this story to life, and helping me make it the best thing I've ever written.

Thank you to Joanne Christenson for always being around to answer my military questions, even if speech to text hates you!

Thank you to CM Foss for answering my horse stable and farm questions, and for fictionally teaching me the correct way to toss a bale of hay.

Thank you to Jessica Prince for months and months of plotting phone calls, and for not wanting to kill me every time I changed my mind about how this story should go.

Thank you to the best beta readers in the world: Michelle Kannan and Stephanie Johnson. People always ask me how they can become a beta reader for me, and I tell them I have only used two people for almost every single book I've written, and unless they get hit by a bus, that will never change. Please, don't ever get hit by a bus. I could never write another story without you kicking my ass when something sucks, and giving me a huge ego when something is good.

Thank you to all of the members of Tara's Tramps for your unwavering support, and for all of your posts that make me laugh when I'm sad, or run out to the store to stock up on eye bleach.

Thank you to the fabulous women of FTN. For your support, your love, your help, and everything in between.

Prologue

How much can a man take before he breaks? Is it measured by how many minutes, hours, days, or years he lives in hell? Is it one too many punches, kicks, or broken bones because he refuses to give in?

I wish I knew. As my head whips to the side when a pair of knuckles slam into my cheek again, I wish I knew the exact moment all of this will finally come to an end so I can count down the seconds and know exactly how much longer I need to hang on. Five years, two weeks, four days, and nine hours of the same thing, day after day, and I'm ready for it to be over. But I won't give in. I won't give them what they want even as the punches turn into kicks and the kicks turn into puddles of blood soaking into the dirt floor around me. Marines never give up.

Ooh Rah!

They scream at me in a rapid-fire foreign language. I've learned just enough in my years here to understand how much they still hate me, my country, and my refusal to give them what they ask for. Just like I've done for 1,843 days, I close my eyes and pretend like I'm not getting the shit kicked out of me. I think of her smile, her laugh, the smell of her skin, and her gentle touch. The punches and the kicks morph into soft hands sliding over my chest and warm palms pressed against either side of my face. The metallic scent of my own blood dripping down my face turns into the sweet, crisp smell of fresh peaches and my mouth waters, wishing I could taste her skin one last time.

I wonder if she'd touch me with the same boldness now that scars disfigure my skin. I wonder if she'd love me the same way when she saw how twisted and confused my mind has become just so I can make it through another day.

I wonder if she still thinks of me as much as I do her.

I wonder if she knows she's the only reason I'm still breathing, still fighting, and still holding on.

Blood pools in my mouth and I spit it into the dirt, wishing the dry, packed earth would swallow me up just like it does with the bodily fluids that drip down off my skin.

"Give us names and this will stop. You will live like king and not like dog."

My torturer speaks in broken English, giving his battered fists a break and squatting down to stick his face close to mine. For five years, they've been under the impression I'm some high-ranking military official and can give them the names of top brass with checkered pasts they can extort for their own agenda in this war. I gave up trying to make them understand after the first year. They'll never understand and they'll never care. At this point, it's just a game to them anyway. They don't care about the names; they just care about having another American under their thumb to torture for sport.

"How about we kill your friend instead? Will that make you talk?"

My eyes flicker to the man shackled to the wall a few feet away from me, and the sorry state of his appearance makes me sick to my stomach. He's my brother. My best friend. Everything dead inside me roars to life and my nostrils flare with pent-up rage. I want to make these people pay for what they've done to him. Since we haven't seen a mirror in over five years, I'm guessing he probably feels the same way when he looks at me. Once, the two strongest Marines in our unit, now just shadows of the men we used to be. Bones and ribs sticking out where well-defined muscles used to be, tattered and dirty rags covering our bodies instead of crisp and clean camo pants and T-shirts, long mangy hair and beards that haven't seen a bar of soap or water in years replacing our close-cropped military haircuts and clean-shaven faces.

Through the mop of dirty hair that hangs down over his face, I see him narrow one blue eye at me in warning, the second one swollen shut from yesterday's beating.

Rylan Edwards. My best friend since high school.

We grew up together, joined the Marines together, and went off to fight a war together. It seems only fitting that we'll die together. God only knows what happened to the other men in our unit that were captured along with us. Rylan and I have heard their screams over the years, listened to their shouts of pain, just like I'm sure they've listened to ours. We haven't heard them in a while, which is almost worse. It could mean they're no longer with us, fighting to stay alive. The quietness just gives you too much time to think about the fact that soon we'll be silenced as well.

"Don't do it, man. Don't you fucking do it," he mumbles angrily around a split lip, the movement of his mouth reopening the scab and letting a trail of blood drip down into his beard. "I can take whatever these fuckers dish out."

I want to tell him to shut the hell up. His words are only going to piss these assholes off, but a part of me wants to tell him to keep going. Don't fucking give up on me and don't let them win. I can't do this alone. I can't survive this alone. If Rylan is still fighting for our freedom, there's no way in hell I'm going to let go and give up.

The piece of scum squatting next to me nods his head in Rylan's direction, the guard standing closest to him slamming his fist into Rylan's cheek, whipping his head back against the wall.

Rylan laughs, like the smart-ass that he is. He laughs loudly from deep in his gut after each punch the little shit levels him with.

"Is that all you got, asshole?" he laughs again, shooting me another look of warning, letting me know he's fine.

He can handle it. He's not giving in. He's not giving up.

How much can a man take before he breaks? When do the dreams stop giving him comfort and he has to accept that he'll never see her again, touch her again or hear her say "I love you" again?

With my knees curled up to my chest and my arms wrapped around my waist to protect my broken ribs from any more abuse, I look into our captor's dark eyes and nod when a particularly nasty punch across the room sends one of Rylan's teeth sailing through the air to land in the dirt right by my face. I've watched them beat the shit out of my best friend for years, and eventually the relentless fists to his face and boots to his stomach turned me numb. But something about this moment shakes me to the core. The determination on Rylan's face, and the pride I feel for him that he refuses to give in, wakes me the fuck up, and one way or another, it ends now.

The monster smiles at me for the first time in five years.

I return his smile with my cracked and bloody lips, knowing it's the first *and* last time.

I feel Rylan's eyes on me. I feel his anger and his disappointment from across the room and ignore his shouts to me in between the *thwacks* of a fist connecting with his face.

Pulling my head back from the close proximity of the animal in front of me, I quickly jerk it forward and spit a mouthful of bloody saliva into his face, wanting to throw my hands up and cheer, feeling victorious that I finally found my balls and remembered how to use them.

I picture her smile and I imagine her laugh as he yanks a dirty rag from his pocket and wipes the blood and spit from his face. I hear the soft cadence of her voice, promising to love me forever when he shouts furiously in his own language. I feel her arms wrapped around my waist when, seconds later, two of his men race into the small room, grab me under my arms, and drag me across the dirt floor.

Shouting, the pounding of footsteps and gunfire sound from outside the room, and I wonder just how many people they need to bring in here to kill two weak men who can barely move.

My hands are quickly shackled to a wall above my head right next to Rylan, my broken body groaning in protest. No matter what happens next, I will not give in. I was born a Marine and I will die a Marine.

"Ooh Rah," we both whisper to each other, not breaking eye contact as a loud explosion shakes the walls, rattles our chests, and rains dirt and rocks down on us from the ceiling.

How much can a man take before he breaks?

How much can a man handle before he forgets all the good things and only has regrets filling his head?

I never should have left you. I'll never stop loving you, even if you hate me for walking away.

Closing my eyes to the chaos around us and waiting for them to finally end this once and for all, I let my mind take me away to warm summer nights, the smell of peaches and a woman who loved me more than I ever deserved. I remember how it felt to be loved, wholly and truly loved. I fill my head with thoughts of her, wanting to die with a smile on my face instead of shame in my heart. My cracked and bloody lips tip up at the corners and I hold on tightly to all the good things, refusing to give them up, and refusing to let them go.

Chapter 1

Shelby

I sigh in frustration when the tiny clasp to the strand of pearls slips from my clumsy fingers yet again. I've been trying unsuccessfully to slip this necklace on for the last five minutes, and my arms are beginning to feel like dead-weights. But when another set of fingers entwines with mine at the base of my neck, my breath catches in surprise. I drop my arms and fold my hands together in my lap as he quickly hooks the two ends of the necklace together before resting his hands on top of my shoulders. His palms are smooth and warm against my skin. His touch is gentle and kind, just like the man he is. It soothes me and erases all my irritation, as it always does.

"The pearls look beautiful on you. I was afraid you didn't like them."

I force a smile onto my face as our eyes meet in the mirror, wishing his compliment made me feel happy and beautiful instead of sad and disgusted with the person I've become. The pearls around my neck feel like a noose, choking the life out of me, and I want nothing more than to rip them off and laugh like a madwoman as the beads scatter across the floor. Instead, I squeeze my hands together as hard as I can until the feeling passes.

"I love the necklace, Landry, it's beautiful," I lie, my eyes flashing to the jewelry box that sits on top of the vanity in front of me before moving back to his face. He smiles confidently, naturally assuming I'm thinking about the countless other necklaces, bracelets, and earrings he's given me recently, neatly resting on the red velvet that lines the inside of the box. He's oblivious to the secret compartment under one of the drawers and that's exactly how I want to keep it.

"Your mother is supposed to be the star of the party tonight, but I have a feeling you're going to give her a run for her money," Landry laughs as I stand up from the chair at my dressing table and turn around to face him.

My stomach churns when he whistles admiringly at the black strapless floor-length dress my mother's stylist picked out for me to wear tonight. Landry McAllister is a handsome man and he loves me. I wish that were enough. I wish I could forget about the life I used to dream of and the plans I used to make. I wish I could stop thinking about those broken dreams, accept my fate and just be happy. All of this wishing and regretting has killed something inside me that I'll never be able to bring back to life. I'll never be able to give Landry what he needs, no matter how hard I try, and I feel a physical ache in my chest, knowing he deserves more.

My hand unconsciously presses against my left thigh when a dull pain throbs through the muscle as I stand. Glancing out the window beyond Landry's shoulder, I see a flash of lightning and the beginnings of a storm send raindrops splattering against the glass. The pain in my leg is never gone, always hovering under the skin, around the muscle and in my bones, making its presence known and reminding me I once had dreams. Dreams that went beyond the walls of this prison I've been exiled to.

Aside from the constant pain, the storm is another reminder of everything I've lost. Everything that was taken from me in the blink of an eye, six years ago, on another rainy night when I lost control. Of my life, my dreams, and my car on that wet and winding road.

Now, I have nothing but memories and regrets. Day after day filled with fake smiles, feigned happiness and pretending like I never hoped for bigger and better things. Twenty-eight years old and every decision about my life is made *for* me, without consideration for what I want, what I need or what matters to *me*.

I wonder if Landry knows how much I want to scream every time he looks at me like I'm the most beautiful woman in the world. I wonder if he notices the guilt clouding my face when he touches me and it never sets my body on fire. I know it would break him if he found out that the only reason I'm with him now is because I have to protect the only person I ever truly loved, and I hate myself for doing that to Landry. I always thought my feelings for him would change and grow. I assumed the love he gave to me would be enough to fix my broken heart and make me whole again, but it's done the opposite. I've become this numb shell of a woman I don't even recognize anymore for a man who probably only used me, but I don't know how to stop. He left this town without saying good-bye and then he left this earth without giving me closure. He left me to pick up the pieces and protect his family and his name and I hate him for that. I've allowed someone else to make all my decisions, rule my life and crush my dreams because I don't know how to stop loving him more than I hate him.

Shouting voices and the pounding of footsteps in the hallway outside my room distract us. Landry walks quickly to the doorway, stopping one of my mother's household staff as she rushes past. With his back turned and his attention focused away from me, I slowly and quietly slide open the bottom drawer of my jewelry box and lift the lid of the hidden compartment. I run my fingertips over the dog tags and wish I could forget how the cold metal used to feel warm against my skin from the heat of his body. How they would dangle down between us, grazing against the skin of my chest when he moved above me. I know I should have gotten rid of them a long time ago, but they're a constant reminder that everything I do is for him, even if what we had was all a lie.

The quiet conversation in my doorway penetrates my thoughts when I hear the staff member tell Landry there's some sort of emergency and it's all over the news.

"Your mother is in a panic and needs all hands on deck."

I close the drawer to the jewelry box right before Landry looks over his shoulder at me. Putting on a smile, I wave my hand at him.

"It's fine, go see what's happening and I'll meet you downstairs," I tell him.

He tells the woman to let my mother know he'll be there in a few minutes, walking back across the room to me when she scurries away. I keep the smile on my face when he grabs one of my hands and brings it up to his mouth, kissing the top quickly and then sighing as he lowers our joined hands.

"I won't be long, I'm sure it's nothing. Your mother panics over everything," he laughs softly.

Landry has been in love with me since I was a teenager

and he worked as an aide for my father, the senator of South Carolina. Ten years my senior, Landry came from a family as wealthy and affluent as my own and my parents never shied away from trying to push the two of us together once I turned eighteen. I wanted to hate him simply because my parents approved of him and because of the pathetic way he followed my father around like a puppy. I spent all four years of high school faking politeness when he'd try to talk to me and every year after that turning down his requests for a date. I'd like to say I did it for the sole purpose of pissing my mother off after my father died and she became obsessed with pushing the two of us together, but I'd be lying. While Landry spent our high school and college years chasing after *me*, I spent those years chasing after someone else. Someone who gave me butterflies each time I saw him, someone whose life was different from mine in every way and someone who took my heart with him when he left, making it impossible for me to ever give it to another.

"And as her financial advisor and the man she's backing to become our new state senator, you're required to panic whenever she does," I remind Landry. "Although considering you have your own things to worry about with your upcoming election, she shouldn't lean on you so much."

Landry chuckles, giving our joined hands a squeeze. "Your mother let me stick around after your father died and helped me make all of the contacts I needed to make a bid for the senate. If I win this thing, it will be because of her. Whatever Georgia wants, Georgia gets."

I paste a smile on my face at his words instead of rolling my eyes sarcastically. Landry kisses my cheek and I watch him leave the room, wishing I had something left to give him. Wishing I wasn't a liar and a fraud. Wishing I could magically glue the broken pieces of my heart back together and give them to him, because I know he would cherish it. He's a good man, even if he *is* one of the sheep in my mother's flock and I was coerced into dating him.

Sitting down on the edge of my bed, I grab the remote from my nightstand and power on the television hanging on the wall across from me, using my free hand to rub the pain from my aching leg. I know I'll be briefed immediately on whatever major crisis my mother is having a conniption over so I won't say the wrong thing if I'm questioned by reporters at her charity event this evening, but since I have nothing else to do while I wait, I might as well get the scoop ahead of time.

When I get to CNN, the reporter's voice fills my quiet room. I'm barely paying attention to what she's saying, busy smoothing down the front of my dress and checking for stray pieces of lint. Every word she speaks runs together in a blur of background noise, until she says a name I recognize. A name I haven't heard or spoken in years, but couldn't stop thinking about every second of every day. A name that makes my heart beat faster and my hands start to shake. My head whips up to stare at the television with wide, unbelieving eyes, and my heart drops into my stomach. They flash a picture of him on the screen from Marine Corps graduation day, but the sight of him in his dress blues isn't what makes my world tilt on its axis. It's the sound of his name coming from a stranger's lips in the quiet room that steals the breath from my lungs, making it impossible to do anything but stare at the television as my hand flies up to cover my mouth and hold back the sobs.

"In a top secret mission yesterday evening, a team of Navy SEALs were sent into the small Afghanistan village of Sangin to rescue Commander Stephen Whit-

> feld, who was taken hostage earlier this month. We have just been informed that during this rescue mission, several United States Marines who were presumed dead have been found alive. Five years ago, only days away from the end of his year-long deployment, Lieutenant Elijah James was involved in an IED explosion that killed several members of his team and only left behind the men's dog tags as identification. There were rumors that a traitor existed on the team who was working with the Afghan army. But those rumors were quickly put to rest just days after the explosion. Now that Lieutenant James has been found alive, we can only hope no truth will come from those rumors."

The rapid thump of my heart sounds like a drum in my ears, making it impossible for me to hear anything else the reporter says. A wave of nausea rushes through me and I press a shaking hand to my stomach as I stand on unsteady legs while a memory from so many years ago rushes through my mind. Even though I want nothing more than to forget about that moment and the day I signed my fate, I'm unable to stop my eyes from closing as I relive it.

"It's a lie. He would never betray his country. You have to fix this, please!" I begged my mother as I stood in her office with my broken heart clutched tightly in my hands.

She scoffed at me. She didn't care about my pain, the tears streaming down my cheeks, or my conviction that he would never do something like that.

"You don't know anything about him. He used you and then threw you away like a piece of trash," she replied as she stuck the knife deeper into my chest.

I didn't need to be reminded of what he'd done. It had

been slowly chipping away my confidence and pieces of my heart every day since he'd left, but unlike my mother, I could separate the man who broke me from the man who fought for his country. The soldier I knew would never do something this appalling.

"He's not a traitor. He doesn't deserve this and neither does his family. Please, Mother, I'm begging you."

She stared at me for a few quiet moments, studying me as I angrily swiped the tears from my cheeks and lifted my chin in the air to show her I wasn't backing down. I would do whatever it took to clear his name.

"I could call in a few favors, but it's going to cost you. Nothing in this life is free, Shelby."

Her words sent a chill down my spine, wondering just how much she would demand as payment, but knowing I would agree to anything in that moment.

"I don't care what it costs. I don't care about anything but making sure he's remembered as a hero. I'll do anything if you just make this go away. Please, I'll do whatever you ask."

The conversation I had with my mother five years ago plays on a loop until I can't stop the voices in my head and I have to grab and tug at fistfuls of hair just to stop myself from screaming.

He's alive.

I promised to do whatever she asked when I feared he'd be remembered as a traitor instead of a hero, and she took everything I had to give as payment. Once she had me under her thumb, it quickly became a slippery slope filled with reminders and threats to keep me in line until I'd fallen so far down the rabbit hole I didn't know how to find my way out.

He's alive.

I can't stop the tears from falling. I can't force back the

sobs of relief that something like this is actually happening. How many people lose someone they love, knowing they'll never see them again, never touch them again, never hear their voice again, only to find out it was all a mistake? How many people wish they could turn back the clock for just one more moment, just a few seconds in time so they could look into their loved one's eyes, run their hands down the side of their loved one's face, and hear them speak? It's a dream that everyone who's lost someone has. A dream that slowly turns into a nightmare you feel like you'll never wake up from. Something you know is impossible, but you can't stop obsessing about. I've prayed and I've screamed and I've cried, wanting the impossible, and now, I have it.

He's alive.

I gave up everything to protect him and to save his sister from a controversy that would ruin her in this town. They'd already suffered enough after their parents died—the rumors, the whispers, the finger-pointing and judgment following them everywhere they went...they didn't need anything else marring their fragile reputation. Especially something so completely absurd as Eli being a traitor to his country.

Every dream I let slip through my fingers, every decision I handed over for someone else to make for me, and every piece of myself I've lost in the last five years was for *him.* No matter how badly he shattered my heart, nothing could erase the good memories he left behind. I've wished on over a thousand stars for over a thousand days for closure and to finally have an answer *why.* My heart never healed and I could never let go because I just wanted to know *why.*

Why he lied.

Why he used me.

Why he left the way he did.

The hardest thing I've ever done was get out of bed the morning after news hit that he was gone and live through the pain of knowing he'd never smile again, never laugh again, never speak again, never *exist* again. It was the hardest thing until now.

He's alive.

I could try and pretend this news will finally set me free, but that would just be a waste of time. I know my mother will find a way to make sure I don't stray from the path she's forced me to take.

The hardest thing I'll have to do is face him again and let him see what I've become, knowing I'll never be able to tell him the truth without repercussions. I'll finally get the closure I need, but I know it will cost me. Nothing in this life is free.

"Oh, good, you turned on the news. Can you believe this?"

Landry rushes toward me and takes the remote from my hand, changing the channel to another news outlet. His preoccupation gives me time to push back my feelings, take control of my mind and my heart, wipe the tears from my cheeks, and remove all traces of the hope and fear and desperation that I know are written all over my face. I stare at Landry's profile and watch a muscle tick in his jaw as he listens to the news. A jaw I've run my fingers over and kissed. My eyes move down to his hand clutching tightly to the remote as he switches back and forth between channels. A hand that I've held tightly in my own and felt roaming all over my body. Seeing him standing here next to me is like a bucket of cold water dumped over my head, bringing me back to reality, reminding me of the promises I made and what my life is now.

He's alive.

"Your mother is losing her mind because a reporter did some digging and called her with this crazy story that you had an affair with that Elijah guy they found and they want her to make a statement," Landry says with a laugh. "Didn't he used to work here on the plantation as a stable boy? Shelby Eubanks, the heiress of the Eubanks empire and daughter of the Queen of Charleston, dating a stable boy! The things these people will come up with to make headlines..."

His voice sounds far away and echoes in my ear like he's speaking inside a tunnel instead of right in front of me, pointing the remote at the television and flipping from one channel to the next, while he drones on and on about the impossibility that I would ever lower myself to have an affair with the hired help.

"Lieutenant Elijah James has been found alive..."
"Presumed dead, Lieutenant Elijah James..."
"Elijah James..."
"Elijah James..."
"Elijah James..."

The name I never thought I'd hear again feels like the stab of a knife into my chest each time another newsperson utters it until my vision starts to blur and my shaking legs finally give out. My body crumples and I stare up at Landry as he drops the remote and quickly turns when he hears me hit the floor. He looks like he's standing in front of a strobe light, his worried face vanishing and then quickly reappearing as my eyes blink rapidly.

I've spent the last five years compartmentalizing things into *before* and *after*. There's a secret place in my head where I've hidden all of my memories of *before* Eli died. I keep those memories buried and refuse to think about them. I refuse to remember that time in my life when I was young and stupid and so foolishly in love and full of dreams. When my leg wasn't made up of shattered bones with pins holding them together. When dancing, and the love I had for a man who was so different from me, were going to be my ticket away from this town and out of this life.

After Eli died, *after* my dreams died...that's who I am now. Moving through life like a robot and locking the door to *before* is the only way I know how to keep moving, keep breathing, and keep waking up each morning.

I never thought *before* and *after* would collide. I never thought I'd have to unlock that door and be forced to brace myself for the explosion of memories, covering my head and shielding my heart from the pain I know it will bring.

I hear Landry shout for help from far away and I close my eyes, letting the darkness take me away from the name that continues to whisper through my ears.

Elijah James.

He's alive.

And it will cost me.

Chapter 2

Eli

I find myself standing in front of the locked door, in a place I remember like the back of my hand.

With my arms folded, the toe of my scuffed and dirty cowboy boot taps against the cement floor in irritation.

I know I saw her head down this hallway a half hour ago, and it's the only place she could have gone. I didn't even know there was a room hidden here in the back of the stables, until I caught her strawberry blond hair disappearing around the corner when I was pretending like I hadn't been keeping an eye out for her ever since I heard she was back in town.

I've been working these stables since I was sixteen years old and thought I knew every nook and cranny of the sprawling barn, multiple tack rooms, practice arenas, and offices. I don't like finding a door I can't get into any more than I like how my heart started beating faster when I caught a glimpse of her out of the corner of my eye.

Shelby Eubanks has been a thorn in my side since she was twelve years old, following me around like a puppy dog, batting her eyelashes and staring up at me with those big green eyes. Flirting with me every chance she got, probably thinking it would be fun to fool around with the hired help and a way to piss off her bitchy mother. I laughed her off and shot her down up until the day she turned eighteen and left for college. The little bird finally flew the coop and here I am, standing around in front of a fucking locked door just to get a glimpse of her for the first time in four years.

"Why are you standing here staring at a door? Jasmine and Belle need to be cooled down."

I ignore my friend and coworker Rylan and try the door handle once more, stupidly thinking it will magically open this time.

"Why is this door locked?" I mutter.

"Who cares? Get your ass back to work so I don't have to pick up your slack," he complains.

"Did you know this room was down here?" I question, looking at him over my shoulder.

He removes the dusty cowboy hat from his head to wipe the sweat from his forehead with his arm.

"I don't know, probably," he shrugs, slapping the hat back on his head. "It's probably just an unused tack room."

Why in the hell would Shelby have locked herself in an empty tack room? And why the fuck do I care?

"Jesus, she's in there, isn't she? One of the guys said he saw her come into the stables a little while ago and we should keep our swearing to a minimum since the princess was in the building," Rylan laughs. "She's off limits, and above your pay grade, even if she is legal and hot as fuck now that she's all grown up."

I turn my body and glare at him. Rylan has been busting

my balls for two weeks, ever since he got a glimpse of her stepping out of the black limo her mother had sent to the airport to fetch her after her college graduation when she moved back home. For fourteen days I've had to listen to him talk about her tits and ass and make tactless comments about her long legs wrapped around his waist.

No, I'm not jealous he got to see her and I didn't. I'm not green with envy that she came out to the stables on my day off and talked to him. She used to race out here every day after school just to annoy the shit out of me. She used to follow me around, asking a million questions about my life and my job. She used to spend every minute of her free time out in these stables whenever she knew I was working, and now I don't even get so much as a wave or a "screw you." I get her sneaking into the barn without a word and locking herself behind this damn door. I don't even know why the hell any of this bothers me. Maybe it's because I thought we were friends. Sort of. In a weird, "I know she has a crush on me, but she's too young and too damn out of my league to even go there" type of way, before I screwed everything up the night of her high school graduation. It's been four damn years, for God's sake. There's no way she's still holding a grudge because of that one stupid night.

"All right, well, good luck with that. I'm going back to work."

Rylan gives me a pat on the back and disappears down the hallway, whistling as he goes. When his whistles fade into the distance, I curse under my breath and pull the small rasp out of my back pocket that I'd been using to file Ariel's hooves earlier, jamming the sharp, pointed end into the hole in the middle of the door handle. This is the stupidest thing I've ever done, but I can't stop myself from doing it. I tell myself I'm only breaking into this damn room to make sure she's okay, but I know that's a lie. I want to see her. I want to talk to her. I want to know everything about the last four years and I'm pissed off she's been ignoring me. If breaking into this room is the only way to get her to acknowledge me, then so be it.

Ten seconds later, the lock pops and I smile to myself as I shove the tool back into my pocket and open the door. My ears are immediately assaulted with the thumping bass of loud music as I step inside and into another long hallway. Closing the door behind me, I wonder why the hell I couldn't hear the music from outside. Glancing around as I move down the dark hallway to where the music is coming from, I notice soundproof padding attached to the walls and the back of the door I just walked through.

The music gets louder as I move, not having any idea what the fuck this place is or why no one seems to know it was here in the back of the stables. I come to an abrupt halt when I get to an open doorway, my eyes widening and my jaw dropping open when I see what's inside.

The room at the end of the hallway is roughly 1,000 square feet in size, with shiny hardwood floors, floor-to-ceiling mirrors all along one wall, and no windows. The pristine condition of the room that is nothing like any of the other dusty, shit-smelling rooms in the stables isn't what keeps my feet glued to the floor in the doorway and my eyes bugging out of my head. It's also not the reason my dick is stirring to life in my pants and my palms are starting to sweat.

Right smack in the middle of the room, with her back to me and bent at the waist with her perfect ass in the air, is Shelby. Her body flies back upright and she twirls around the room, her hips moving erotically to the beat of the music while she spins, leaps, and dances like a goddamn angel. A hot, sexy angel in a pair of the smallest black shorts I've ever seen, a white sports bra, and bare feet, her body glistening with a thin sheen of sweat and pieces of her long, wavy hair sticking to her cheeks and her chest as she whips her head around to the music. She combines moves that would make a stripper proud with steps that would make a ballerina bow at her feet, her left leg extending above her head as smooth and easily as one would throw their arm up to wave at someone.

She's beautiful.

She's breathtaking.

And she sure as shit isn't a little girl anymore.

The music comes to a stop and so does Shelby, poised with her arms draped over the top of her head, breathing heavily. Her chin comes up and her eyes meet mine in the mirror before I can back out of the room and pretend like I was never here.

"What the hell are you doing in here?"

Her green eyes are filled with fire as she whirls her body around and presses her hands to her hips.

"How did you get in here? That door was locked."

Forcefully moving my eyes up from her tits straining against the thin cotton material of her top, I give her a smirk and lean casually against the doorjamb, pretending like I see shit like her standing in front of me half-dressed every day and it has no effect on me at all. She doesn't need to know that I'm suddenly feeling the four-year absence of her from my life like a punch to the gut, because I feel like I missed out on so much. She also doesn't need to know the memory of that kiss she gave me the night of her high school graduation is suddenly flashing through my mind, wreaking all sorts of havoc in my head. Soft lips, bold tongue, the smell of peaches filling my nose as I fought the war raging inside me to push her away when all I wanted to do was strip her naked and fuck some sense into her.

"Shelby Eubanks, all grown up, a fancy college graduate and a dancer to boot. How 'bout that?"

She rolls her eyes at me, her bare feet moving her across the room toward me. Right when I think she's going to hug me in greeting, she turns and grabs a towel from the small wooden table right inside the door.

"You're not supposed to be in here. *No one* is allowed in here," she tells me irritably, dabbing the fluffy white towel against her cheeks.

"Nice to see you, too, Legs."

She presses the towel to her chest and raises one perfectly sculpted eyebrow.

"Really?"

"I'm sure all those college boys you hung around for four years showered you with plenty of compliments on those long legs of yours," I tell her with another sarcastic smirk, ignoring the jealousy coursing through my body at the idea that any guy got close enough to those gorgeous fucking legs and the hot body attached to them. "How come I never knew this room existed? Or that you could dance like that?"

Shelby tosses the towel onto the table and mirrors my casual pose, crossing her arms in front of her.

"There are a lot of things you don't know about me, Eli James. I'm not a stupid little girl anymore and I'm not going to fall at your feet, so you can go ahead and wipe that smirk off your face."

Four years in New York City didn't diminish the Southern twang in her voice, and if anything, her annoyance with me brings it out even more. At least one thing is still the same in this fucked-up scenario where the tables have turned and she seems to want nothing to do with me.

I open my mouth to ask about the room again, when suddenly, I feel something drip down the side of my face. Bringing my hand up, I swipe my fingers against my cheek, holding them in front of me to find them covered in blood. Pain explodes through my head and I cry out, my hands clutching on to handfuls of hair.

Shelby calls to me, but her soft Southern voice speaks in a foreign language. One that churns my stomach with nausea and fear and hate. I cry out again when my stomach explodes with pain, like someone just punched me right in the gut. Bending at the waist, I drop my body forward and feel my mouth filling with the salty, bitter taste of blood. I spit it out onto the floor, noticing I'm no longer standing on shiny hardwood, but roughly packed dirt. My head whips up when a burst of searing pain explodes through my ribs, catching my reflection in the mirror across the room. My face is filled with bruises and cuts, the blood dripping down from my head making bright red rivers trickle through the mud and dirt caked on my face.

I open my mouth and scream at the man in the mirror. The broken, dirty, ruined man staring back at me with so much pain on his face that it hurts to look at him.

"Eli, wake up!"

I close my eyes, refusing to look at the ugliness in the mirror and scream louder.

"ELI! WAKE UP!"

My eyes fly open and I jerk myself upright, my arms and my fists swinging as I go.

"ELI! IT'S ME! IT'S ME, IT'S OKAY!"

My fist pauses in midair when I realize where I am, and that it's been three months since I was rescued. I'm holding my hand an inch away from the woman sitting on the edge of the bed next to me, her eyes the same chocolate brown as mine, her tangled mess of hair from being woken up in the middle of the night, once the same shade of dark brown as mine, but now filled with fancy blond streaks, her face as white as the sheet tangled around my sweaty body, and probably the same hue as my own face after that fucking dream.

I pull my knees up under the sheet and rest my elbows on them, dropping my head in my hands.

"Jesus, Kat, I'm sorry. I'm so sorry," I whisper softly, trying to get my heart rate back to normal and slow my breathing as the pain in my heart and the guilt swarming through my head amplify, hating myself for what I'm putting my family through.

My younger sister scoots closer to me on the edge of the bed, wrapping one arm around my shoulder. I immediately flinch when she touches me, looking up from my hands to see tears pooling in her eyes when she nervously jerks her arm away and clenches her hands together in her lap. My baby sister. The one I used to take care of and provide for after our parents died when we were teenagers and the responsibility fell on my shoulders, is all grown up. She's a wife and a mother and now she has to take care of *me*. She has to listen to my screams in the middle of the night, deal with my shitty attitude and my refusal to talk about what happened. I want to scream and rage at the unfairness of it all, but that would make things worse. It would just make Kat sadder and want to do even more than she already is trying to help me.

Three months since I was pulled out of that hellhole. Three months of interviews and debriefing and countless sessions with enough military headshrinkers that if I wasn't crazy already, they sure as shit would have pushed me right over the edge with their endless questions and need to know everything I went through for five years. I used to love going to sleep at night. It was the only time Shelby and I were ever left alone and I could dream about *her* without the memories being tarnished. The dream I just had was one of my favorites. The day she came back into my life with an attitude and a backbone that made me finally wake up and *see* her for who she really was. She burrowed her way under my skin and never left. And now that's ruined, too. I can't even dream about her anymore without the hell I lived through coming back to haunt me and taint the only good thing I still have inside me.

"I thought the dreams were getting better," Kat says softly.

They've never gotten better; I've just gotten better at keeping my screams to a minimum when they wake me up in the dead of night.

"They have. They are," I lie, giving her a tight-lipped smile. "I'm fine now, Kitty Kat, go on back to bed."

Kat smiles when I use the nickname I gave her when we were kids. She leans forward, probably to kiss me on the cheek, but quickly thinks better of it and pulls herself away from me and slides off the bed.

"Get some sleep. We'll talk in the morning, okay?"

I nod, even though we both know that talk will never happen. I've been back in Charleston for two weeks, staying with my sister and her family until I can figure out what the fuck I'm going to do with my life. I can't stay here any longer. I can't keep putting her through this night after night. I only came back here for one thing. The only thing I know that will help me heal and keep the nightmares away. I know she's probably long gone, living her dream far away from this town, and I know it's shitty of me to burst back into her life after what I did to her, but I have to try. All my shrinks have told me I need to find a hobby. Something to focus on other than the torture and the pain, something to keep me grounded to the here and now and not stuck in the past, reliving every moment of hell. It's probably not healthy that I've decided finding Shelby and convincing her to love me again is the perfect hobby for me, but that's too damn bad.

I'm broken and scarred and half the man I used to be, but if she'll let me explain, I hope to God she can put me back together again.

Chapter 3

Shelby

I jerk awake with a scream dying on my throat and my body covered in sweat. Taking a few deep, calming breaths, I stare up at the slowly turning ceiling fan above my bed, wondering if I'll ever get a good night's sleep again. I haven't been sleeping well since the night I fainted, making up a lie about low blood sugar so Landry wouldn't know my mind and my heart had shattered into a thousand pieces as soon as I heard that name. In the three months since the story broke, I can count on one hand how many hours I've been able to close my eyes and not see him, feel him, or hear his voice.

Knowing I'll never be able to get back to sleep, I slide out of bed, wrapping a short, silk robe around my body as I open the door to the guest house where I live, and head out for a walk across the grounds.

Sitting down on a bench under a particularly large oak tree on the front lawn, I stare up at my family home with the moon shining bright above it and a chorus of cicadas chirping all around me. Located on sixty acres in South Charleston, it was once a cotton plantation before the Civil War. The 10,500-square-foot historical home is your typical updated Southern plantation home. It's a two-story white wood-framed house with black shutters, a sprawling front porch, and an expansive terrace on the second floor that extends the length of the house. With a pecan grove, saltwater marshes, two ponds, orchards, a 35,000-square-foot horse stable, and numerous live oaks draped with Spanish moss around the property, it really is one of the most beautiful places to live.

If only the beauty on the outside could make up for the ugliness on the inside.

Checking the face of my silver watch, which I haven't taken off since Meredith gave it to me for my birthday a few months ago, the perfect gift to hide the markings on the inside of my left wrist from prying eyes, I realize I've been sitting out here for two hours. Ever since I woke up from a dream and couldn't fall back to sleep. In the daylight hours, I can put on a brave face, don a happy smile, and push away the thoughts that have been plaguing me since that night in my room a few months ago when I listened to the news report and collapsed to the floor in front of a completely shocked Landry. At night, when the sun goes down and darkness fills my room...that's when I forget how to shut everything off. That's when my mind and my memories take over and refuse to let me forget, and it's only gotten worse in the last few weeks. My best friend, Meredith, has been checking on me nonstop ever since the news broke. She's the only person in my life who knows everything about Eli. Well, everything that happened *before*, at least. No one knows about *after*, especially not Meredith. I'd never be able to handle her disappointment and anger about what I've done and the choices I've made.

For three months I reassured Meredith I was fine, happy with Landry, and couldn't care less about what was happening on the news, but Meredith knew me better than that. It was easy to pretend my life hadn't changed when I didn't know where he was. When I'd only caught one grainy glimpse of him on the news and didn't even recognize the man they claimed was him. He was too skinny, had too much hair, and didn't smile. It wasn't the Eli I remembered. Maybe they were wrong. Maybe they misidentified him and it was all one big joke. They screwed up once before, claiming he'd been killed in action, what's to say they couldn't do it again?

When I found out he'd come home, when I heard he was living with his sister, a few miles away, breathing the same Southern air as me, walking the same streets I frequented, I couldn't pretend anymore. In the midst of a panic attack the other night, curled up into a ball on my bedroom floor, I called Meredith and begged her to come for a visit. I needed my friend. I needed my rock to get me through this.

He's alive and he's home.

Every time I go into town, I'm afraid I'll run into him. Every time I turn around, I'm afraid I'll see his face, once a face I knew like the back of my own hand. A face I used to love to touch and kiss and hold in the palms of my hands, now a face that I'll never be able to look at without being reminded of all the things I've done. It won't matter that those things were all for him. It won't matter how much I've died a thousand times over the years, all for him. Nothing will matter to him but the fact that I'm still here, still where he left me, following in my mother's footsteps, unable to move forward. While unspeakable things were being done to him, every day for five years, I had good things, *wonderful* things right at my fingertips, and I let them slip away. It won't matter how or why; it will only matter that I let them go.

Pushing myself up from the bench, I walk with determined steps through the wet grass, to the one place I can still escape and forget the world around me until Meredith gets here tomorrow and talks some sense into me. It cuts me like a knife each time I walk in there and see the floor and the mirrors covered in dust, unused and forgotten, but it's still *my* place, my sanctuary and the one thing that is still one hundred percent all mine, that no one, not even my mother, can take from me.

She's taken it all, and still, it's not enough. She'll continue to take and demand and I'll continue to fold, because it's the only thing I know how to do. Over the years, we developed a quiet understanding that has served us well. I did as she said without complaint, and she continued to make sure Eli's sister and the rest of the world would always remember him as a hero. Now that he's alive, now that old rumors resurfaced, that quiet understanding has been destroyed. I've had to beg and plead with her every day, I've had to show weakness and bite back my anger because, once again, I needed her popularity with all the heavy hitters in the town and government that carried over from my father, and the power that reputation brings to fix things. And once again, she named her price and I paid in full to make sure Eli and his sister were protected.

I rub the tips of my fingers against the band of the watch on the inside of my wrist, as I make the two-acre walk across our land to the stables. I can see a few lights streaming from the windows in the distance, guiding me through the dark cover of night. My mother and the household staff are fast asleep in the main house, and the stable workers went home to their families hours ago. Just like I've done every night for the last three and a half months, I quietly walk through the open archway into the stables, letting the soft whinny of one of the horses and the stomping of hooves against the dirt calm my racing heart.

I head past the stalls and turn down the hallway that leads to the very back of the stable, pausing in front of the locked door. Closing my eyes, I try and stop the memories, but it's pointless. I continue coming to this room, night after night, because I need the pain. I *need* the sharp stab of agony in my heart and the overwhelming ache of sadness, because even though it hurts, underneath all that pain is a reminder that I used to be happy. I used to be a different person, a stronger person, a confident person.

Slowly opening my eyes, I unlock the door, and walk down another dark hallway, my hands shaking with nervous energy as I flip the switch on the inside of the room. *My* room. The place I love and hate equally. Leaning my back against the wall right inside, I slide to the ground and let the memories consume me, slicing my heart open to leave me bleeding on the floor.

Chapter 4

Eli

"You're sure you'll be okay home alone?" Kat asks for the hundredth time in the last twenty minutes since her husband, Daniel, left to drop my niece off with a sitter.

God forbid they leave a two-year-old home alone with her crazy uncle. It's not like I know the first thing about kids, or would even *want* to be home alone with one, but it would have been nice to be asked. To be considered. To feel *normal.*

Fuck, I have a niece. A beautiful, chatty, spitting image of my sister, niece.

"Kat, I'm not a child, I'll be fine. Plus, I have Rylan to keep me company."

The man in question lifts his arm next to me on the couch and gives my sister a wave. She ignores him, like always. Aside from having to put up with my bullshit, she's also had to contend with my best friend also living under her roof until he can get acclimated to not being chained to a wall and not having to ask permission every time he takes a piss. Although his problems lean farther away from screaming nightmares in the middle of the night to being a slob of a houseguest with no respect for anything around him. Rylan grew up in the system, bouncing around from one foster home to the next until we graduated high school and he convinced me to join the Marines with him. He spent more time in our tiny apartment at the edge of town when we were kids than he did at any of his numerous foster homes, finding more comfort with us even though we had two drunks for parents who never cared about our well-being, than he did in the homes he moved around between during that time. Kat had the unfortunate experience of having not one, but two, older brothers to stick up for her and kick anyone's ass who dared mess with her. I probably should have asked if it was okay that Rylan shack up in her house instead of just bringing him home with me when we were rescued, but it's not like my sister would have ever said no anyway. Rylan was part of the family, and he always would be, end of story.

"Did you take your medication today?" Kat asks softly, grabbing her purse from the side table by the front door when we hear Daniel's car pull into the drive.

"We got your uppers, we got your downers, we got your Xanax and your Prozac, your Lipitor for high cholesterol from the shit they made us eat, when they remembered to feed us, and every antibiotic known to man to make sure we didn't bring any funk home," Rylan rattles, ticking off the long list of medicines we both came home with. "We're covered, sis."

I snort and Kat sighs.

"We won't be gone long. Just dinner with one of Daniel's clients," she tells me.

Her husband, Daniel, is surprisingly a really nice guy, considering he's an investment banker with slicked-back hair and his closet doesn't have one pair of jeans or cowboy boots in it. I know, because I checked when Kat told me I could borrow anything I wanted from him until she could go to the store and pick some things up for me. I turned down her offer and spent fifteen minutes fighting with her about how I could damn well go to the store and buy myself a pair of jeans and a few T-shirts. And then I spent an hour sitting in the driveway, keys in the ignition of Kat's SUV that she let me borrow, with shaking hands, sweaty palms, and an undeniable urge to throw up all over the front seat at the idea of driving a car down a busy highway and then attempting to interact with a mall full of people, bumping into me, asking if they could help me, and filling my head with too much noise.

After I threw up in the driveway, I stormed back into the house, threw the keys on the kitchen table, and told Kat I'd make her a list. She gave me that same pitiful, sympathetic smile she always gives me and never batted an eye at my request for peach-scented candles that I scribbled at the very bottom under *boxer briefs*.

I have been reduced to letting my sister buy my underwear. I thought I'd gone as low as I could get, but obviously I was wrong. Not only did she go out and buy shit for me, she did it using her own money, which pisses me off even more. Every time I even mention the idea of getting a job, she tells me to take it easy and that we can talk about all that once I've had time to adjust. It's demoralizing needing your baby sister to fulfill all your basic needs.

Kat gives me a smile and a small wave, heading out the door to her husband. I breathe a sigh of relief when the door closes behind her.

"She's too easy to tease. It's almost not even fun at this point," Rylan complains, grabbing the remote from the coffee table in front of us and aiming it at the television.

"When are you going to shave that shit off your face and cut your hair?" I ask, taking in his full beard and the mess of hair he piled on top of his head with one of my sister's hair ties.

It didn't take long, with the assistance of hospitals and round-the-clock care and IVs full of nutrients, for both of us to gain back a lot of the weight we'd lost over the years. Once our major injuries like broken bones and cracked ribs were healed and we were given the okay, we immediately hit the gym to start building muscle mass. We were nowhere near the tip-top shape we were in after our year of deployment, right before we were captured, but at least we no longer looked like prisoners of war, half-starved and wilting away to nothing, like we did when they first found us.

"I don't know, I've kind of gotten used to it," he muses, scratching the hair on his cheeks before pointing to the disaster on his head. "The hair is definitely staying. What you see here is called a man bun. I guess it's all the rage with the ladies now, according to Google."

I laugh, shaking my head at him. It feels good to laugh, even though I can't joke as easily as he can about what we endured. That's how Rylan is, though. That's how he's always been. He doesn't dwell on the past, no matter how bad it was. It doesn't make a difference that we were used as human punching bags every day for five years, it doesn't matter that we never thought we'd come home again, and it doesn't matter that we were seconds away from dying and had made peace with it and were ready for it to be over. We didn't die, and that's all that matters to him now. He's the only reason I've been able to wake up every morning and keep moving forward, keep building myself up for the only goal I've had my mind on since we were pulled out of our prison.

"So, how long are you going to pussyfoot around before

you go find her?" Rylan asks casually, flipping quickly through the channels. "Or are you still thinking about taking down her mother first?"

I've had plenty of sleepless nights in the last few months to think about what I should do. Plenty of hours of lying awake after a nightmare, wondering if what I heard in the moments before we were rescued was real.

"You heard it, too, I know you did," I mutter quietly.

Rylan switches off the television and turns to face me on the couch.

"We were both out of it, man. Shit was exploding, men were screaming, and the goddamn building was falling down around us when the cavalry charged in. Who knows what the fuck we heard?"

I look away from him and stare at the wall across the room, filled with pictures of Kat and Daniel from when they were dating, on their wedding day, on their honeymoon, and on the day Lilly Elijah was born. I wonder if all of this will ever stop feeling bittersweet. I'm proud of my sister and happy for her that she's created such a great life for herself, but it kills me I missed out on all of it, and it makes me feel like shit that I'm jealous of her life and her beautiful little family. It's a reminder of all the things I don't have. I also wonder if Lilly Elijah will want to change her name when she's older, when my sister tells her the story of how she was named after her dead uncle, who turned out not to be dead at all.

These are the sick and twisted thoughts that float through my mind on a daily basis. These are the things bumping around in my twisted brain that have kept my ass on this couch for two weeks instead of looking up Shelby's name on the Internet and finding out where she is now. These thoughts and the memory of what I heard that last day in Afghanistan.

"Why in the hell, when the shit was hitting the fan, would those fucks say what they did?" I ask quietly, remembering the words as clearly as if I'd just heard them yesterday.

"Kill him. Now! The money will stop if we don't do as we were ordered."

I continue staring at the photos of all the things I missed, knowing there could only be one person responsible for making me miss them.

"Maybe they were just hangry and didn't know what they were saying. That's another new word I learned from Google," Rylan smiles, attempting to make a joke.

"She got our unit bumped up for deployment long before it was our turn," I remind him. "She pulled some strings and got down on her knees for whatever politician she had in her back pocket just to get me away from her daughter and uncover the truth about my parents. Don't you think it's a little coincidental that on the day we're rescued, they say shit like that?"

I'll never forget those final moments for the rest of my life. Closing my eyes, knowing our time was up and ready to feel the sharp sting of a bullet in the middle of my forehead before I finally felt nothing at all. No one will ever understand what it's like, knowing you're about to die and coming to terms with it. Mentally saying good-bye to everyone you love, knowing you'll never see them again, and forcing yourself not to be afraid and be okay with letting go. I remember the walls shaking against my back, I remember the gunshots *rat-a-tat-tatting* all around us, and I remember our captors, standing right in front of us, *their* eyes finally filled with fear while in between their rapid shouting at each other in their language, those words were spit out, clear as day.

The money will stop if we don't do as we were ordered.
The money will stop if we don't do as we were ordered.
The money will stop if we don't do as we were ordered.

Georgia Eubanks is the only person I can think of with enough money and power to make something like that happen. The woman never gave a rat's ass about her own daughter's happiness. She only cared about the embarrassment it would bring if anyone found out her little girl had been having an affair with the stable boy. The same stable boy whose parents were killed in a drunk driving accident that might not have been an accident after all. It didn't matter that I was a damn good Marine who'd received hundreds of recommendations and accolades while working part-time at the plantation to put my sister through college. It didn't matter that I proudly served our country. Nothing mattered but her precious reputation in this town and not letting anything interfere with that. Her only daughter, refusing to date any of the filthy rich, pedigreed men she paraded in front of her, as well as putting her foot down about following in Georgia's socialite footsteps, were interferences she wouldn't tolerate. Having the poor, lowly stable boy her daughter had been sleeping with all summer put two and two together and confront her with it, and then find himself on a plane out of the country a few hours later, followed by all the shit that happened over the next six years, only to end with something like that on those asshole's lips, wasn't a coincidence.

I walked away when it came down to a choice between Shelby's future and my own, my sister's security over mine, and it's a choice I would make a hundred times over again for both of them, but especially for Shelby now that I know my sister found her own security by way of Daniel. Just knowing Shelby was happy and doing what she'd always dreamed and her mother would finally let her be to live her life was all I needed.

Maybe I should leave it alone. Maybe I should just find Shelby, get down on my knees, and beg her to love me again, but I know it's not that simple and I know I'll never be able to move on until I find out the truth, once and for all, about the night my parents died. It was one thing when it was just a year of deployment I agreed to. It's a whole other thing to suspect the darling of Charleston of conspiring with the enemy to make sure I never stepped foot on U.S. soil again to protect her reputation and wrongdoings.

Pushing myself up from the couch, I head over to the small table in the foyer and grab the set of keys out of the bowl on top.

"Where you going, man?" Rylan asks, getting up from the couch and following me to the door.

"I need to get out of here, go for a drive and clear my head."

I twist the ring of keys to Kat's SUV in my hands nervously, thinking about the one place I want to be right now, but knowing it's probably the worst idea in the world considering where it's located.

"You're going to the fucking stables, aren't you?" Rylan asks with a shake of his head, reading my mind with just one look at me. "If Mrs. Eubanks sees you out there, she'll have you arrested for trespassing. I still don't know how the fuck we managed to get them beyond that traitor bullshit they tried to pin on us again and I don't like how fast they switched their tune five minutes after we got to D.C. You walking onto her turf is the equivalent of poking a hibernating bear. One look at you and she'll chew our heads off and make sure our asses fry."

I chuckle, twisting the handle on the front door and

pulling it open, a blast of heat from outside hitting me in the face.

"Like Georgia Eubanks would ever get her feet dirty by stepping foot out in those stables," I tell him with a smile and a shake of my head. "I'm just going to pop in and pop out. See how the horses are and see if any of the same guys still work there." Especially one man in particular, who I know had something to do with the anonymous police report I received just days before I was deployed.

And hopefully one of them knows Shelby's whereabouts so I don't have to bang my head against the wall trying to find her.

I know I made the decision to walk away from her, and I'll regret it for the rest of my life. I've had nothing but time to think of her since I was rescued, and now that I've been given a second chance at life, I'm not going to fuck it up. I've spent the last three months getting my body and my mind stronger, with thoughts of Shelby and getting her back spurring me on through the pain of rehabilitation and the shock and fear of learning how to be a civilian again after so many years in captivity. I know I have a long way to go and I'm nowhere near back to normal, if that's even possible at this point. But I've waited long enough. Shelby is the main reason I'm still here, alive and kicking, and it's time she knows that. It's time for me to take back what was always meant to be mine.

Chapter 5

Shelby

As I'm locking the door to the studio, I hear a soft, whispering voice echoing down the hall. Shoving the key into the pocket of my green-and-white-striped drawstring pajama pants, I cross my arms across my chest to cover up the fact that I'm wearing a tank top and no bra. I came out here in the middle of the night in my pajamas specifically because I knew no one would be in the stables.

Coming to the end of the long, dimly lit hallway, I quickly round the corner with an irritated scowl on my face, my flip-flops smacking against the cement floor. I should probably just sneak back up to the house and attempt to fall asleep, but my curiosity has gotten the better of me, wondering which one of the workers is out here at such a late hour. Hopefully none of the mares are sick. I don't need my mother catching wind of it from the property manager and ordering it to be put down without bothering to call the vet, just like the last time. She usually never bothers with the stables, the horses, or the barn staff, unless she feels like her control around this place is slipping and she needs to prove the point that she's still in charge. With everything that's happened in the last few months, I wouldn't put it past her to do something stupid where the horses are concerned just to make herself feel powerful.

As soon as I turn the next corner into the main stable area, my body comes to an abrupt halt. My stomach drops down to my toes, my shaking arms fall limply to my sides, and my chest begins to ache like it's made of glass and someone just took a sledgehammer to it. I would recognize him anywhere, even with all the time that has passed and what he must have gone through for all of those years in captivity. I feel like I'm standing in a dream, unable to believe what I'm seeing. The edges of my vision blur and I feel like if I lift my foot to try and walk, it will feel like I'm sinking in quicksand, unable to move, unable to get closer and reassure myself that I'm really awake and this isn't a dream. How many times did I wish for a moment like this? One moment in time where he was standing right here in front of me, alive and breathing and smiling. Just a few seconds where I could look at his face, watch a dimple pop out of his cheek, and not have it disappear like a puff of smoke when I woke up.

"I missed you, Belle. My pretty girl…I missed you something awful. Have they been feeding you enough sugar cubes?"

The black Arabian snorts, butting her head against the forehead of the man in front of her, and he chuckles softly. The sound hits me like a bolt of lightning, making my scalp tingle and my heart beat double time. I squeeze my hands into fists as hard as I can, my fingernails digging into my palms, the pain reminding me this isn't a dream. He's really here, standing in front of me, smiling, talking, breathing…*alive*.

I stand here in complete silence, my legs refusing to move even though if they did, I don't know if I'd want them to take me out of here as fast as possible, or race me toward the man speaking in hushed tones to the beautiful beast in front of him.

If I could find my voice, I'd tell him the animal he's petting isn't his beloved Belle, who died the year after he left. She died giving birth to the animal he's currently showering with attention. It would break his heart to know that isn't Belle, always his favorite among the thirty or so horses we own. He raised her and helped train her when she came to this plantation, a wild and unforgiving horse who wouldn't let anyone near her until she heard *his* soft commands and felt *his* gentle touch.

My vision blurs with tears as I stand perfectly still, taking him in from the top of his short, spiky dark hair to the tips of his scuffed cowboy boots. The arm he holds up to pet the side of the horse's neck flexes as he runs his hand down her flank, his bicep no longer large enough to snap a tree trunk in half, but with enough muscle definition that I can see it from where I stand, a hundred yards away. He's not as skinny as he was that day I saw him on the news, but he's also no longer the hulking beast of a man he was six years ago. He's lean, with just enough muscle definition to fill out the shirt and worn, tattered pair of jeans encasing his long legs.

I stare at him through my tears, drinking in every inch of him, wondering if at any minute I'm going to wake up and this is all going to be a dream. Him being alive, and home, and within touching distance.

I want to call out his name and see if saying it out loud breaks the spell.

I want to run into his arms and see if I can feel them wrapped around me or if he'll disappear as soon as I get to him, like a puff of smoke.

I want to turn and leave these stables, forget that I ever saw him and pretend like standing here right now isn't breaking every piece of me apart all over again, knowing I can never have what I want.

His face turns slightly in my direction as the horse tries to head butt him again, and that's when I see the scar that runs down his clean-shaven cheek from the corner of one eye to his jaw, which looks like it came from a knife. I choke back a sob and tightly press my hand to my mouth when I notice his nose is slightly crooked, most likely from being broken more than once. My eyes travel the length of his arm and I see an assortment of faded scratches and scars dotting his forearm as he continues to whisper and pet the horse in front of him.

Everything he's been through, things I'll never know or understand, hits me like a ton of bricks, threatening to make my knees give out from under me. I'm standing here feeling sorry for myself when this man literally went through hell and came back from the dead.

He's here. He's alive.

No matter how tightly I clamp my hand over my mouth, I can't keep the muffled sob from escaping and his head whips in my direction. His deep brown eyes lock on to mine and his hand slowly drops from the side of the horse as he turns to face me fully.

I want to run to him.

I want to run away and hide.

"Legs," he whispers softly.

So softly I almost don't hear it over the thunderous beating of my heart, but my eyes are locked on to his lips and I see his mouth form the words, the nickname making me wince and die a little bit more inside.

"Are you real?" He speaks softly, his eyes widening in wonder as he takes a tentative step toward me.

I've wished for this moment, every day for six years, and now I just want to close my eyes and disappear. I don't want him to see me like this. I don't want him to know anything about the woman I am now. I want to click my heels together like Dorothy and go back to the way it was before. I want to close my eyes and go back to a time when everything was easy and perfect and I was worthy of the amazement shining in his eyes as he stares at me and takes another step toward me. I don't care about the pain he caused me, I don't care about the heart that he broke, I don't care about all the reasons why, I just want to hold on to him and never let go.

As much as I want to run in the opposite direction, I can't do it no matter how hard I try. Being in the same room with him has always made me feel like we were magnets, unable to deny the pull and unable to do anything but slam together as soon as we were close enough. My feet move before I even realize they've remembered how. We move toward each other, our eyes never breaking their hold, both of us picking up the pace at the same time until we're running, unable to stop the magnetic tug now that we're this close. Now that we both know this is real, it's not a dream, and we're both really here, together.

Our bodies collide, my arms flying around his neck, his arms wrapping securely around my waist, both of us clinging to the other like at any minute something will try and rip us apart. He smells like soap and fresh hay and I breathe him in as I bury my face in the side of his neck, letting the smell take me back six years ago when everything was easy and perfect and amazing. His arms tighten around me, so tight I can barely breathe, but I don't even care. I don't need to breathe when he's my oxygen and everything I need to live.

"Fucking hell, Legs," he whispers brokenly as I squeeze my eyes closed to keep the tears at bay.

He nuzzles his face into my hair and breathes deep, cursing again under his breath.

"Peaches. Fucking peaches... goddammit, I missed this."

I'm dying.

I'm suffocating.

I'll never survive this.

"Am I dreaming? Fuck, tell me I'm not dreaming," he mutters. "You feel so warm and so real and so perfect."

I sob against the skin of his neck, the tears falling so fast and so hard that I don't know how I'll ever get them to stop. I take a deep breath, one last smell of his clean skin. I hug him tighter, one last touch of his warm body against mine, one last second of feeling his heart beating with mine. I take it all in and shove it into the compartment in my brain reserved just for him, where I can take it out whenever I want and remember this moment. This one moment where I could pretend, for just a few seconds, that this could be my life. Wrapped up in this man who went through hell and found his way back to me.

My arms slide from around his neck and I press my palms to his chest, pushing against it gently until he finally loosens his hold and lets me move back. I feel the loss of his warmth immediately, my skin pebbling with goose bumps, and I tell myself this is how it has to be. I remind myself that I can live through the cold as long as he's okay.

I can't handle the questioning look in his eyes when I take another step back from the comfort of his arms, still suspended in the air, held out for me and just waiting for me to fit back inside them. Swiping the tears from my cheeks, I lift my chin and put the mask back in place before crossing my arms in front of me.

"Legs?" he whispers in confusion, taking a step toward me to try and close the distance I've created.

My hand comes up between us and he stops immediately.

"Please, don't call me that."

A muscle ticks in his jaw when I speak, firmly and with authority, all signs of the relieved and weepy woman from moments ago long gone.

"I know this is crazy and you probably have a thousand questions. I shouldn't have just shown up here like this, but I didn't think you'd be here," he says, his arms finally dropping to his sides when he realizes I'm not going back into them.

"Of course I'd be here. I live here."

His mouth drops open in shock and he slides one of his hands through his short hair, something he always used to do when I said or did something that pissed him off.

I'm sorry, oh, God I'm so sorry.

"What the fuck do you mean you *live* here? You mean you're just visiting, right? You live in New York, like you planned, and you're just here for a visit. Tell me you're just here for a visit, Legs."

I let out a frustrated breath, my fingernails digging into the skin of my arms to stop myself from screaming.

"Don't call me that!" I shout angrily, hating myself for yelling at him, but unable to stop the hurt and animosity I feel whenever I so much as *think* of that name. Hearing it from his lips, after all this time, will break me in two. If I hear it one more time, I will crumple into a ball on this floor and never be able to get up again.

I take another deep, calming breath, looking at a spot over his shoulder. I can't look at him and do this. I can't see the eyes I've dreamed about, the mouth I've wished to kiss more times than I can count, and the face my hands are dying to touch and do what I have to do without breaking down.

"I'm sorry, fuck, I'm sorry," he speaks softly. "I don't know what to say. I've thought of this moment every day for six fucking years, and now that you're here, standing in front of me, I don't know what the fuck to say."

"You don't have to say anything," I cut him off. "And you don't have to apologize for anything. I'm glad you're okay. I'm glad you made it back to your family. Your sister must be so relieved to have you home."

He tries again to move toward me, and I take another step back.

"Talk to me. Tell me what's going on," he urges, dipping his head down to try and get me to look at him. "What happened to New York? Are you just taking some time off? Did you knock their socks off and they couldn't handle how bad you made everyone look?"

He laughs softly at his own joke and I dig my nails harder into my skin.

"New York didn't happen, okay? It was just a stupid dream. I work for my mother as her assistant," I tell him quickly, hoping he'll drop it and let me leave with a tiny shred of dignity.

"You've got to be fucking kidding me," he mumbles irritably, one hand flying through his short, spiky hair again. "You were supposed to get away from here. The only reason I left was so you could get away from here and away from *her*. The only thing that kept me going all of these fucking years was knowing you were out there, living your dream and happy. What the fuck happened, Shelby?"

And I thought hearing him call me by my nickname cut like a knife. My name flying out of his mouth in anger and disappointment hurts a hell of a lot worse.

I'm sorry, oh, God I'm so sorry.

"Life happened, Eli!" I shout. "You weren't here and life happened! Things got messy and dreams got broken and I moved on!"

"You didn't move on, you fucking gave up! You had *everything* right there for the taking and you gave up because of HER! The minute I leave, you turn into one of her little sheep! How the fuck could you just *give up*, Shelby? Goddammit, how could you throw it all away?"

I move farther away from him, each step hurting worse than the one before when all I want to do is tell him. Tell him everything, show him everything, and make him see I had no choice, but I can't, because he's right. I gave up. I threw my life away and I gave up because I didn't care about anything but him. My happiness meant nothing if his name was being dragged through the mud and his sister's life was ruined because my mother couldn't handle not being in control of everything around her, including me.

"You don't know anything about me," I tell him through clenched teeth. "You've been gone for six years and I'm sorry. I'm sorry for everything that happened to you, but I'm not sorry for the choices I've made. I have a good and happy life now and I've moved on."

I'm sorry. I'm so sorry. Please don't hate me. I'm not happy, I hate this life that I'm barely living.

"Bullshit. You didn't move on. You stayed in the exact same fucking place, never moving forward because you were too goddamn scared to take that leap. The only way I managed to stay alive in that fucking hellhole for five years was knowing you jumped, when all along, you stayed here and turned into *her*."

I'm dying.

I'm suffocating.

I'm sorry.

I say the last two words out loud, so quietly I'm not even sure he hears them, before I turn and walk away from him. I wait until my back is to him before I let the tears start to fall again. I hear him calling my name, but he doesn't come after me.

He lets me go, just like he did six years ago.

It's what I deserve. He lived through hell hoping he'd come back to the same woman he left behind, maybe to apologize, probably to make amends for how he left me, but that's impossible.

That woman died a long time ago, along with her dreams, and it was all for him. *Everything* was always for Eli, and seeing him alive, knowing he'll be okay as long as he stays away from me, reminds me that I made the right decision. Knowing his sister is happily married with a family of her own without my mother tainting their life in any way reminds me that I would make the same decisions all over again, even if it kills everything inside me.

Chapter 6

Eli

Are you okay?"

I try not to let my irritation show when my sister asks me the same question for the tenth time today as I grab a bottled water from the fridge and take a seat next to her at the kitchen table.

Going for a five-mile run through her development this morning was meant to clear my head. All it did was give me too much quiet time to think about what happened last night. For a few seconds, I had Shelby in my arms. Just like I'd dreamed about for six brutal years. Clinging to me like her life depended on it, her body so warm and perfect pressed against mine, her breath puffing along the skin of my neck and her heart beating against my chest...until suddenly, she was gone. Replaced with a stoic, hard woman who didn't want anything to do with me. I'd like to say I didn't even recognize her, but I did. One look at her with her chin raised and all the tears dried up like they'd never been there in the first place, staring at me like I wasn't even good enough to shine her shoes...I damn sure recognized *that* woman because she looked exactly like her mother and made me think about the last conversation I had with that bitch of a woman six years ago.

> "You need to get out of my daughter's life and you need to get out now. If you want Shelby to fulfill her silly dreams of being a dancer and your sister to finish college and have a secure future, you will leave and never look back."

"I'm fine, Kat," I sigh, taking a drink of my water and pushing that damn conversation out of my mind. "Just working through some stuff."

She reaches across the table, resting her hand on top of mine as I nervously spin the bottle cap around the wooden top.

"Daniel saw you threw those candles away when he took the garbage out before work," she whispers softly. "Were they the wrong smell?"

I close my eyes and sigh, not wanting to talk about this with her, but feeling a huge amount of guilt that I haven't shared *anything* with her since I've been home, no matter how hard she's tried to pull it out of me. She never knew about Shelby and me back then, and there's no way I want to burden her with it now. Telling her to buy those damn candles so I could fall asleep to the smell of peaches was an asinine decision on my part. It was one I quickly fixed after what went down last night at the stables, by tossing the stupid glass containers filled with pale orange wax so hard into the cans out by their garage that they shattered all over the bottom of the empty container.

"Don't worry about the candles, Kat. They're the least of our worries."

Moving my hand out from under hers, I grab the letter that came in the mail earlier and pull the piece of paper with the United States Marine Corps insignia stamped at the top closer to me. I knew it would happen. I knew they'd be sending a letter like this; I just didn't expect it to be so soon.

"You had another bad dream last night," she tries again.

I wince, turning my head away from her so I don't have to see the sadness in her eyes. I can't handle the expression of pity on her face whenever she looks at me. I love my sister, and I thank God that I'm getting a second chance to be here with her, especially when I never thought I'd see her again, but I can't stand her feeling sorry for me. I can't have her worrying about me all the time when she has a family to take care of. After what happened last night, I woke up screaming louder than I ever have, once again bringing Kat flying into my room to take care of me, when she had other priorities that should come first.

"I'm sorry. I'm gonna find my own place as soon as I can."

Kat lets out an irritated huff. "That's not what I mean and you know it. I'm worried about you, Eli."

My eyes lift from the paper and I try to soften my features. I don't want to hurt her, but that's all I seem to be doing lately. My baby sister has done well for herself and here I show up, threatening to ruin it all. I did what I could while we were growing up to shield her from the shittiness of having two parents who never really got the hang of parenting, did their own thing, and put their children at the bottom of their list of importance. I helped her with her homework, packed her lunch, and made sure she had something good to eat for breakfast and dinner, threatened any boy who came sniffing around for a date, shielded her from the drunken fights our parents always had by taking her out for ice cream, helped her pick out a dress for her first dance, and always made sure I was there for her when she had questions or needed advice. When our parents took their selfishness and excessive partying too far and got themselves killed, I worked my ass off to make sure she never suffered. To make sure she always had what she needed and never forgot how much she was loved. She moved on from me and found herself a good man in her husband, Daniel Evans. One who I can tell just by being in the same room with them for five minutes would give up his life to make sure she and their daughter were safe. I hate that I wasn't here to see this happen, to see her turn into such an amazing woman, wife, and mother. I hate that so much of our time was stolen from us, and I hate that I have to be the one to knock her back down again.

Kat would never tell me how hard it was on her when she thought I'd been killed. She'd never admit how much it broke her and how difficult it'd been for her to keep moving forward and get on with her life without me in it, because she wouldn't want to hurt me. Daniel, on the other hand, had no issue with sitting me down over a beer after Kat had gone to bed a few nights ago and laying it all out on the line for me. He didn't treat me like I was a piece of glass, ready to shatter if I heard something upsetting, and that made me like him even more. He was protective of his wife and he worried about how strong she was trying to be for me, when he was there with her five years ago, holding her up and letting her cry on his shoulder when she'd thought she lost me. Making her get out of bed every day, shower, and face the world. Telling her I would kick her ass if I knew she was wasting her life, spending every day crying over me.

Daniel Evans is the exact opposite of me, and I thought for sure when I first met him, I'd hate him. With his slicked-back, perfectly styled, short blond hair, expensive three-piece suits, and evidence of his fancy college background hung in frames in the hallway among family photos. He might dress like a spoiled rich boy, he might do business with all the spoiled rich folks in this county that I despise, but he worked hard to get where he's at. He gave my baby sister a nice home in a private, gated community with a sprawling, manicured lawn, and he treated her like a princess—all the things I dreamed of for her when we were growing up.

Yeah, I liked Daniel Evans.

I liked him even more when I confided in him about the report I received anonymously in the mail and how I confronted Georgia Eubanks with it right before she shipped me out of the country, and Daniel became protective of my sister once again. He wanted me to make absolutely certain I had all of the facts before I told Kat. He wanted me to know, without a shadow of a doubt, that everything I was suspecting was true, before I gave this heavy burden to her. He wouldn't let anything, even her brother who was back from the dead, hurt her or upset her in any way. You gotta respect a man for that, even though I know she's going to kick my ass for keeping it from her for so long.

"I don't want you worrying about me, Kat. I'll be fine. It's gonna take some time, but I'll be fine. I hate that this letter is going to make things hard for you guys," I explain, tossing the paper across the table angrily. "It's bad enough you have to put up with me; now you gotta put up with *this* shit."

Kat's eyes follow the letter as it skates across the top of the table before fluttering to a stop right before it falls off the other side.

"Eli, we need to—"

"Hon? You home?" Daniel calls from the front of the house, the sound of the door slamming closed behind him and his dress shoes smacking against the hardwood as he heads in our direction.

I give him a confused look as he rushes into the kitchen, nods in my direction, and bends to give Kat a peck on the cheek.

"Sorry I'm late. Damn meeting with an investor took a little longer than I thought it would," he explains quickly, pulling his suit coat off and flinging it over the back of the empty chair next to Kat as he sits down. "Did you tell him yet?"

He loosens his tie with one hand as he scoots his chair closer to Kat and slides his other arm over her shoulder, pulling her close to his side.

Even though it pains me to know I wasn't around to take care of my sister, at least the mix-up with my death provided them with a good nest egg they could both build on, and that gave me a little bit of comfort knowing I had helped her in some small way while being imprisoned for five years. Daniel did right by her, and I owe him everything for it. Having to sit here in their beautiful kitchen, with all new appliances, in their home that he worked so hard to give her and discuss that damn letter is not what I want to be doing right now.

"You didn't have to leave work early for this shit," I tell him, jerking my head in the direction of the letter. "I've already put in a few inquiries about work, so I should be hearing back from someone this week. That money was yours, free and clear, and I'm going to handle it. This isn't your problem, so don't even worry yourselves about it."

When I was declared dead by the U.S. government, my

military life insurance policy of $100,000 was immediately given to my next of kin. Even though they screwed up, they still aren't going to let them keep that money now that I'm alive. I get it and I understand it, but that doesn't make me any less pissed off that I have to give my sister and her husband one more thing to worry about. I don't know what they did with that money, and I don't give a fuck. Maybe they used it to buy this house, maybe they used it to buy the small clothing boutique my sister owns and runs downtown, or maybe they put it toward the three other stores she opened up throughout the state. When Daniel and I had our little talk the other night, he let it slip that a few years ago, my sister almost lost her business and he almost lost his job because of some tax fraud bullshit. He reassured me it wasn't a big deal and that the problems went away in a few days, so maybe they used the money for that... it doesn't matter, as long as they used it. It was theirs to do with as they wished, and now having to ask for it back isn't something I have any intentions of doing, even if I have to take the rest of my life paying it off. It's my problem, and I'll handle it.

"You didn't tell him?" Daniel asks Kat softly.

She shakes her head and gives him a small smile. "You know I don't understand all that financial crap you go on and on about all the time. I figured I'd wait for you to tell him."

My eyes narrow as I look back and forth between them and they turn their heads at the same time and smile at me. I don't like the way they're looking at me, like they have a secret they can barely handle keeping quiet about. Kat is practically bouncing in her seat at this point, and I can hear her bare foot smacking against the floor under the table in excitement. And I call bullshit on her not understanding "financial crap," since she singlehandedly takes care of the accounting and the books for all of her clothing stores.

"You're not paying it back," I tell them through clenched teeth. "It's my problem, and I'll handle it."

Daniel laughs and shakes his head at me. "You're right, *we* aren't paying it back, *you* are."

Finally, we're on the same page.

"And you're not going to have to bust your ass working a shitty job for years to do that," Daniel goes on to explain.

"We never spent the money," Kat quickly adds.

My hands clench into fists on top of the table, and Daniel, noticing that I'm starting to get a little pissed off, continues with his explanation before I blow a gasket.

"You know your sister, man. Do you honestly think she would touch one cent of that money, thinking you lost your life for it?" Daniel asks quietly.

"Dammit, Kat!" I shout. "It was *yours*. Yours to spend, yours to save for a rainy day, yours to do whatever the fuck you wanted to do with it! I don't care if you still have it in your damn bank account, you're not giving it back. It. Is. YOURS."

Kat shakes her head at me, tears pooling in her eyes. "Daniel's right, Eli. That money made me sick. I couldn't even touch the stupid check when it came in the mail. The things you did, the things you went through… it wasn't my money to do *anything* with and you know it. You earned that money, and now I'm thankful I didn't want anything to do with it. I'm thankful I have a smart husband who knew what to do with it, and Eli, you're going to be pretty thankful, too. You took care of me when Mom and Dad died. Hell, you took care of me all our lives, even before they died. You worked two jobs to keep a roof over my head and put me through college. Now, it's my turn to take care of you, so shut the hell up."

Daniel moves his arm from around Kat's shoulders and leans down to the side of his chair, pulling up a briefcase I didn't even notice he walked in with. He smacks the leather case on top of the table and flips the two snaps by the handle, lifting the lid and pulling out a manila folder. Sliding the folder across the table to me, he leans back in his chair and puts his arm back around his wife's shoulders, both of them staring at me with those damn matching smiles.

"I can't believe you didn't use that money, and of *course* I took care of you. You're my family. That was my job," I mutter, snatching the folder and pulling it closer. "What is this?"

Opening the folder, I see a pile of bank statements inside, each one in my name. Glancing down to the bottom of the top statement, my mouth drops open and my eyes widen in shock.

"What the fuck," I whisper, my eyes glued to the balance of the account.

"My husband is a very smart man, Eli," Kat informs me with pride in her voice. "And now you're a very *rich* man."

Sliding the top piece of paper aside, I move on to the next one, another account in my name with another balance that makes my head spin.

"I repeat. What. The. Fuck?"

Daniel laughs, and when I get through all the papers in the folder, each one for a different account with more money in it than the previous one, I finally look up.

"What can I say? I'm good at my job," Daniel tells me easily. "I invested your life insurance money, and since we never had any intentions of using it, and never thought in a million years you'd suddenly show up again, I took a lot of risks I wouldn't normally take with a client. I know you're pissed, but get over it and see it from my point of view. I take care of my own, Eli. I know she's your sister, but she's *my* wife. I can provide for her and our daughter just fine, and even if I couldn't, her clothing stores more than make up for that. We didn't need your money. I'm grateful the money was there, in case something happened, but it didn't, and now it's all yours and then some."

And then some is right. One minute I'm worried about getting a job, *any* fucking job, just to be able to at least pay my sister back for the food she's provided and the clothes she's bought, and now I find out I'm a goddamn millionaire.

Yeah, I definitely like Daniel Evans.

"So, how about dinner tonight to celebrate? We can go somewhere nice, get dressed up, and Eli can treat," Kat announces with a laugh.

I laugh right along with her, feeling lighter than I have since I got home, my eyes unable to move away from the stack of paperwork in front of me as I continue to flip back and forth through the papers. Not only can I pay the government back in full, but I don't have to worry about getting a job for a very long time. I can buy my own place, do whatever I want, and have one less thing hanging over my head to worry about.

"Can't tonight, babe. I've got that stupid charity function at the Eubanks Plantation," Daniel reminds her.

My head jerks up from the paperwork at the mention of the plantation.

"Damn, that's right. I forgot you were invited to that thing," Kat sighs.

"What charity function?" I ask, feigning nonchalance.

"Honestly, I have no idea. There's always something going on at that house, and since half of my clients go to these things, I always wind up getting invited," Daniel tells me. "And since kissing ass is part of my job description, I go. At least I usually get a few new prospective clients out of it, so there's that."

The conversation Rylan and I had when he followed me out the door this morning, and annoyed the shit out of me during my run, flashes through my mind. Rylan is the only person in my life who knew about Shelby and what she meant to me. He knew it when it happened six years ago, and he had to listen to me talk about it all through our deployment and when we had moments of peace in the five years of hell after. He knew how I felt about her, he knew she was the one thing that kept me alive, and he knew as soon as he saw me chucking candles into the garbage can this morning, cursing and kicking the shit out of the damn thing, that our first meeting didn't go as planned.

> "You've been out of her life for six years. You have no idea what she went through or what's gone on in her life during that time. You say you love her, carried this torch for her all these years, then man the fuck up and do something about it. Make her talk to you, find out what the hell is going on and stop being a pussy."

A few hours ago, I had no intention of going back to her. Not after I'd seen what she'd become, knowing all the guilt I felt over the way I left her and the reasons *why* I left her were all for nothing. I gave up everything to keep her safe, and almost gave up my life because of my involvement with her. Before last night, every minute of my time away from her had been worth it when I'd thought she was happy and following her dreams. Even if that whole scene in the barn never happened and I was still oblivious to the woman she'd turned into, I was still plagued with doubts about finding her again, knowing I had nothing to offer her. Being a broken man living with his sister and with no clue what the hell he was going to do with his life isn't exactly a position of strength. Now I can walk into that room, with her rich-ass friends and her mother's rich-ass supporters, hold my head high, and not be ashamed and feel like I have a right to be there. A part of me wanted to walk away and never look back after my first encounter with Shelby out at the stables. I was hurt and pissed that something I'd been holding on to for so many years was gone, and it made me wonder if it had ever been there to begin with.

I'm still hurt, and I'm still pissed, but I'll be damned if I just walk away without making her talk to me and tell me what the hell happened. I need to see that *my* Shelby is still in there somewhere, and I don't give a shit if I have to do it in front of all of Charleston. Bonus points for also being able to rub it in Georgia's face and let her see that I'm back, and I'm not going anywhere. Her days of bullying and blackmailing me are over.

"How about you let me be your plus-one?" I ask Daniel. "I'll even let you dress me up in one of your monkey suits."

Daniel laughs. "I hate to break it to you, but it's black tie. Which means you're going to need a tux, my friend. Good thing I have an excellent tailor always on standby and you have enough money to buy something that fits you better than anything in my closet."

While Kat rushes out of the room to get my niece when she starts crying from her afternoon nap, Daniel calls the office and takes the rest of the day off, then immediately places a call to his tailor to book us an emergency appointment for within the hour. As all of this takes place, I wonder if this is the dumbest idea I've ever had, walking into the lion's den and facing Georgia Eubanks on her turf. I tell myself I'm not a hypocrite for having more confidence now to face Shelby again, knowing damn well that having a few extra zeros behind the balance of my bank account doesn't make me a better man. All this money does is give me access to her world, a place where I'd never been welcome before. A place where I can confront her on equal footing and prove that everything she said to me in the stables was complete bullshit.

It's also a place where I can show Georgia Eubanks once and for all that I'm not backing down, and there's not a damn thing she can do to keep me away from Shelby now, especially in front of all her people. With a thumbs-up from Daniel as he speaks to his tailor, at least I know I'll look damn good when it happens.

Chapter 7

Shelby

Dr. Eugene Stanford, and his wife, Maribell. Large plastic surgery practice in Charleston. Donated two hundred and fifty thousand to the Leatherback Turtle Endangered Species event last year," I say softly in my mother's ear before pulling back and pasting a smile on my face as the couple moves forward in the reception line.

"Dr. Stanford, Maribell, so nice to see you again," my mother tells them with a bright smile, shaking both of their hands and expertly using the information I just fed to her. "Thank you so much for coming this evening."

I glance behind them in line to prepare myself for the next guest while they chitchat about the charity event, ironically being held for wounded veterans. Ironic because the one wounded vet that *should* be at this event would never be important or wealthy enough to be added to my mother's guest list. And it's not like I want him here, especially after our confrontation last night and how much it drained me to be in his arms one minute, and have to pull away from him the next. To see the disappointment and anger in his eyes and feel the sharp sting of his accusations, cutting deeper than any knife possibly could.

Rubbing the watchband on the inside of my wrist, I know I deserved every insult he threw at me, but that doesn't make the hurt go away. It doesn't help me rest easy at night knowing he's sleeping just a few short miles away and I can't go to him, can't touch him, can't kiss him, and can't tell him *why*.

A man in a crisp white Navy uniform, walking with a cane, moves forward in line as my mother says her goodbyes to the doctor and his wife. I'm spending an evening in a room filled with military personnel and it's the worst form of torture. I've seen at least a dozen men in Marine dress blues come through this line tonight, and each one reminds me of Eli and the one time I got to see him in his uniform. He had just come home from a funeral for the wife of one of his commanding officers. Even though it was a somber event, his face lit up as soon as he let me into his apartment and that uniform was quickly ripped away by my own hands.

Shaking myself out of my thoughts, I lean forward, closer to my mother's ear once more and speak quietly.

"Lieutenant Anthony Michaels, son of Virginia state senator Brandon Michaels. Wounded in Afghanistan six months ago," I inform her as Anthony moves forward and my mother kisses both of his cheeks and thanks him for his service.

Running my hands down the front of my dress, I glance at the soft fabric covering my body. It's a Versace gown the color of emerald green and perfectly matches my eyes. The soft jersey material clings to every curve of my body and drapes around the floor at my feet, a slit up the side showcasing one long leg—the good one, of course. It only has one strap over my shoulder, held together with a gold filigree brooch, leaving my other shoulder completely bare. It's a beautiful dress and it fits me like a glove, but I saw this dress on the runway a few months ago. I know the original style of this dress was intended to be cut short, several inches above the knee. I know my mother had her stylist send it to get altered, because God forbid I ever show myself and my scarred leg in public, around people who respect her.

"No one likes to be reminded of tragedy, Shelby. These people see enough ugliness in their lives."

The only concession I made tonight was refusing to put my hair in a fancy updo. It took fifteen minutes of arguing with my mother's stylist before she finally gave up, left the room, and I petulantly curled my long, strawberry blond hair into soft waves framing my face and hanging halfway down my back.

Brushing my hair back over my bare shoulder, my smile quickly dies from my face when I realize it's more than a little pathetic that my hair is the only form of rebellion I'm brave enough to fight for tonight. I'm here at this charity function, held at my family plantation, because I was told to be. I'm wearing this floor-length Versace dress because it was chosen for me. I'm whispering in my mother's ear because it's the job I was forced to take. I feel like my mother's doll. One she dresses up in a pretty package to hide the truth on the inside.

"Have I told you lately how hot your ass looks in that dress?"

I smile, barely containing an unladylike giggle as I step away from my mother's side while she's busy talking, to turn and look at Meredith. Unlike me, Meredith is wearing whatever the hell she wants, her curvy body showcased in a tight red halter-style dress with a deep vee in the front showing off a generous amount of cleavage that has most of the men in this room tripping over their own feet when she walks by.

My mother shoots a quick, annoyed look at the two of us over her shoulder and Meredith raises her champagne glass in the air toward her in a silent toast, giving her a huge, fake smile.

"Let me guess, she's still pissed I helped you move out into the guest house today?" Meredith asks out of the corner of her mouth, bringing the crystal flute to her lips and taking a sip.

Okay, so I might have managed to perform one more rebellious act today, but that's only because of the woman standing next to me. Meredith took one look at my face when she walked into the house this morning after she landed, dragged me upstairs, and started packing my things.

> "You need your space. Especially with all this shit going on. You can't think clearly living under the same roof as Lucifer and I'm not going to stand here and watch you take her crap day after day. Even if you move back after I'm gone, at least we can have some privacy out there and I can knock some sense into you without her walking in on us, demanding something from you every five minutes."

To say my mother was flustered when she came home from a few meetings this afternoon and found out from one of the household staff that I'd moved out was the understatement of the year. Luckily, I was in the shower at the guest house when she stormed over and Meredith handled that confrontation. All she had to do was mention her father, and my mother shut her mouth, turned, and walked back to the main house.

"Of course she's pissed, but she'll keep her mouth shut and continue glaring at us throughout your entire stay just in case you might have the urge to tell your father she's being difficult," I tell her softly, grabbing my own glass of champagne from a passing waiter.

"Lucky for her, I try to avoid speaking to my father as much as possible, but she doesn't need to know that."

Meredith and her father have always had a rocky relationship. Even though he lets her make her own choices in life, he's never quiet about his disappointment in those choices. He doesn't understand Meredith's free spirit and artistic nature. While I've been stuck here in Charleston, Meredith has been flourishing as a romance author in New York. The first book she published after we graduated from college soared to the top of the bestseller lists, and every book she's penned since then has been no different. Her nonstop upward movement since that first book is probably the only reason her father has stopped trying to pressure her into moving to D.C. to work for him as the head of Homeland Security. That, and the fact that she writes under a pen name, never makes public appearances even though two of her books have been made into popular movies, and the whispers and rumors about who she really is continue to increase her fame each time she puts out another book. As long as she continues showing up to his social functions to fake her support for him, her father is perfectly fine to let her be. It's no wonder he and my mother get along so well.

"Shelby, there are a few people I'd like you to meet."

Meredith and I both turn to look at Landry as he walks up to us and kisses me on the cheek, before giving a curt nod in Meredith's direction. Landry, being of mostly the same mind as my mother, isn't Meredith's biggest fan either and has made his complaints loud and clear about my moving out into the guest house because of her influence. One would think he'd be happy that I had my own place, so to speak, so the two of *us* could have some privacy, but one would be wrong. If something upsets my mother, it gets back to him and he has to deal with the backlash. My mother spent the entire evening chewing his ear off about letting me make such a stupid decision.

I should be offended neither of these people seem to think I can make my own decisions, but what would be the point? I can't and I don't. I do what I'm told, like a good, obedient daughter. I used to be headstrong and confident, ready and willing to take on the world, and it makes me sick to my stomach that I've let that part of me slip away.

"We're a little busy here, Lando, how about you come back in a few minutes?" Meredith informs him with a cheeky smile, tossing back the rest of her champagne.

Obviously there is no love lost between these two, indicated by Landry's annoyed sigh when she uses the nickname she gave him years ago that he absolutely hates.

While the two of them quietly bicker back and forth, I take a minute to look at Landry. He looks handsome in his black tuxedo, just like he always does. Hair perfectly styled at the salon in town, nails manicured, clean-shaven, and smelling of expensive cologne. With my four-inch gold heels, we're exactly the same height. I've never had to crane my neck or stand on my toes to kiss him. We're perfectly matched in every way.

Every way but the one that counts. I'll never love him. I'll never be able to give him what he wants. I stand here looking at him, so handsome and well dressed and full of so much love for me, and all I can think about is a man who towers over me, looks just as amazing in jeans and a T-shirt as he does in a uniform and who doesn't need to bother with fancy cologne because the smell of his body mixed with his soap is the most intoxicating scent I've ever experienced. If I had a fully functioning heart, it would be breaking for Landry with the way I'm betraying him with these thoughts of another man. As it is, my stomach is tied in knots every time I look at him and my head is full of regret every time he smiles at me because I can't give him more. I can't give him all of me, because the man that has always filled my thoughts, a man I never thought I'd see again, is now alive.

I hear Meredith softly curse beside me and I look over to see her eyes trained on the wide open front door. When my gaze moves in that direction, the gaslight lanterns hanging outside on either side of the door flicker and cast a warm golden glow of light in the doorway and my champagne glass slips right out of my hand.

The feel of liquid splashing against my arm and Meredith fumbling and bumping into me makes me realize her quick reflexes must have caught the glass before it shattered to the floor, but all I can see is the man standing in the open double French doors. The clear, starry night behind him makes a perfect backdrop and I hold my breath as he moves around a few people milling about. His eyes meet mine from a few feet away, and I press my hand to my stomach to quell the butterflies flapping around as I watch his eyes move over every inch of me, from head to toe, as he continues walking in our direction.

"Isn't that the Eli James fellow from the news?" Landry asks. "I don't remember him being on the guest list."

He definitely wasn't on the guest list. My mother would rather set her hair on fire in front of all these people than invite him to our home. Him being here can only mean one thing and that one thing does not make the nerves taking over my stomach calm down. Eli was never a fan of my mother, even before we started seeing each other. As our relationship advanced and I started trusting him enough to open up about my life, his dislike for her grew tenfold. There's no way him showing up here tonight is for any other reason than to make her nervous and put her on edge and I know it will not end well. He has no idea that just by being here, my mother could assume I had something to do with it and go back on every promise she made me and ruin everything for him.

What the hell is he thinking?

By the time he gets to the table right next to my mother where people can pay for their tickets for dinner if they haven't already done so, a small commotion has begun in the entryway. Everyone knows who Eli James is, thanks to the news blasted across every television station the last few months. Not only is he a hometown hero, he's a national hero, and his presence here is not going unnoticed. People whisper and point in his direction, a few walk up to him and pat him on the back, welcoming him home and thanking him for his service. I watch in awe as he casually shakes the hands of strangers, his eyes always coming back to mine, until my mother finally notices what is happening right in front of her.

I take back everything about how I thought Eli looked better in jeans and a T-shirt. I've never seen him in a tuxedo, and especially not one that looks like it was made especially for him. Unlike most of the men in the room who are wearing bow ties, Eli has paired his black suit with an emerald green necktie and coordinating pocket square sticking out of his left breast pocket. In a sick twist of fate, we look like we match. Like a couple who planned their outfits to complement each other, but I know it's just a fluke and I won't allow myself to wonder if he did it because his favorite color is still green. The color of my eyes.

"What's your favorite color?"

"It used to be blue, but I'm more partial to green these days, because it's the color of your eyes. A man could completely lose himself in those eyes of yours."

"Are you a lost man, Eli?"

"Not anymore, Legs. Not anymore."

"Mr. James, welcome home," my mother says, pulling me out of my thoughts when I hear the fakeness in her voice, carrying loudly over the hushed conversation so that everyone can witness what a welcoming and wonderful person she is, when I know just how much she must be seething inside at the sight of him. "I wasn't aware you were on the guest list, but I'm sure we can make a concession."

I move forward to stand next to her, feeling like I want to throw my body in between the two of them to protect Eli from whatever my mother might say or do.

"I hope you don't mind me crashing the party," Eli tells her, his baritone voice warming my chilled skin. "I'm sure you know this charity is very near and dear to my heart."

My mother nods, clasping her hands together low and in front of her body.

"The more the merrier, but I regret to tell you the tickets are quite expensive. I'm sure you understand. It's for charity," she tells him with a tight smile as a few flashes from the media's cameras go off.

And there it is. With a polite smile and a sweet voice for everyone who stands around us listening in, my mother just put him in his place by inferring that he can't afford to buy a ticket to an event that should benefit *him*. After everything he's gone through, she has the nerve to deny him entry.

As I try to formulate some valid excuse as to why he doesn't need to pay for a ticket without making either one of them look foolish, Eli reaches into the inside pocket of his suit jacket and pulls out a black leather wallet.

"Sorry, I found out about this fancy function a little late, so I didn't get the memo on the cost. How much is it again?" he asks, flipping his wallet open and waiting for her to respond.

She laughs at him like he's a silly little boy who just told her a precious joke, adding in a pitying shake of her head

"It's one thousand dollars," she whispers dramatically, widening her eyes to emphasize the steep price.

Eli whistles and I have to bite down on my lips to stop a hysterical giggle from escaping. "Wow, that's pretty steep."

A few people standing next to him chuckle uncomfortably at his reply.

"It was very nice of you to stop by," my mother tells him, confident that she's made her point, made him look like a fool, and is just waiting until he scurries back out the door with his tail between her legs.

"Oh, I'm not leaving," he informs her, pulling a huge wad of cash out of his wallet and tossing it on the table in front of him. "A thousand, you said? How about I give you six? A donation, of course."

The woman from the charity gasps loudly when she sees the money, quickly picking it up and sticking it into the lockbox next to her and ripping off six tickets to hand to Eli.

He takes them from her hand and gives her a wink, sticking the tickets and his wallet back into the inside pocket of his coat, his eyes moving over my mother and latching on to mine. My heart stutters in my chest and I feel my palms start to sweat as he keeps his eyes locked on mine and walks past us, finally turning away as he enters the ballroom.

Landry steps away from Meredith and me and goes to my mother's side. I watch as the two of them share a quick, whispered conversation before my mother quickly resumes greeting people as they enter, pretending like nothing happened, but I know it won't be that easy.

"Jesus Christ, what the fuck just happened?" Meredith whispers in my ear.

I can't speak as I turn away from my mother and Landry and watch Eli disappear into a crowd of people, his eyes staying glued to mine as he goes, the fire and determination I see in them burning a hole straight through me, making goose bumps break out on my skin and butterflies swarm in my stomach. I stand rooted in place, watching him shake more hands and smile at strangers until the feel of my mother's hand clamping down around my elbow and her nails digging into my skin pull my eyes away from him and I feel like I can finally breathe again.

Oh, no. This won't be easy at all. This will definitely cost me.

Chapter 8

Eli

"Well, that went well. Very inconspicuous," Daniel sighs, flagging down the bartender in the corner of the giant ballroom and ordering a scotch and soda. "Tell me again why you wanted to come to this thing? And felt the need to ruffle Georgia Eubanks's feathers five seconds after you walked through the door?"

I feel like an asshole telling Daniel earlier that I wanted to tag along to this thing because it was time I get out of the house and start socializing, and there was no better way to do that than attending a charity function to support my brothers in arms. Daniel's snort at my explanation proved he wasn't buying the bullshit I tried selling, but he kept his mouth shut and let me do my thing.

"I'd appreciate it if you tone down the stink eye you keep shooting in her direction, considering her right-hand man and our future senator, Landry McAllister, sends clients my way."

This news comes as a shock, but I don't let it show as I continue to take casual sips of my bourbon on the rocks. I know Daniel represents half of the people in attendance tonight, but I had no idea the man standing possessively next to Shelby a few minutes ago helped Daniel with clients. After what Daniel's done for my sister, taking care of her and giving her the love she so badly needed when I was gone, I feel guilty for the thoughts swirling through my brain, wondering if because of his association with Landry that he's privy to any illegal activity Georgia has been conducting behind the scenes. There's no way that woman had the power to send an entire unit out on deployment a year before they were due without throwing money around or having some sort of allegiance with the wrong people. I don't want to involve my family in this mess, any more than they already are, but Daniel could be my ticket to finding out the truth.

My thoughts are put on hold when the woman in question steps up to the mic on the portable stage in the front of the room. I throw back the rest of my bourbon in one swallow as all two hundred people in attendance listen with rapt attention, hanging on her every word as she drones on and on about how special and important our military is to this country. When she finishes, the room erupts in a chorus of clapping, whistling and cheering while she goes on to introduce the band that will be playing music until it's time for dinner, inviting everyone to have some fun out on the dance floor.

Setting my empty glass on the bar next to me, I see a flash of green out of the corner of my eye and my head turns to see Shelby walk gracefully into the room, shaking hands and talking to people as she moves, one of her long gorgeous legs sliding out between the material of her dress as she goes. She's every bit the professional ass kisser, just like her mother, smiling politely and laughing at whatever bull-shit these rich assholes are saying to her. Part of me wants to hate this woman I see before me, behaving nothing like the firecracker I knew six years ago. The one who refused to follow in her mother's footsteps, the one who hated every part of this life and wanted nothing to do with it, and the one who worked her ass off night and day to get as far away from this place as possible. In the time I spent with her, I saw another side of her, one that made me regret ever thinking of her as a spoiled princess, unable to make a decision for herself to save her life. She had hopes and dreams and a fire inside her that burned brighter than anything I'd ever witnessed and it was the hottest fucking thing I'd ever seen.

She quickly made me feel like an ass for what I did to her the night of her high school graduation. I'd spent the next four years while she was away at college, dreaming of that damn kiss she gave me in the stables, her small body pressed against mine, her fingers clutching the hair at the back of my head and her tongue tentatively pushing past my lips until I lost myself in her. Four years of jerking off to thoughts of that kiss and four years of remembering the hurt in her eyes when I called her a princess, pushed her away, and accused her of slumming it with the help for a cheap thrill. She came back to town a different person, a grown woman with attitude and determination, and I'm not gonna lie, the way she tried to ignore me that first week was like waving a red flag in front of a bull.

I wanted to know *that* Shelby. I wanted to find out why she kept her dancing a secret when it meant so much to her and she was so fucking amazing at it that I kept sneaking back into that damn studio day after day just to watch her.

I'm alive and standing here right now because of *that* Shelby. I brought myself back from the brink of death for *that* Shelby. Now there's not even a trace of her left. I know things change and I know the news of my death would have affected her and never left her untouched by sadness and pain, but why did it have to be like this? Why did she have to give up everything she'd worked so hard for and turn into her mother? It's like she never existed even though I have six months filled with memories of us, lying naked in bed while she told me about her dreams, dancing together in her studio, doing whatever I could to make her laugh and watch her face light up, feeling her breath against my lips when I moved inside her and she gave me everything I never knew I wanted and more. Her dreams became my dreams, her hopes became my hopes, and I was determined to do whatever I could to make her happy and make all those things come true for her. I put in a transfer request for a base in New York so I could be close to her because I knew without a shadow of a doubt she'd nail that audition she spent all summer practicing for, I made plans for our future, and I did it all for her because I thought she was different.

I know I hurt her when I left. I know I could have handled it a thousand different ways than how I did, but when someone is threatening your family and the woman you love, it's hard to put things into perspective when you're given less than an hour to pack your shit and get the fuck out of the country. It only took me a few weeks to get my head out of my ass and try to make things right. Every day for the next three months, I tried to make things right by her, and she never responded, but I never gave up hope. Thoughts of her following her dreams and being happy kept my heart going through every beating, every day without food and water, every month without her touch, and every year without knowing if I'd ever make it out of there alive and make it back to her to beg for her forgiveness for the way I let someone else control me.

She wrote me off, turned right into that spoiled princess, making me now wonder if those six months were all a lie, and yet, I still can't take my goddamn eyes off her. Even in a fancy dress that probably costs more than I made in a month with the Marines, I know there isn't another woman in this room who can even come close to her beauty. Standing here, wanting to hate who she's become, I clench my hands and lock my knees to stop myself from stalking over to her, dragging her into the nearest empty room, pushing her up against the wall, and fucking her until she magically turns back into the woman I loved once upon a time.

"This is the dumbest idea you've ever had and I have a feeling it's going to end in bloodshed. Try not to get arrested, I haven't saved up enough bail money yet."

Rylan's voice echoes through my head from earlier tonight when he lounged against the door to the spare bedroom at Kat and Daniel's house and watched me get ready. He didn't like the idea of me putting myself right on Georgia Eubanks's radar, but at least he didn't try to stop me. He knew how determined I was to get to the bottom of everything. He knew I wouldn't be able to move forward with my life until I got answers as to why Shelby stayed here to work for her mother and until I made Georgia pay for what she did to us. He might be able to let things go, but this is personal to me. She fucked with my life and she fucked with my best friend's life. She got half of our unit killed because of her low opinion of me and because she knew I was getting close to something she wanted to keep buried. My *brothers*. My fucking brothers lost their lives because one woman abused her power and influence to get me away from her daughter and the truth. Men who will never see their wives again, who will never kiss their children good night again, who will never get to spend another holiday with their families or grow old, all because of *her*. And now Shelby, the woman I loved more than my own life, follows her around like a fucking puppy, dresses like her, acts like her, and has erased any trace of the woman I gave everything up for.

"I've got some ass kissing to do. Will you be all right by yourself?" Daniel asks as he slides his now empty glass across the bar behind me.

I give him a pat on the back and a smile. "Just gonna ruffle a few feathers. I promise to keep my stink eye to a minimum."

Daniel chuckles and shakes his head at me before he moves forward into the crowd. Smoothing down my tie, I slide my hands into the front pockets of my tuxedo pants and head in Shelby's direction.

As I make my way through the dance floor, moving around couples locked together and swaying to the music, I see Landry McAllister walk up to Shelby's side, wrap his arm around her waist, and pull her closer. He looks like every other douche bag in this place with slicked-back hair and a bow tie and I hate him on sight. When he leans forward and whispers something in Shelby's ear and she pulls back and smiles at him, pressing one hand to his chest in a familiar, easy way, something violent churns in my gut and my feet start moving me faster across the floor until I'm standing right in front of the happy fucking couple.

I smirk at her when her eyes widen as she looks up at me, quickly dropping her hand from douche bag's chest and pulling away from his possessive hold on her.

"How about a dance, Princess?" I ask, holding my hand out toward her with my palm up.

For just one second, so quickly I would have missed it if I hadn't been staring into her eyes, I see a flash of something that looks like hurt, before it's quickly masked with irritation.

Knowing if she refuses me, it will most likely cause a scene since a few people are standing close by and heard me ask her for a dance, Shelby has no choice but to put on a brave face in front of them, tell the fancy-pants jerk-off next to her she'll be right back, take my hand, and let me lead her to the dance floor.

I came here tonight because I wanted to show Georgia Eubanks that she couldn't push me around anymore. I wanted to make Shelby admit she was lying when she told me she'd moved on. I wanted to see that she missed me as much as I missed her; I wanted her to take back everything she said in those stables and tell me she still felt everything as deeply as I did, and that she never let me go. Being here tonight, seeing her interact with all these assholes and watching her with another man, just makes the anger inside me grow and fester until there's nothing I can do to hold it back.

I want her to feel the same searing pain that has settled inside my chest, taking root and taking over all my thoughts and actions.

I want her to know what it feels like to be stabbed in the heart and forgotten.

I want her to hurt as much as I do right now.

Chapter 9

Shelby

I smile and nod at everyone we pass as we make our way to the center of the dance floor, not seeing faces, not recognizing anyone, just blurs of hair and eyes and colorful expensive gowns as we move. I can't think, I can't focus, and I don't want to be here, but I can't make myself drop his hand and walk away, walk back to the safety of Landry and the security of what I know. I don't know this man, gripping my hand so tightly I can feel my bones rubbing together under my skin. I don't recognize this man who called me by a name he swore he never would again because he knew how much it hurt.

> "All my life, people have looked at me like I'm a spoiled princess. The poor little rich girl, living in one of the biggest houses in town, able to buy her happiness with just the snap of her fingers. I hate the way they look at me. I hate the way they see me."

"I see you, Shelby. Who cares what they think? I see you, and you are nothing like that person. You couldn't be even if you tried."

I close my eyes when he finally stops walking and turns to face me, still hearing that voice and those words from what seems like a lifetime ago. His words gave me wings back then. They made me feel like I could do anything I set my mind to when he whispered them as he kissed his way down my body.

"Open your eyes and dance with me, Princess."

I feel that one word like a punch to the face and it's impossible to hide the wince this time. I covered it up the first time he used it with a fake smile and an angry stare, but I'm not that strong. I'm not that person anymore who could fight her way out of any situation, argue until her point was made or give a damn about being hurt.

I deserve the hurt. I deserve the pain of his words and the smirk on his face while he stands here in front of me, watching me wrestle with my decision. He knows I won't storm off in a huff in front of all these people. He knows I won't tell him to go to hell. Not because I'm worried someone will hear me, because I know he's already been there. The scars that mar his beautiful face and the hardness in his eyes are proof that he's lived through torment I'll never understand, so I let him have this moment. I let him call me *Princess* even though it breaks off one more piece of my heart and tosses it into the pile of shattered fragments. I let him tug me roughly to him and I let him dig his fingers into my lower back as he holds me close and we begin swaying to the music.

Glancing around us, I give a few more polite smiles to other couples as they dance their way around us. I crane my neck to look through the crowd and make sure my mother is occupied and not getting a front row seat to this... whatever this is. I know she'll hear about it. One of her many minions will make sure to scurry over to her and whisper in her ear, wrongfully assuming I'm doing something good for the charity tonight and expect her to be grateful. Presume I instigated this dance, in front of all these people, to show our support for the military hero who finally came home. They don't know how much it will anger her. They have no idea I'll be paying for this moment later after everyone has gone home to their happy homes with their happy families.

"Was it worth it, Princess?"

My eyes move away from the distractions all around us and I finally tip my head back and look up at his face. He's scowling at me, his eyebrows clenched together and a curl in his lip indicating his disgust at what I'm doing, how I'm dressed, and what I've become.

"Was what worth it?" I ask, hating the quiver in my voice that lets him know I am not comfortable with this situation or with his question.

"Giving up. I just want to know if it was worth it, letting go of everything you'd ever wanted just to be one of her little fucking sheep."

You're here, you're breathing, and you're alive. It will always be worth it.

I swallow past the lump in my throat and force myself to continue looking into his eyes that feel like laser beams, burning a hole into my flesh.

"Don't make this more difficult than it already is," I beg, my hand slipping from his shoulder to rest over his heart, hoping the thump of it under my palm will give me the strength I need to hold my head high and not collapse into his arms and beg him to forgive me.

He laughs, but the sound doesn't match the anger in his eyes.

"Princess, you wouldn't know difficult if it walked in here and smacked you across the face. While you were sitting here all nice and cozy in your fancy castle in your perfect, pathetic world, helping your mother toss her money around, I was fighting for my life. Fighting for one more fucking breath just so I could come back here to you. But there's nothing left, is there?"

I bite down on the inside of my cheek before the sting of his words fills my eyes with tears. My eyes leave his to glance at my left hand, which is still resting against his chest, to stare at the watch on my wrist. I wish I could let go of his hand so I could run my fingers over the inside band. It's my security, my reminder, and the only thing that keeps me grounded and stops me from losing my sanity. I try not to focus on what he said about fighting his way back to me. I can't allow myself even a moment of weakness to believe that's true. The hurt and anger over how he left me are the only things I have left. They're the only things stopping me from wrapping my arms around him and telling him the truth.

"You're right," I finally say, my eyes still on my watch. "There's nothing left. Maybe it wasn't even there to begin with. I chose a different path because it was easier."

There's nothing left because you took it all with you. And now that you're back, I can't even reach out and grab it without ruining both of us.

"I have an easy life," I lie, forcing my eyes away from my watch and back up to his furious ones. "I have a good man who makes it easy to love him and won't leave me. I have a good job that's easy to do. It's all good and I'm happy."

He scoffs and shakes his head at me, his arm tightening

around my body until I realize we're no longer dancing. We're standing in place in the middle of the dance floor and I want to run. Dancing with him, even if it was just moving from side to side, brings back too many memories of other times we moved like that. Times when I laughed and loved and *felt* something, anything.

"You're not happy, you're miserable," he growls, lowering his head closer to mine until I can feel his breath on my face. He smells like bourbon and peppermint and I want to drown in that smell until it washes everything away. "You're sad and miserable and pathetic. I can't believe I fought so hard to come back to *this*. I can't believe you can stand here, supporting that woman, when you know what she did."

He finally drops my hand, removes his arm from around me, and takes a step back as the band finishes their song and everyone claps for them. A chill of fear works its way up my spine, wondering what he means about knowing what my mother did. Does he know about the threats she's held over my head? It doesn't make sense. How could he? Why would he still be so angry with me if he knew?

I let his words of hate give me the strength I need to take my own step away from him. Everything inside me is screaming to deny what he said so he'll look at me with love instead of hate, but I can't do that. I can do nothing but let him have this moment and this anger that he so rightfully deserves and hope to God he doesn't know about the bargains I've made with my mother to keep him safe. He'll never be able to keep quiet if he knows, and she'll stop at nothing to make sure he does.

"I'm sorry," I whisper. "I hope you can find your own happiness and move on, like I have."

I see him clench his jaw before I turn and walk away, gently pushing my way through all the people as the band starts back up again. I hear people say my name but I don't stop moving through the ballroom. I see Meredith out of the corner of my eye, her hands on her hips and fire in her eyes as I move quickly past her, out into the foyer and across the hall to a small office with the door closed. I just need a moment alone, to remember how to breathe and to remember how to push the hurt away so I can go back out there and do my job. Hold my head high with a smile on my face and pretend like dancing with Eli, being close to Eli, and letting him rain insults down on me, didn't cut me in half.

As soon as I turn the handle and push open the office door, I feel something solid slam into me from behind, moving me faster into the dark room. I trip over my feet and an arm slides around my waist to steady me before whirling me around. I smell his soap and recognize his firm hold on me before the moonlight shining in the floor-to-ceiling windows behind me illuminates the shadow of his face, but that doesn't stop the rapid thumping of my heart as the door is kicked shut with a *slam* and my body is turned and pushed roughly against the wall next to it. With the first touch of his hands, the first feel of the heat from his skin against me, I'm lost. I'm drowning in a pool of desire I've only ever felt with him, and I never want to come up for air. Every inch of my body is on fire, begging for more, needing everything I've been missing, but knowing everything about this moment is wrong. This can't happen. I can't want this and I certainly can't act on what I'm feeling.

Before I can shove him away, shout at him, and tell him to let me go, his mouth is on mine. His chest pins my arms between us and I clutch a fistful of his dress shirt in my hands when my lips automatically part for him. His tongue quickly pushes into my mouth and I feel tears prickling behind my eyelids when I taste him, so familiar and so beautiful it breaks off yet another piece of my heart. One of his hands moves from around my waist and I feel the heat from his palm as it slides against the side of my neck to the back, his fingers gripping tightly to the hair at the base of my skull to hold my head in place. His kiss is punishing and hard and I can do nothing but hold tightly to the front of his shirt as our tongues battle together and I try to remember how to breathe.

His arm that holds me close loosens slightly until I feel his hand skim down my spine, clutch my ass, and pull the lower half of my body up and against his hips. His hardness presses into me and every nerve and cell in my body I thought had long since died suddenly fire back to life as I push myself into him, wanting to feel more, needing to feel everything as our tongues swirl together and push deeper.

This kiss is killing me.

This kiss is bringing me back to life.

His fingers dig into my ass as he moves me against him and his hand in my hair tightens, the pain immediately replaced by the pleasure only *his* mouth and *his* lips and *his* tongue can give me. My body loses all of its stiffness and I melt into him, molding my body to his from thigh to chest until I can't tell where he ends and I begin. That's how it always was with us when we came together and it's no different now after years of being apart, no matter what kind of hurt lies between us. He makes me feel whole, he closes up wounds while at the same time ripping them wide open...and I never want it to stop.

I match the intensity of his kiss, sucking his tongue into my mouth after he does the same to me, biting his lower lip after he nips at my own, letting his breath with a hint of bourbon on it and his lips tasting faintly of peppermint breathe me back to life even though I know, somewhere in the back of my mind, that I'm not allowed to have this. I'm not allowed to be this person who loses herself in this man. As our tongues blend together and our heads move from one side to the other to get the best angle for the kiss, I feel myself getting wet for him, I feel my legs shaking with the need to wrap my thighs around his waist and let him sink inside me. It's been so long since I've felt something like this, only with him and never with anyone else, that I can't stop a gentle moan from floating out of my mouth and into his.

The muffled music and murmur of voices on the other side of the door feel like they're a million miles away, and my soft moan sounds like an explosion in the quiet room, suddenly so loud and needy.

Eli immediately pulls his mouth away from mine, drops his hold on my hair and his hand from my ass, stumbling a few feet away from me, putting so much distance between us I feel like I'll never be able to reach him. I have to lock my knees and press my back as hard as I can into the wall behind me just to stay upright and not collapse on the floor at his feet. I'm light-headed and I can't stop my hands from shaking as I reach up and brush my hair out of my face that his quick departure caused.

My head thumps back against the wall and I wrap my arms around my body to try and hold myself together.

"It's all good and you're happy, huh? You want me to move on, just like you have?" Eli asks in a low, angry voice.

He moves back to me in a rush and I shrink away from him as much as the hard wall at my back will allow. Without his mouth on mine and his body pressed into me, all the reasons why I can't let myself have him come rushing back, the coldness seeping into my pores and taking root in my heart.

His face is right in front of mine, our noses almost touching as his eyes search mine and I hold my breath.

"Bullshit," he whispers. "Does your *boyfriend* who's so easy to love make you moan like that when he fucks you? Does walking around with a stick up your ass acting like you're better than everyone else just like your mother really make you happy? You acted like you'd rather be skinned alive than move around on that dance floor. And don't try to tell me it was because of your dance partner when that goddamn kiss proves otherwise. I remember a woman whose entire face lit up as soon as she heard music. Who could lose herself in dancing and it was the most beautiful fucking thing I'd ever seen in my life. She came alive when she danced and those fucking legs of hers that went on for days defied the laws of gravity."

He holds my stare for a few more seconds until he finally moves away and I can let out the breath I was holding. My bottom lip shakes with the need to scream and cry when he turns from me, grabs the handle of the door, and yanks it open so roughly it slams into the opposite wall.

"You're not happy. Best thing about you right now is that at least you still have the most beautiful damn legs I've ever seen. Too bad you chose to stop using them."

I watch him walk out into the brightly lit hallway and turn toward the double French doors that will lead him out of the house, my body sliding down the wall until my butt hits the ground. My bad leg is straight out in front of me and I bend my good leg, wrap my arms around it, and bury my face in the material of my dress that covers my knee. Eli's parting shot hit its mark right in the center of my chest, breaking off the last remaining pieces of my heart as the memory of another night, one filled with thunder and tears and pain, crashes through my mind.

Chapter 10

Shelby

Six years ago...

Rain.

Thunder.

Lightning.

Flashing headlights blinding my already blurry and puffy eyes from so much crying.

Spinning and sliding through the flooded section of road, the wheel slipping from my hands and turning so quickly I can't hold on.

Screams.

So many screams and I realize they're my own. I can't hold on. I can't stop. Before I squeeze my eyes closed, the sky illuminates outside my window, lighting up the handwritten note resting on the passenger seat and I watch it slide across the leather and onto the floor.

I don't need to see the words to know what they say. I

memorized them and they've been playing on a loop in my head since I got in my car. This car that is careening out of control. This car that he always insisted on driving when I would sneak away and pick him up. This car that he loved because it wasn't flashy and new, but safe and reliable and I paid for it with the money I earned waiting tables. This car that he loved to pull off on a secluded road, pull me over onto his lap, light my body on fire with his hands and his mouth, and whisper in my ear how much he loved me.

The words from the note play on a loop as this car, the one he loved to drive and tell me lies in, spins off the road.

"It was fun while it lasted. I'm in love with someone else. Good luck with your dancing."

Even through the squealing of tires, the crash of metal, the breaking of glass, the words in my head are louder and demanding to be heard.

"It was fun while it lasted. I'm in love with someone else. Good luck with your dancing."

My body jerks and my head hits the side window before that, too, shatters in a shower of glass, and still, the words won't stop.

"It was fun while it lasted. I'm in love with someone else. Good luck with your dancing."

The vehicle finally crashes into something that stops it, but it doesn't stop my side of the car from collapsing in like it's made of a thin piece of paper, pinning me in place. My left leg explodes with so much pain that my screaming grows louder, ringing in my ears as the car hisses and creaks and the remaining few pieces of glass from the windows tinkle down on top of the twisted metal all around me.

I try to move, but I can't. I scream even louder when I feel the burning, the crushing, the stabbing, the agony, shooting from my hip down to my knee. I move my shaking hands to where the pain is and I feel something sharp and hard sticking out of my thigh where it shouldn't be. My hands are immediately covered in warm, wet blood and I choke on my tears and my screams when I realize what I've done.

"It was fun while it lasted. I'm in love with someone else. Good luck with your dancing."

Good luck with your dancing.

Good luck with your dancing.

My screams of pain start to die, right along with my vision... and my dreams.

Chapter 11

Eli

"Get in the car, asshole."

My feet stop in the middle of the turnaround where I've been pacing since I stormed out of the plantation house and away from Shelby thirty minutes ago. I look up to see a sleek, silver BMW idling right in front of me with the passenger window down and an irritated woman leaning over the center console, glaring at me.

"Not in the mood right now, Meredith," I reply as I start to turn away from the vehicle.

"I don't give a shit what kind of a mood you're in. Get in the car."

I hear the locks *click* as she releases them and leans back against her seat, her hands on the steering wheel and her fingers tapping against it while she waits for me to do as she says.

Fucking Meredith Prescott. There was a time when I thought the two of us might be friends when Shelby introduced me to her that summer six years ago. Friends who constantly bickered with each other, insulted each other, and couldn't be in the same room together more than five minutes before we were throwing sarcastic comments around like a baseball, but we had the love of Shelby in common and that always made us try to get along for her sake. It didn't always work, but we tried. I liked that she was so protective of Shelby, even if it sometimes pissed me off when she would make comments about how she'd kill me if I ever broke her heart. Going by the look on her face and her cheerful greeting, she's come to collect on that death threat.

Realizing I'd rather be anywhere than standing in front of this fucking plantation with a woman inside who I can't keep my hands off even when I'm pissed at her, I huff out an irritated breath and stalk to the car, throwing the door open none too gently and climbing inside.

The engine revs and Meredith presses down on the gas before I even get my door closed.

"If you're taking me somewhere to dump my body off a cliff, I came with my brother-in-law and he might get suspicious when I disappear," I inform her, quickly buckling my seat belt as she takes the corner of the turnaround entirely too fast and then opens the car up on the long driveway to the main road.

"Don't worry, I introduced myself to Daniel and told him I'd be giving you a lift home. He was quite pleased he wouldn't have to leave early, so he won't consider you a missing person for at least twelve hours," she tells me with a straight face, her eyes never leaving the road in front of her.

Meredith has no reason to hate me, unless she's still mad about the way I left Shelby all those years ago. But she also knows damn well I explained why I did that in all the letters I wrote to Shelby after I got my head out of my ass. It's clear she's still very good friends with her and is out to right whatever wrong she thinks I might have done.

I clench my hands in my lap thinking about that fucking kiss and how quickly her shock and anger turned to hunger. The softly playing music in Meredith's car quickly reminds me of other kisses, of pulling Shelby's car off the side of the road, turning down the car stereo until it was just background noise and losing myself in her. The wind rushing through the open car windows and ruffling my hair sends me back in time to riding horses with Shelby through the back acres of her family property, tying them up to a tree, and spreading a blanket out on the ground where we could touch and taste and do whatever we wanted to each other without anyone finding out.

I close my eyes as Meredith drives, listening to the quiet sounds of the local jazz station on the radio and feeling the warm Southern air on my face, and I think about how quickly Shelby's body melted into mine tonight and how quickly she opened for me and let me in. She still tasted the same, smelled the same, and kissed the same, pouring everything she felt into me and it messed with my fucking head until I couldn't take it anymore. As soon as I heard that little moan of need vibrating into my mouth, I pushed her away so I could breathe. She always had that power over me. With just a touch of her lips and the feel of her tongue gliding against mine, I forgot everything around me and all I cared about was *her*. Her pleasure, her happiness, her life. A few minutes in a dark room and there I was again, forgetting that the woman I loved no longer existed.

"Care to tell me where we're going at such a high rate of speed?" I question, my eyes flying open and my hand grabbing on to the door handle when she suddenly makes a sharp left-hand turn onto another road.

"Care to tell me why I saw you go into an empty office with my best friend and then, a few minutes later, watched you stomp out of it all pissy and found her in there crumpled on the floor looking like someone just killed her dog?" she fires back.

I don't answer her, not because I'm angry she's calling me on this shit, but because I suddenly have that image of Shelby in my mind and it does something funny to my heart. I want to hate her for what she's become. I want some time to be furious that I had a moment of weakness. I can't do that when Meredith is giving me this image and making me wonder if there really is a little bit of *my* Shelby left inside there somewhere. I can't let that penetrate my brain. I won't allow it, because if it's true, if she really is in there, buried underneath all the similarities to her mother, the things I said to her tonight would be really shitty and that would make me an asshole, just like Meredith called me.

Maybe I *am* an asshole and the things I said were a little out of line, but they were *right*, dammit. She can lie all she wants about how happy she is and how good her life is, but all I had to do was take one look at her to know the truth. She's still here, in the same fucking spot I left her, because it was easier than trying for something more.

Neither one of us says anything else as Meredith continues into downtown Charleston, turning down a familiar road right on the opposite end of town. It's the road my old public high school is on, and the school is the only building located on this stretch of road. A half mile down from the turnoff, Meredith turns into the school parking lot, killing her headlights in the middle of the empty lot and slowing the car down until she finally stops. I notice we're on the south side of the sprawling, one-story brick building and it's pitch dark over here, all the streetlights and spotlights located around the front main entrance, a few hundred yards from where we are now.

Turning my head, I see Meredith's profile in the glow of the dashboard lights as she stares out the front windshield.

"You've been gone a long time, Eli," she says softly, the sound of the idling engine forcing me to lean closer to hear what she's saying.

"I'm glad you're okay, but you've been gone a long time," she says again.

"I think I know how long I was gone, Meredith. I have the scars to prove it."

My hands clench into fists as they rest on top of my thighs, pissed off that I got in the car with her, just to listen to her tell me what an asshole she thinks I am. She has no idea what I went through to get back home. She has no idea the kinds of horrors I saw or lived through. Who the hell does she think she is? I get it. She's Shelby's best friend and she's looking out for her, but give me a fucking break. Shelby doesn't need a guard dog. She seems to be doing just fine in her happy little bullshit life.

Meredith laughs, but it's hollow and there's nothing funny about the serious look on her face as she continues staring at something in the dark out of the front windshield.

"You're not the only one with scars, Eli. And I'll say this again, you were gone for a long time. Maybe you should stop and think about the fact that she thought you were dead for five years. She *loved* you. She gave you *everything*. You broke up with her in a shitty note and then you died without giving her any kind of explanation or closure and she's had to live with those thoughts in her head all this time. You gave her a kind of strength that I never thought possible for her, and then you left and she had to figure out how to pick up the pieces without that strength she so badly needed. I did what I could, Eli, but I couldn't fill up the holes in her heart that your dying left behind," Meredith says quietly, twisting the knife in my heart a little harder as she continues.

"A lot of things happened while you were gone. Things you know nothing about. So before you decide to rip my best friend apart again, maybe you should know about at least one of those things."

Her arm closest to the driver's side door reaches out and she presses a button that turns her headlights back on, flooding the area in front of us with bright light. My heart starts thundering in my chest and my palms start to sweat, but I don't really know why. The image in front of us that is suddenly on display thanks to her headlights makes me cringe. I've seen things like this before, similar displays on high school lawns—a mangled vehicle with a sign warning students not to drink and drive or not to text and drive. An excellent scare tactic for new drivers so they know what could happen if they make stupid choices.

Something about the image in front of me tugs at the back of my mind and my hand blindly reaches for the door handle and I push it open. My eyes never leave the crushed pile of metal and glass as I unfold myself from the car, move around the door, and walk slowly across the asphalt, unable to stop until I'm just a few feet away from the wreckage.

My heart is beating so fast I wonder if Meredith can hear it as she gets out of the car herself and I hear her heels clicking on the ground until she stops right next to me and we both stare at the image in front of us. The car, if you can even call it that anymore, is just a pile of twisted metal with the driver's side door completely collapsed in on itself. I can only assume whoever was driving this thing wrapped it around a tree with the way the vehicle is now in the shape of a U. All the windows are gone, save for a few jagged pieces of glass still attached to the door frames and the roof has been completely peeled back like someone took a can opener to it.

I walk closer, my feet leaving the asphalt and stepping onto grass, my hands starting to shake when I see something stuck to what's left of the back bumper. It's scratched and faded and detaching at the edges but I know what it is. I know what it says and I should know, since I put it there before she left for New York for her audition.

Dance Your Ass Off!

A stupid little bumper sticker I found. A cheesy gift I gave her to make her smile and take away her nerves about her audition. She threw her head back and laughed that beautiful laugh of hers that always made my stomach drop like when you go down the first hill of a roller coaster. She jumped into my arms, wrapped her legs around my waist, and told me it was perfect. Made me walk over to the back of her car, with her still clinging to me, while I slapped it on the bumper. Then I opened the backseat and tossed her inside with a squeal, following right behind, climbing on top of her and getting rid of her nerves another way.

My scalp tingles with sweat and my stomach rolls with nausea as I stare at what's left of the red Honda Civic in front of me. She was so proud of that fucking car that was five years old and had a hundred thousand miles on it when she bought it. And I was so proud of her for refusing to use any of her mother's money to buy it, waiting tables in the next town over so her mother wouldn't know, working her ass off in between preparing for the audition and spending time with me, just so she could save enough to get it on her own.

I hear a noise in the quiet night, and realize it's coming from me. I can't stop the grunt of pain that flies out of my mouth thinking about her being in that car when this happened to it. There's nothing left of that fucking red Honda Civic that I always made her let me drive and always loved pulling off somewhere secluded so I could hear her shout my name and listen to her loudly proclaim how much she loved me. We could do and say whatever we wanted in that car, however loudly we felt like it, without me having to sneak her into the apartment I shared with Kat after she'd gone to sleep or creep into an empty tack room at the stables without anyone seeing us.

"After the accident, the high school called and asked if they could use it for this display. She wasn't drinking and driving or texting and driving or any of that shit, but the car was enough of a mess to get the point across to their students," Meredith tells me quietly.

Being tortured and beaten for five years hurt like a bitch, but this is worse. This hurts deep down into my soul and it feels like someone is reaching into my chest and pulling my heart out with their bare hands.

"When?"

I choke the word out roughly, not wanting to know when or how or why, but unable to stop myself from asking. I feel my body swaying from side to side as I stare at the twisted metal and broken glass and the driver's side door that is so bent it's a wonder she's still standing and breathing.

"The night you left."

Meredith's words hit me like a bullet to the gut and I have to press my hands into my hips and lean forward before I throw up.

"She got the acceptance letter from Montclair Dance Company and the first thing she did was drive to your apartment," Meredith continues, oblivious to me dying inside right next to her while I listen to her talk and hear the words I said to Shelby earlier, screaming through my head.

"Best thing about you right now, at least you still have the most beautiful damn legs I've ever seen. Too bad you chose to stop using them."

"Your sister had no idea what she was doing there, didn't know anything about the two of you. Knew you'd left a letter behind for Shelby and assumed it was a letter of resignation from the stables," Meredith goes on. "Handed that piece of shit good-bye letter over and shut the door in her face. It was raining pretty hard that night, and she was upset. She'll tell you until she's blue in the face it was all her fault. She'd been crying, she wasn't paying attention, she was going too fast, but that's bullshit. There's only one reason she was crying and not paying attention."

Because of me. Because of me and that fucking letter I wrote her. No good-bye, no real explanation, if I wanted my sister to finish college and continue to have a roof over her head, and Shelby to have her dance career, I just had to leave and forget the police report I'd seen. I had to make it so Shelby wouldn't ask questions and she wouldn't try to come after me. Telling her I was in love with someone else was the only way I knew how to guarantee that. The only way I knew for sure that she would hate me and want nothing to do with me, move on with her life, forget about me and have the future she'd always dreamed of.

I'd rather be anywhere but here right now. I'd rather be back in that hellhole getting the shit kicked out of me than standing here in front of the wreckage I made of Shelby's life.

"She hydroplaned, lost control of the car, and slammed into a truck. The force of that collision sent her off the road and slamming into a tree," Meredith explains.

I can hear the tears in her voice and I see out of the corner of my eye as she wipes the wetness off her cheek and continues talking while staring at the car in front of us.

"When she hit the tree, it pinned her leg against the door. They called it a comminuted femur fracture—the bone was broken into more than two distinct fragments," Meredith explains through her tears, which have now turned into full-on sobs as she spits out the words that make me wish I could take back everything I'd said to Shelby.

"You didn't move on, you fucking gave up!"

My knees give out and I fall to the wet grass, pressing my hands into the ground to keep my body up when all I want to do is curl up and die, knowing all the hateful things I said to her.

"Goddammit, how could you throw it all away?"

"Parts of the door broke off, slicing right through her thigh," Meredith continues to speak. "Those parts cut off the blood flow to her leg."

I sit back on my legs and bring my hands up to my face, trying to block out all the images racing through my mind of Shelby driving that car. Shelby crying and upset because of that fucking note I left behind. Shelby losing control and being in pain. Shelby losing *everything* because of me. Because I tried to stand up to her mother and it backfired. Because I wrote her a note and broke her heart, thinking I had no other choice.

"She had two emergency surgeries to fix the artery, and had to wait two weeks before they could try and fix the fracture," Meredith explains through her tears. "For a while they thought they might have to take the leg because it had atrophied so badly. Then, weren't even sure she'd be able to walk again."

> "Best thing about you right now, at least you still have the most beautiful damn legs I've ever seen. Too bad you chose to stop using them."

I claw and clutch at my hair to try and get my words to stop, but they won't go away. I said them to her with such anger and disgust that it sickens me. Even while I said them to her, I saw the devastated look on her face but it didn't register. I just wanted to hurt her because it hurt me so much that I came home and the woman I loved wasn't there.

This is why. This pile of broken metal is why. I left her alone and I left her broken and then I came home and accused her of giving up. She stood there in front of me, so proud and trying so hard not to let it show how much my words must have cut like a knife. My words would have killed her. She wanted to dance more than anything else in this world and I yelled all that stupid shit about throwing it all away. I fucking *yelled* at her.

I hear Meredith move across the grass and I drop my hands from my head as she squats down next to me. Our eyes meet and I'm sure we both have similar looks of grief since I can still see the tears falling down her cheeks and my heart feels like it's breaking in two.

"I know you went through a lot of shit while you were gone," she tells me softly. "Shit I can't even comprehend, and I'm sorry for that. But Shelby went through a lot, too. She's *still* going through a lot, so give her a fucking break. She's excellent at hiding her pain, pretending like she's fine, but she is *not* fine. She is *not* okay. She's going to kill me when she finds out I told you about this, but I don't care. Because she. Is not. Okay. I don't like you very much for what you did to her when you left and I *really* don't like you very much for what you did to her tonight, but I can't keep standing around, watching her do this to herself. Jesus, do you know how hard it is to stand by and watch your best friend just give up? She's the most important person in my life, Eli, and she's killing me. She's breaking my heart."

Meredith quickly swipes at the tears that have fallen down her cheeks as she stands up and I push myself from the ground to stand next to her, both of our eyes moving to the car, even though I know neither of us want to look at it anymore and have to think about what happened inside of it.

"There are things going on in that house that you don't understand. Things *I* don't even understand," Meredith whispers. "I know I shouldn't be such a bitch to you, when I actually have a shoe box full of proof that you really did care about her, but I can't help it. She's my best friend and that's my job. I don't like you very much, Eli, but the only time I have seen any kind of spark in our girl's eye in the last six years was when she was out on that dance floor with you tonight. Get your shit together, quit being a dick to her, and bring her back."

She turns and walks away from me and I hear her car door open and close. I take a few quiet minutes and force myself to continue looking at the car and wish I could go back in time. Wish I could take away all of her hurt and pain and especially take away all the things I accused her of.

I'd go through a thousand more years of hell just to erase this from her life.

I'd die a thousand deaths just to make it so that accident never happened.

With one final glance, I turn and walk back to Meredith's

car and she drives me back to Kat and Daniel's house in silence.

I'll get my shit together and I'll bring her back.

Goddammit, I will bring her back because I can't live in a world where Shelby Eubanks isn't okay.

Chapter 12

Shelby

"You're losing focus, and your little dance tonight in front of all of Charleston forced me into a corner. You have no idea what you've done."

My mother slams a drawer closed, glaring at me over the top of her desk. I refuse to fidget or show her any sign of weakness. I meet her stare head-on as she continues berating me.

"You have no idea how much trouble I went through to bring that man home. I hope you realize that with a snap of my fingers, he can be hauled back to Washington and his involvement in the explosion can still be brought into question again," she informs me.

I've heard these threats a hundred times before. Words meant to scare me and keep me in line. My folded hands resting in my lap start to shake and I squeeze them more tightly together, wishing I could tell her to go to hell, but I can't. I didn't spend all these years stuck under her thumb and miserable just to screw it all up by being defiant now.

"I understand, Mother. It was just a dance. A dance with a veteran, at a charity function *for veterans*," I remind her.

"Don't get smart with me. You have no idea what you've done," she mutters again, shaking her head at me.

I've done nothing but what she's asked of me, again and again, at the cost of my own happiness, but she doesn't care. All she cares about is that Eli didn't give a shit about showing up at one of her charity events. She couldn't stand the idea that he wasn't afraid of her and what she could do to him, and I wish I had *half* of his confidence.

"I'm telling you this for the last time. Stay away from him, or everything I've said will become a reality. Do you understand me?"

I understand you're a cruel human being. I understand just how little you really care about me. I understand you'll do whatever it takes to get what you want, even if it means your only daughter suffers in the process.

"Yes. I understand. Are we finished here?"

I push myself up from the chair in front of her desk without waiting for a reply. I turn and walk away, ignoring her when she says my name as I keep moving right out the door of her office, down the hall into the foyer, and out the front door.

A few hours later, as I stand in the living room of the guest house staring over at the stables, my mother's words won't stop ringing in my ears.

Meredith has been sitting on the couch ever since I walked through the door, grilling me about what happened when she found me in the office and I've tried to brush it off, but she's not buying it. She's not buying anything I've tried to explain away to her since she's been here.

"I don't understand why you won't just talk to me, Shelby," she tells me softly as I turn from the window and look over my shoulder at her.

How can I explain anything to her when she'll never understand? She never liked Eli all that much when we were together and happy, and she definitely didn't like him after he left me that note and I had the accident. Trying to explain to her that I've stayed here in Charleston, never moving forward because of him and the debt owed to my mother, will never fly. She'd want me to pack up all my things and be on the next plane out of here, not because she's controlling like my mother, but because she loves me and would lose her mind knowing all the things I did to protect a man who hurt me.

"There's nothing to talk about, Mer. It's just hard seeing him again when I thought he was gone," I explain, looking away from her and back out the window so I don't have to see the sadness on her face and she won't see the lies on mine.

I didn't tell her about the kiss and I didn't tell her about the things he said to me, but I didn't need to. Meredith could always tell my state of mind just by looking at me. Being curled up on the floor of the office with red, puffy eyes was a dead giveaway that my state of mind was not good. Coming back here to the guest house after listening to a lecture from my mother, to find her waiting up for me on the couch, was even worse. On top of all of this, I've been hit with an onslaught of guilt after that kiss with Eli. I know I didn't instigate it, but I also did nothing to stop it. I lost myself in that kiss, I craved it, and I needed more, knowing full well that I had a boyfriend waiting for me back in the ballroom. A man who loves me in spite of my not being able to return his feelings fully, one who is always there for me and has never broken my heart.

"Is he really worth all of this?" she whispers. "Is he really worth your happiness?"

I try not to jerk in surprise at her words. I've never come

right out and told her my reasons for working for my mother and her hundreds of charities, for starting a relationship with Landry when I kept him at arm's length for so many years. But Meredith is my best friend and she knows there's a reason I suddenly changed my tune on everything I believed in and fought against for most of my life. I know I'm a horrible person for not confiding in her, but I don't know what else to do. How do I tell her I gave up my life for a man who threw me away, just because I know, deep down, he's not a bad person? How do I explain to her that I'm doing everything I'm told for a woman I despise?

I hear Meredith push herself up from the couch and walk across the hardwood floor until she's standing right next to me as I stare off into the distance at the stables.

"I know you loved him and I know you feel like you lost everything after the accident, but you didn't, Shelby. You could have still come to New York. I would have done everything I could to help you find another way to be happy so it didn't come to this," she tells me softly, bumping her shoulder into mine.

I love her for caring about me so much but it kills me at the same time that I can't be honest with her. Meredith is a pit bull and she's protective of me. If she knew the things my mother has threatened me with, the things she's threatened Eli's family with, she'd march out of this house and chew my mother a new asshole. She'd call her father even though she can't stand him and she'd chew *his* ass out for his association with my mother. She'd never be able to keep quiet about something like this and it would ruin everything. My mother would make sure it would ruin everything and then where would I be? I would have sacrificed five years of my life for nothing. She'd ruin Eli and she'd ruin his family and it would all be for nothing.

"You know New York would have never worked if I couldn't dance."

Meredith scoffs and I turn to see her shaking her head.

"You're the only person who thinks you can't dance. When was the last time you tried?" she asks.

"Seriously? I have pins and screws in my bones and half of my thigh is missing. How exactly do you think I'd try?" I fire back, trying to keep the anger out of my voice.

We've had this argument a number of times over the years. She always refused to believe the doctors when they told me I'd never dance again. She always blamed my mother and thought she had something to do with this, but that's one thing I know for sure she didn't touch. I've seen the X-rays, I have copies of the MRIs, and I've met with enough specialists and physical therapists over the years that I know it's impossible. Barely a day goes by without my leg hurting in some way and that's just with me walking around doing office work. I'd never be able to withstand the grueling work of a professional dancer. Meredith knows this and I'm so tired of fighting about it.

I'm so tired of keeping everything inside. I'm so tired of not being able to scream and cry and rage at the unfairness of everything. I'm so tired of being this person who just doesn't care about anything, and after what happened tonight and Meredith's insistence that I talk, I'm finding it harder and harder to keep everything bottled up inside.

"Jesus, will you just get mad at me for once?" she complains, practically reading my mind, throwing her hands up in the air. "Call me a bitch, yell at me, tell me to go to hell. Tell me I'm nosy and annoying and to leave you the fuck alone. Do something, goddammit! I don't know how to help you when you won't let me in! I don't know why you stay in this prison day after day, year after year, doing everything you hate with a woman you can't stand who treats you like shit. I don't know if it's because you feel like you have nothing else and I don't know if for some fucked-up reason it's for Eli...I don't know anything because you won't let me in!"

I bite my lip to keep from crying, refusing to look at her. I should never have asked her to come here. I knew she'd see too much and I knew she'd question everything, trying to get to the bottom of things. I thought just having her here with me would give me strength to get through the days, knowing Eli was alive and home and out of my reach, but I should have known better. All it's done is make me angry and make me hate my life even more than I already did. Seeing myself through Meredith's eyes makes me even more disgusted with myself and thinking about my mother's threats after the party makes me realize nothing will ever change.

After what happened tonight with Eli, the kiss we shared, and how badly his words hurt me, I feel lost. I feel like I'm tumbling around in the ocean in the middle of a hurricane, having no idea which way is up. I hate that with just one kiss, he made me feel alive and made me remember what my life could have been like. I hate that he's making me want to lose control and forget about everything I've done to protect him, just to be close to him again.

"There's no point in getting mad. This is my life and nothing is going to change," I remind her.

"I'm not an idiot, Shelby, so don't play me for one. You called me, in the middle of the night, in the middle of a panic attack, because you needed me. And I'm supposed to, what? Just sit here and watch you throw your life away without doing something? Give me one good reason why? Why should I stand by and watch you keep moving through life not caring about yourself and not caring about your happiness? You know that's not my style. You know I have no trouble telling Georgia to go fuck herself."

My body turns quickly to face her and I wrap my hands around her upper arms, unable to hide the panic on my face.

"Please, Meredith," I beg softly. "Just leave it alone. You have no idea...there are things you don't..."

I falter, knowing I can't tell her without repercussions and wanting to tell her so much at the same time that the words on the tip of my tongue are choking me.

"I knew it," she whispers fiercely, her eyes staring angrily into mine. "She's holding something over you. Something to do with Eli, isn't she?"

I don't say anything, which is probably worse than spitting it all out. Meredith has no trouble reading between the lines.

"I'm going to ask you one more time, and for God's sake, don't fucking lie to me. Is. He. Worth it?"

My chin trembles and I clench my teeth to stop myself from crying.

"He's a good man. I know you don't believe that. I know you saw what his leaving did to me, but that's not who he is. Being a Marine meant everything to him. Fighting for this country meant everything to him, and his sister is his entire world. You don't know him. You don't know what could happen to him if..."

Dropping my hands from her arms, I take a step back and cross my own arms in front of me, knowing I said too much. Knowing that even if I still believe with everything inside me that Eli would never betray his country, I'm still wounded and bruised from the way he left things. It's become even more raw and painful now that he's back and I'm living it all over again. I'm torn between protecting him and wanting to lash out at him for the way he hurt me.

"Is that why you're hiding a tattoo under your watch, on the inside of your wrist?" she suddenly asks, her eyes flickering to my left arm tucked against my stomach. She smiles when my eyes widen in shock and my stomach drops to my toes. "I saw you get out of the shower the other day when I was brushing my teeth. Guess I should have bought you a waterproof watch, huh?"

Meredith sighs, running her hands through her long, dark hair.

"I've seen you run your fingers over the inside band every time your mother speaks to you, every time Landry touches you, and every time you get upset. Now I know why. You gave yourself a permanent fucking reminder."

The ink on the inside of my wrist suddenly feels like it's burning under my skin and I have to clench my hands into fists to stop myself from doing what Meredith so keenly noticed and running my fingertips over the band covering it to put me back on solid ground so I don't feel like I'm spinning out of control. She's right. Touching the inside of my wrist is my own personal safety net. It's a way to remind myself that the life I'm living and the dreams I've had to say good-bye to are for a reason. A very important reason. Something bigger than my wants and needs, my hopes and dreams. I feel guilty that I've kept this from Meredith, but I knew she'd never understand.

"Just so you know, I told Eli about the accident."

The breath I was holding and the guilt I was feeling leave me in a *whoosh*, and I can hear the thundering of my heart in my ears. I have to lock my knees together before I collapse onto the floor and curl myself into a ball, wishing I wasn't hearing these words come out of her mouth. I know I haven't been completely honest with Meredith, but she's the only person in the world I trust, and she betrayed me. She shared something personal about me and she had no right to do that.

"I don't give a rat's ass if you're pissed at me, it needed to happen. I will not allow him to come back here, worm his way into your life, and shit all over you when he doesn't know the truth," she tells me in a low voice. "Maybe you're okay with him thinking you made the choice to end your dance career, but I'm not. I'm not okay with him assuming there's nothing left of the old Shelby in there, fighting to get out. I'm not okay with him ripping you to pieces because he doesn't know what happened to you. I'm telling you right now, I still don't know if I like the guy after what he did to you, but he lost it when I told him. Completely lost it. I've never seen a man so gutted before, knowing he said things to you he shouldn't have and things he couldn't take back. I hope to God he's worth it, because I'm placing all my bets on him. I'm hoping maybe he can get you to pull your head out of your ass and do something about this shitty life you think you deserve or you think you need to keep living to protect him, because it's obvious I can't do that."

With those words, she turns and walks away from me and down the hall, the slamming of the spare bedroom door making me jump, close my eyes, and wish I could just disappear.

* * *

I shouldn't be here.

Every time I walk through this door, I tell myself it will be the last time. It hurts so much to look around this room, see the dust clinging to the floors and the foggy floor-to-ceiling mirrors that haven't been washed in years. I stand in the middle of the hardwood floors, staring at my distorted reflection, and I hate the woman looking back at me.

After Meredith laid it all out for me and stormed off into the spare room, I lost track of time. I stood in front of the living room window, staring over at the stables until the last car of workers from the party had long since pulled away and the main house was shut down for the night.

I don't even remember leaving the guest house. I don't remember walking across the acreage to the stables, and I don't remember unlocking the door and walking into this room, but here I am. The studio always seems to pull me back, even when I don't want to be here. Being here hurts too much. I want to be angry with Meredith for telling Eli about the accident, but I can't. I'm honestly surprised he didn't know, what with the power of Google and all. My mother managed to keep the accident out of national news, but it was plastered all over the front page of Charleston's small local paper for weeks. It was only a matter of time before someone told him or he found out on his own.

I stare into the dirty mirror in front of me and lower my hand to the long, clingy green skirt that hangs down around my ankles, not having the energy or the care to remove the gown from the party before I came out here. I clutch my hand into the material by my thigh and slowly begin lifting it up, exposing my bare feet, my shin, my knee, and finally my thigh. My nose burns with tears and my eyes fill with them as I hold the material of the skirt, bunched into my hands by my hip and stare at my scarred leg. The indents and ripples where once there was smooth skin and powerful muscles are always so shocking to see. My sobs echo around the room as I stare at the image in the mirror, my other hand coming up to my mouth to try and quiet them. There's no point in crying over something you can't change, but I'm unable to stop once I've started. I never look at my leg. Not when I'm getting out of the shower, not when I'm changing...never. What's the point? Why should I stare at something so ugly that I can't fix? Why should I torture myself even more, looking at a piece of my body that used to be so graceful? Remembering how easily I could lift it above my head when now, I can barely walk from the guest house to the stables without it hurting.

I drop my hand from my mouth and, with a closed fist, thump my knuckles against my thigh.

"I hate you," I whisper brokenly.

I force myself to open my eyes and look at the damage. I force myself to remember that it used to be beautiful. It used to be my ticket out of this life and it used to be the one thing Eli loved most about me, so much that he gave me the nickname *Legs*. Now, it's a mangled piece of flesh that hurts when it rains, my mother always demands I keep hidden because no one likes to be confronted with ugliness, and Landry never touches and visibly winces when he gets a glimpse of it.

I smack my closed fist harder against my broken thigh, ignoring the pain on the outside since I'm too consumed with the hurt on the inside.

"I fucking hate you," I sob, staring at my hideous leg through the reflection of the mirror.

My head drops forward as I let myself cry for what I've lost. My shoulders shake and I move my hand from my thigh and press it against my stomach to try and hold the hurt in, but it's no use. It's pouring out of me, dripping down my cheeks and screaming to be let out. My anger and my pain are bubbling right under my skin, clawing to the surface, wanting to be heard.

I feel his presence before my eyes fly up to the mirror and

see his face. His arms wrap around my body from behind and I feel myself being pulled back against his hard chest. I let his strong arms soothe me for just a second...just one moment in time to feel protected and loved, and then I pull away, and unleash everything inside me.

Chapter 13

Eli

As soon as I get back to Kat and Daniel's after my road trip with Meredith, I rush into the office and use their computer to pull up Google. I immediately find a bunch of articles about the accident in the local paper. Seeing the devastation of it in print, reading the truth of the words Meredith spoke to me hurts like a son of a bitch and I have to rub my palm across my chest to ease the ache in my heart.

"Wow, you're an asshole."

Rylan chuckles and I take a few calming breaths instead of turning around in the desk chair and punching him in the face.

"First you manhandle her, then you insult her. She's definitely going to come running back to you now."

I'm now regretting the fact that I shared everything that happened tonight with him as soon as I walked in the door. I shake my head in frustration, sitting down on the edge of the desk and staring at the screen in front of me like the answers will somehow magically appear.

"Fuck off, I didn't know about the accident. Jesus Christ, you should have seen the car. She'll never forgive me for all that shit I said to her," I tell him, clicking away from the article and slamming the laptop lid closed.

"You've got a lot of sucking up to do, man. I know your endgame is to nail Georgia Eubanks's ass to the wall, but is it really worth it to put Shelby through even more bullshit? You said it yourself—she kept you alive when we were in that shithole. For five years you kept fighting the good fight because of her. Sitting here on your ass, feeling sorry for yourself, isn't going to prove that to her. Being a dick because you hate her mother isn't going to make her see what she means to you."

Resting my elbows on the edge of the table, I put my head in my hands and close my eyes, trying not to think about the look on her face when I accused her of giving up.

"She's not even going to let me get close to her after what I said and did, and I don't blame her," I mutter, rubbing my hands down my face and glancing up at Rylan as he pushes off the desk and stands next to me with his arms crossed over his chest.

"Yeah, she's gonna be pissed at you and you need to let her. You need to take it like a fucking man, let her rip you apart, let it hurt like a bitch, and then show her you aren't walking away. Marines don't give up, so stop being a pussy and go to her," he tells me with a pointed glare.

"Since when did you become a fucking love guru?"

"Since I had to listen to you mutter in your sleep for five years about peaches," he says with a roll of his eyes, always finding a way to make light of our situation when it was anything but that.

"Now, get the fuck out of here and give me the laptop. I've got porn to catch up on."

Before I know what's happening, I've snagged Kat's keys from the table by the front door, left Rylan to his porn, and the next thing I know, I'm pulling up behind the stables and walking mindlessly to the hidden room in the back of the building in the middle of the night.

My hands shake as I turn the handle of the door, shocked that it's unlocked. I don't even know why I'm here, torturing myself like this. I push open the door, remembering all the times I've done this before. A few times picking the lock to get inside, and then one day, suddenly finding it open, knowing she wanted me in there. Knowing she liked seeing me in the back of the room, quietly watching her dance. Walking down the narrow hallway, I stick my hands into the front pockets of my tux pants, having left the jacket and tie back in the spare bedroom at Kat's. My feet move faster when I hear a muffled noise in the room at the end of the hallway, stopping abruptly when I get to the doorway and see the cause of the sound.

My eyes quickly take in the state of the studio, dusty and unkempt after what I now know has been years of disuse, and it hurts something deep inside me knowing why it's in this state. My heart thunders in my chest when I see her standing in the middle of the room. Gone is the woman I saw earlier tonight, with her head held high and an elitist air about her. She's still wearing the fancy, body-hugging green gown, the same color as her eyes, and she still looks just as stunning in it as she did earlier in the night. But in the cloudy reflection of the mirrors in front of her, I see her clutching one side of her long skirt up by her hip, her head bent forward and her shoulders shaking with sobs. She presses a hand against her stomach like she's trying to hold herself together and it completely wrecks me. I shouldn't be standing here, watching her in this private moment, but I can't turn away. I deserve to see her so broken and devastated. I deserve to feel the pain of her tears and her hurt after the things I said to her, the things I accused her of.

My feet start moving me through the doorway and across the floor in her direction, my eyes never leaving her reflection in the mirror, bouncing back and forth between her beautiful scarred leg and the misery on her face as she continues to whimper and sob, so painfully that it breaks me in half. My footsteps falter as her body rocks forward and back with the force of her crying and I can't stop my own eyes from welling up with tears, wishing I could take away all of her pain.

I move faster, acting without thinking as I silently wrap my arms around her and pull her back to me, wanting to take every ounce of her hurt and pull it inside me so she no longer has to feel it.

Closing my eyes, I tighten my hold on her, feeling her body shake in my arms, and I just want to go back. I want to go back to the night I wrote that fucking letter, back to the night I walked away from her and make it so it never happened. Make it so she never has to feel even an ounce of the pain that I can feel so acutely as it travels from her body to mine. Right when I open my mouth to apologize, say something—anything—to make this better for her, she yanks herself out of my arms so roughly I stumble forward as she whirls around to face me.

Seeing the pain on her face through a distorted image in the mirror is nothing compared to seeing the stark agony face-to-face as she glares at me with tears streaming down her cheeks.

"I HAVE NOTHING!" she shouts brokenly, dropping the hold she has on her skirt to press her palms against my chest and shove me away.

"It was all I had and now I have NOTHING!" she screams through her tears, shoving against my chest again.

"It hurts! It hurts so fucking much I can't breathe!"

"I know, baby," I choke out, trying not to cry right along with her as she continues coming at me, pushing and shoving me backward.

"I can't stand being in this room, remembering what I used to be, but I can't stop coming here. I can't stop staring in that fucking mirror, wanting it all back so much I can't breathe…I can't breathe," she sobs, her hands dropping from my chest and wrapping around her waist as she bends forward.

Every bit of anger that I felt toward her disappears in an instant. I can't stand seeing her like this. My heart can't handle knowing she's in so much pain and all I can think about is taking it away.

I move in a flash and wrap my arms around her once again. I move one hand up to cup the back of her head, sliding my fingers through her hair and pushing her face against my chest and kissing the top of her head, smelling the scent of peaches that clings to her hair, the smell that got me through so many days and nights and made me want to keep fighting.

"I can't breathe…" she whispers against me brokenly. "I can't breathe."

My body starts swaying the two of us gently back and forth as I hold her and let her cry. I wish I had the words to tell her how sorry I am, but I can't find them as I tighten my arm around her waist, knowing nothing I say will take away her pain. Having her in my arms again, so soft and warm and *real*, feels like a dream that I never want to wake up from. I'm the biggest asshole in the world for loving how she feels against me while she's dying inside.

"I can't even hear the music anymore," she says softly in between gasping breaths when her sobs start to wane. "I used to hear it everywhere I went. I used to hear melodies that weren't even playing, choreograph entire routines without even knowing it was happening, and now, I can't even hear the music and it hurts so much."

I run my fingers through her long, soft hair and continue rocking us back and forth. She's rambling, speaking so quickly and so unlike the fierce woman with an attitude I've encountered the last two times I've seen her that I'm afraid to say anything, afraid to stop her from letting this all out. Finding out what happened to her and realizing how deeply she's kept all of this inside, I know she needs to let it out before it destroys her more than it already has.

"I just want to be able to look at myself in the mirror and not hate everything I see. I hate it. I hate it so much. And I hate myself for feeling like this when you're here, so strong and perfect after what you went through."

I want to laugh at her words. I'm not strong and I'm not perfect. I'm a fucking mess. Moving my hand from the back of her head, I slide it to her cheek and tip her face up so I can look into her eyes. Her skin is so soft under my palm and the flush on her cheeks from crying is so warm against my hand that I have to swallow a few times to find my voice instead of just standing here, holding her face in my hand and forgetting about everything I need to say to her.

"Don't you dare," I whisper. "I'm not strong and I'm not perfect. I'm barely holding on and I'm so sorry. I'm so sorry for what I said to you. I know you, I know you'd never give up, and I never should have said those things to you. You are stronger than you even know."

I stare deeply into her eyes and I pray to God she can hear the truth and conviction in my words. I need her to be okay. I would give anything right now to take away her pain.

She shakes her head at me, and fresh tears fall from her eyes and down her cheeks.

"You came back here for the girl who could dance. The girl who fought to make her dreams come true, and I'm not that person anymore. I don't even know who she is."

I shake my own head in disagreement to her words.

"I was wrong. All of it was wrong, everything I said, and everything I've thought since I saw you again was bullshit and I should have known it the first time I touched you again out there in those stables. I came back here for *you*, Shelby. YOU. Not the dancer. I didn't fall in love with your dancing, I fell in love with *you*. The person *you* are. I don't care if you're not dancing, I don't care about anything but *you*."

She turns her face and presses it against my hand as I pull her body closer, hold her tighter against me.

"I'm not her anymore. I'm not Legs anymore and I never will be," she murmurs with her eyes closed, her breath whispering against my palm.

"I don't need Legs. I just need you," I tell her quietly. "I never should have left you the way I did, but I'm here now, and I'm going to make everything right again."

I feel her stiffen in my arms, and before I can even blink, she's shoving away from me, leaving my arms empty and cold without the feel of her body in them. I watch her swipe angrily at the tears on her face and take a few steps away from me, her eyes narrowing in irritation. The moment of her letting down the wall she's built up around her and letting me in has passed and it fucking hurts. I can see it written all over her face that she regrets having even one minute of weakness with me. I feel raw and vulnerable and pissed off that she's dismissing me so easily.

"Don't shut down on me, Shelby, please," I beg softly.

"That shouldn't have happened," she says with a shake of her head, gesturing between the two of us. "It's this damn room. It makes me emotional and I...I'm with someone else, Eli. You need to understand that and just stop. I don't need you to comfort me and I don't need you to think you need to make it all better. You can't. Just let it go and move on."

She moves to walk around me and I quickly reach out and grab her arm to stop her from leaving.

"Bullshit," I argue, watching her eyes widen with even more anger. "You can't just give me something like that, let down your walls and let me see you, and then pull away like it's no big deal. You can't kiss me back like you did in that fucking office tonight and then tell me you don't need me and you don't still want me. I can't leave you alone and I can't move on because you're *everything* to me. You always have been and you always will be, and I know damn well you feel the same, even if you want to stand here, look me right in the fucking eyes, and lie to me."

She pulls harder against my hold on her arm, but I refuse to let go. I hate that she's hurting and I hate that I'm the cause for all of it, but I'm not about to let her leave and pretend like what she gave me when I had her in my arms just moments ago wasn't real.

"I don't give a shit if you're with someone else, he'll never love you the way I do. He'll never fight for you the way I do and he'll never fucking *see* you the way I do!" I shout, knowing the words I say will piss her off and not caring one fucking bit about it. I want her fired up. I want her to get angry and let go and prove my point that she hasn't moved on any more than I have.

"I'm standing here in this room, alive and breathing and

fighting because of YOU! Because in between the torture and the beatings and the fucking hell, year after year, I couldn't get you out of my head. I didn't WANT to get you out of my head. Your smell, your smile, your laugh, your taste, your touch…it's the only fucking thing that made me want to wake up every damn day and go through that shit again and again. Thinking about you and fighting to get back to you is the only way I could fucking survive, so don't stand here and tell me to move on! Don't fall apart in my arms and then lie to me!"

"YOU LEFT!" she screams at the top of her lungs, finally giving me what I want and I quickly realize Rylan was right. She's going to rip me apart and it will hurt like a bitch.

"You left me here because you were in love with someone else and then you died! I mourned you and I can't do this again! I'm sorry! I'm sorry for what happened to you and I'm sorry you came back here for nothing but you need to listen to me and just GO! Just leave and move on with your life and forget about me!"

Her body shakes with anger and I know I shouldn't push this any further, but I can't stop. She needs to understand and she needs to stop pretending.

"I lied, Shelby! Jesus, you have to know it was all a lie. You have to know after those months we spent together that there never was and never will be anyone else for me. You know I never would have left you if I felt like I had another choice," I tell her, not wanting to get into everything about her mother and upsetting her more, but it's the only way I know how to apologize. It's the only way I know how to make her see that I felt like I didn't have any other option and get through to her.

"You had a choice!" she shouts, tossing her hands in the air in frustration. "ME! I was your fucking choice and you threw it away with that goddamn note! You couldn't even be honest with me. Is that supposed to make me feel better? After everything I gave you, everything I shared with you... you couldn't even be honest! You always had a choice and you chose wrong! I would have done ANYTHING for you, Eli. So no, you didn't know me at all. You left without a fight because you were in love with someone else and now you're back, wanting everything to be the way it was and I can't do that. I can't go back there. I can't be here with you, I can't erase everything that's happened since you left. Just GO. Leave me alone and let me live my life!"

I stalk closer to her and she moves backward again, trying to put distance between us, but I'm not going to let her. I did what Rylan said, I let her have her moment to be hurt and give me hell for what I did to her, but I'll be damned if I let her walk away thinking any of this shit is true. We both keep moving until her back hits the mirrors behind her and she has nowhere else to go. Bringing my hands up, I smack them against the glass on either side of her, caging her in.

"I will never forgive myself for leaving you, Shelby. EVER. I'll never forgive myself for the part I played in what happened to you," I tell her, leaning closer and softening my voice even though I want to scream right back at her and make her fucking hear what I'm saying and believe it.

"I lied to you in that note, I made a mistake, and I spent six fucking years wishing I could go back and do it differently. Wishing I could touch you and hold you and tell you I love you, take back every stupid decision I made that took me away from you, but I can't do that. Don't stand here and tell me I didn't fight for you, when we both know I fucking did. It might have taken me a few weeks, but I fought for you, dammit! I wrote you, every day for three months when I got to Afghanistan and woke the fuck up. Every goddamn day I wrote to you and I apologized and I begged for you to forgive me and you didn't. I take full responsibility for the shitty way I left things and how much I hurt you, but don't you dare stand here and lie to my face, telling me I didn't fight," I argue. "I wrote to you, every day, and I fought for you, every fucking day, for MONTHS!"

She moves quickly, bending down and sliding out from under my arms, shaking her head at me as she goes.

"I don't believe this," she mutters. "Are you seriously *Notebook*-ing me right now? You are UNBELIEVABLE!"

Now it's my turn to shake my head, having no idea what the fuck she's talking about.

"You have a lot of nerve. And you're calling ME a liar? You didn't write me any letters. You're just saying that because you came back here and can't get what you want, saying whatever you can to make me give in."

"Look, I don't know what notebook you're talking about and I don't give a shit. I'm telling you I tried to fight for you and you didn't respond. But it doesn't fucking matter. I didn't give up then and I'm not about to give up now. I don't care about the letters, I don't care if you threw them away or burned them or you want to pretend like you never got them. I'm here and I'm not going anywhere, so get that through your head!"

She turns away from me, stalks across the room, and I let her go, knowing she's done listening to me and realizing I need to stop while I'm sort of ahead before this escalates even more and I completely lose my footing. I have no problem letting her leave right now and be pissed at me. Having her pissed and angry is much better than having her indifferent and pretending like she doesn't care. If she didn't care, everything I'm feeling would be a waste of time and energy. Every regret and every broken piece of my heart wouldn't mean a damn thing.

"Go away! Take your lies and your fucking Ryan Gosling references and shove them up your ass!" she finishes, rounding the doorway and moving out of sight.

I chuckle to myself when I hear the door slam shut at the end of the hallway outside the studio. I have no idea who Ryan Gosling is and what he has to do with what just happened here, but I don't care. She just proved to me that she hasn't moved on, no matter how hard she tried to convince me otherwise, and there's no way I'm giving up now. At least my therapist will be happy I've found a hobby.

Chapter 14

Shelby

I'm sorry, I should have told you."

Slamming a folder full of e-mails down on the desk in my small office in the guest house, I look up at Landry and glare at him.

"You're damn right you should have told me!" I fire back, watching Landry's eyes widen in shock.

I never curse in front of him. I've never even raised my voice in his presence, and going by the look on his face, he has no idea what is going on.

"It's bad enough ninety percent of my communication with my mother is done via her assistants through e-mail. You knew what she was planning to do for a week and you didn't say one word to me. I thought we were friends, Landry."

The shock on his face is immediately replaced with hurt and I know I should feel bad and want to take the words back, but I don't and I can't.

"*Friends?* Really, Shelby? I'm pretty sure we're more than friends," he tells me, moving farther into the room to stand directly on the other side of the desk.

He rests his hands on top of the polished wood and leans forward, his voice getting softer.

"What is going on with you lately? You're acting differently, you're dressing differently, you're speaking to me in a way I've never heard before, and you flinch every time I come near you."

I reach down deep inside me to find the part of myself that should feel upset and guilty, but all I find is anger and the only part of his speech I zone in on is about how I'm dressing differently and it pisses me off.

Pushing the computer chair back, I stand up and round the desk until I'm standing right next to him. I tap the foot of my left leg against the hardwood floor, the sound echoing around the room, daring him to look down at my leg and wince. For years I've never worn skirts unless they went well past my knees, or I've done away with them altogether and chosen tailored dress slacks to hide my scars. Ever since my fight with Eli a few days ago, I've worn nothing but skirts. Sure, they're not super short or indecent. They still cover most of my scar, the hems stopping a few inches above my knee so only a hint of the bottom of my scar shows, but it's still out there, for anyone to see.

That damn fight with Eli broke apart something inside me, and now I can't get a handle on it and pull it back inside. I can't calm my nerves, I can't tamp down my anger, and I don't want to hide.

Landry's eyes never leave my face even though I'm standing here, silently daring him to look down. Trail across my body until he notices the scar and makes his usual grimacing face of disgust. I want him to do it. I want him to give me a reason to lash out even more and I'm not even sorry for feeling this way. I try to remind myself that he's a decent man and he's good to me, but it's not working. All I see when I look at him right now is a sad little puppy who does everything my mother tells him, using her popularity and my father's past political connections to get his seat in the state senate. He doesn't defend me, he doesn't stick up for me, and he never disagrees with any decision she makes, including the most recent one of taking me off all the charity boards, removing me from almost all of my duties, and basically demoting me to being a receptionist answering the phones for the next few weeks.

"I don't want to leave for this campaign tour fighting with you, Shelby. Talk to me. Tell me what's going on?" Landry asks softly, resting his hand on my shoulder, his eyes still firmly glued to my face like he has to physically force himself not to look down.

I want to tell him that I'm itching for a fight and he won't give me one. The louder I get, the more placating his smile becomes and the softer his voice gets. Where something like this used to put me at ease and make me feel safe and cared for, now it just makes me want to grab on to handfuls of my hair and tug on it until my eyes water from the pain. I want to scream even louder, curse even harder, and stomp my foot like a toddler throwing a temper tantrum. I don't do any of this and I don't say anything I want to say. I take a deep breath and a step back away from him, forcing his hand to drop from my shoulder.

"My mother just basically fired me and you're honestly asking me what's wrong?"

Landry lets out a big suffering sigh and I can't stop myself from rolling my eyes.

"She didn't fire you. She's giving you a little break to

get your head on straight. We've all noticed how stressed you've been lately. This campaign is very important to me, you know that, Shelby. Your mother has worked hard to help me get here and she just wants to make sure you're taking care of yourself. Giving you some time off so you'll be raring and ready to go to be back on my arm for the media when I get home in three weeks," he informs me with a smile.

Bullshit, I want to scream right in his face. My mother's e-mail this morning had nothing to do with making sure I was okay or looking out for my well-being. It was all about making sure I took this time to remember what's at stake and make sure I made it loud and clear to Eli that he needs to stay far away from me. Knowing Landry would be out of town and I wouldn't have to continue lying to him about what's going on with me meant in her mind that I would have plenty of free time to get my life sorted and back on track.

"I still have a few hours before my flight leaves," he informs me quietly, moving back into my personal space and pressing his hands on either side of my face. "Meredith is gone for the day and I don't have to worry about her giving me dirty looks or attitude. We have plenty of time to test out the bed in your new room."

I have to bite down on my bottom lip to stop myself from laughing at his suggestion.

God, I'm such a bitch.

He's trying so hard to be smooth and seductive and it's just falling flat. Especially after I woke up this morning covered in sweat, the tail end of a dream about Eli and one of the many times we had sex leaving me feeling needy and wanting to burrow myself deeper under the covers and touch myself until I came. I stand here looking up into Landry's blue eyes and all I see are bright brown eyes staring back at me. I feel his smooth, soft hands on my face and all I can think of are rough, hard ones against my skin. Why can't I just let go of the past and look forward to a future with this man? I hate that I can't just open up my heart to him and give him everything he deserves.

I've done nothing but think about Eli since I stormed away from him in the studio. I've done nothing but replay that entire interaction, wondering what the hell happened. I let him hold me. I let him comfort me, and I let him have it. I let him have all of my pain and misery and he just stood there and took it...until he didn't and he fought back. I made a mistake and I tried to fix it. I tried to push him away and I tried to make him believe I'd moved on. I tried to protect him the only way I knew how, but he wasn't buying it and then he made up some bullshit lie about letters he wrote me and that just fired me up even more.

I stand here looking at Landry, so good and kind, and his eyes shining with love for me. When all I want to be doing is standing in the middle of my studio, fighting with Eli, I know I can't do this anymore. I know I can't continue to hurt Landry like this anymore.

"I think we need to take a break," I blurt out, before I lose my nerve.

Landry laughs, but the smile on his face quickly dies when he sees I'm not joking.

"What are you talking about?" he asks with a disbelieving shake of his head, his hands falling from my face.

"I care about you. I really do, but—"

He lets out a small laugh of annoyance, cutting me off as he takes a step back from me.

"Don't. Don't even finish that sentence with, *It's not you, it's me.*"

Thankfully, I hear the front door open and Meredith

shouts my name, saving me from saying the exact clichéd statement Landry knew I was about to speak.

Landry tries to hide his disappointment when he hears Meredith come back from shopping and interrupt us, and I try to hide my excitement that my best friend always seems to have the perfect timing.

"You're serious, aren't you?" Landry asks.

"I'm sorry. I'm so sorry," I whisper.

My stomach churns, knowing I'm hurting a good man, but I have no other choice. I can't keep doing this to him. I can't keep stringing him along, giving him hope that someday I'm going to return all of the love he has for me. I truly believed that eventually my feelings for him would grow, but now that Eli's back, I know that's never going to happen.

Landry doesn't say anything else; he just turns and walks away.

The only thing I can feel as I watch him walk through the doorway is relief. I no longer have to pretend like I'm a meek, quiet woman who always does as she's told. I no longer have to worry about Landry's feelings while I figure out a way to make Eli take back everything he said and change his mind. As badly as I want him to fight for me and prove to me that he really never fell in love with someone else, as much as I'm dying inside for him to touch me and argue with me, I can't let that happen. I have to keep him safe, and pushing him away is the only thing I can do to accomplish that.

* * *

I've lost track of how many times this week I've given in to yet another sleepless night, tossed back my covers, and quietly made my way across our land to the stables. Tonight is no different. At three o'clock in the morning, I'm standing in front of Ariel's stall, using my fingernails to scratch the white diamond shape in her fur right between her ears on her forehead. I avoided going into the studio to feel sorry for myself and came right down the main hall to my favorite horse, feeding her sugar cubes and muttering to her about how stupid I am.

Her response is a snort and the jerk of her head as she cranes her neck toward the hand I have resting on the gate by her chest, looking for more sugar.

I've come out here in the middle of the night, after all the stable workers have gone home, hoping to see Eli sneaking around somewhere inside. I keep telling myself I'm only doing this so I can tell him once and for all to move on with his life and leave me alone, but I know that's not true. I'm out here for one reason and one reason only—I want to get close to the fire. I want to fight with him and yell at him and feel alive and I don't care how badly I get burned. I want to tell him I tore apart my mother's office earlier tonight, looking for those stupid letters he claims he sent me, wondering if maybe she intercepted them and hid them from me, and tell him I didn't find a single one. I want to see if he'll keep going with that lie just to make me feel bad and to try and pull me back in under his spell.

It's stupid and it's pathetic, because I'm already under it. He cast that net around me through the television screen the day I found out he was still alive and there wasn't a damn thing I could do to stop it. Everything inside me is at war, screaming at me to be careful, to protect him and get him as far away from me as possible, while at the same time, craving his touch and his lips on my skin and longing to hear him tell me again that he's going to fight for me.

A loud *thud* sounds from behind me and down the hall,

making my head jerk back to look over my shoulder in the direction it came from. I hold my breath and wait for another noise, hoping to God one of the workers isn't still here. In my haste to get out of my bed and head to the stables, I didn't bother throwing on a robe or covering myself up. I'm wearing a pink ribbed tank top with no bra and an old pair of gray cotton boy shorts left over from my dancing days. I've never walked out of the house in something like this, something that puts the scars covering my leg on full display, but it's the middle of the night and I figured no one would be here.

My heart beats faster when I hear the sound again, followed by a strangled cry. Turning away from Ariel, I walk toward where it came from, pushing my bare feet up onto my toes as I go so I can move as quietly as possible. Stopping outside the closed tack room door in the middle of the long hall, I try to calm my racing heart as I stand here waiting for another noise. The silence on the other side of the door lasts long enough for me to wonder if I was hearing things and I drop my hand from the wood and start to move away, when a sound even louder and more painful rips from the other side and makes me jump.

Without thinking, I quickly grab the handle and fling the door open, stopping in the doorway when I see what's inside.

With just the light of a small, antique lamp on a table in the corner of the room, I see someone lying on the hard, cement floor, curled up in a ball, wearing nothing but a pair of low-slung black cargo shorts with his naked back to me. A back that is littered with long, white scars, old burn marks, and other signs of abuse that bring tears to my eyes as soon as I see them.

"NO! LEAVE ME THE FUCK ALONE!"

I gasp when I hear Eli's tortured voice shout from underneath his arms, which he has wrapped around his head. For a minute, I think he knows I'm standing here and he's yelling at me, but I quickly realize he must be dreaming. His body starts to jerk and he curls himself up into an even tighter ball as he continues to shout and curse at something unknown.

"FUCK YOU! HIT ME AGAIN! I'M NOT TELLING YOU ANYTHING!"

Every thought I've had the last few days flies from my mind as I listen to him yell, watch him tuck his body in on itself, and continue to make slight jerking movements like he's being repeatedly hit or kicked by whoever he's dreaming about. Every irritation I have with him, every vow I made to push him away and be pissed at him for lying about those stupid letters, flies right out of my mind, knowing his dreams aren't fantasy. They're real, they're memories, and even in sleep he can't let go of what was done to him. Seeing him like this, watching him relive something so horrific and awful that he experienced every day for five years makes me forget everything. It makes me sick to my stomach that I yelled at him, pushed him, and did anything but speak to him with a soft, caring voice and shower him with the love and kindness that he missed out on for so long.

"FUCK YOU, YOU PIECE OF SHIT!"

His voice comes out strangled and full of so much pain that it almost brings me to my knees. I move quickly across the room, dropping down on my knees behind him and bringing my hand up to his back, pressing it softly against his warm skin so I don't startle him. I just want him to wake up. I want this nightmare to end. I can't stand seeing and hearing him in so much pain.

"Eli, wake up," I whisper softly, trying to keep the tears out of my voice as I rub my hand in small circles against his spine.

I barely get the words out when he suddenly twists his body, vaults up from the floor, and tackles me. My back slams into the cold, hard ground and I feel the wind get knocked out of me when his body falls on top of mine, pinning me to the floor. He quickly grabs my arms when I try to push against his chest, wrapping both of my wrists tightly in one hand and yanking them up over my head to hold them above me. I gasp and cough as I struggle against him until I'm finally able to drag in air. My eyes fly up to his face, and even though it's covered in shadows from the dimly lit lamp over in the corner, I can see the whites of his wide open eyes. They stare at my forehead, unblinking and unseeing. He's still asleep even though his eyes are open. He doesn't see me, he doesn't know it's me he just took down like a linebacker, the sting from hitting the ground still radiating up my spine as I tug on my arms to try and get them free.

"Fuck you," he growls under his breath, his eyes still staring at my head.

I know those words aren't meant for me, but they still break something apart inside me, knowing he's lost in a nightmare and he's angry and hurting. I want to touch his face, slide my fingers through his hair, and make him look at me, but I still can't get my arms free. I need to wake him up and get him to look at me and see me.

"Eli, wake up," I whisper again. "It's me, it's okay."

He growls again, low in his throat, as he pushes the full length of his body harder against mine, making it unable for me to even wiggle or move an inch to get out from under him.

The only part of my body I can move is my head. I lift it up and lean it forward until my lips are right by his and I speak softly against his mouth.

"Wake up, Eli. It's me. It's Shelby."

He grunts in pain, the grip he has on my wrists getting tighter as he continues to hold them in place above my head.

I crane my neck and press my lips to his, holding them there for a few seconds before pulling back just enough so I can look into his eyes. They've moved away from my forehead and are staring right at me as he blinks and tries to focus.

"It's me," I whisper against his mouth, closing my eyes and praying that I can get through to him. "It's Shelby. It's me, it's me, it's me."

I repeat myself quietly over and over, doing whatever I can to soothe him with words since I can't do it with my hands.

He starts to loosen his hold on my wrists and I open my eyes to find him still looking at me, this time much clearer than before, but still wary.

"It's me," I whisper one last time, tipping my chin down to rest my forehead against his lips, my heart finally beating normally instead of racing inside my chest.

"Goddammit," he mutters under his breath against my forehead as he finally lets go of my arms.

I quickly bring them down and press them to his cheeks as I move my head back and look up into his eyes.

"I'm sorry. Jesus Christ I'm so sorry," he curses brokenly, his eyes rapidly moving all over my face as I rub my thumbs against his cheeks.

One of his hands glides over my shoulder and down my side, sliding under my back and pulling me against him as he continues to look at me and check to make sure I'm okay.

"I'm fine. I'm okay," I reassure him quietly. "Are you all right?"

I watch his Adam's apple bob as he swallows thickly and shifts his body on top of mine, making me suddenly aware of how little clothing I'm wearing and how good it feels to have him on top of me now that I know he's okay and wide awake. My legs part just enough for him to fit perfectly between my thighs as I bring my knees up, hugging them on either side of his hips and cradling him against me.

"Did I hurt you?" he asks, ignoring my question about his own well-being.

I can see the worry clouding his eyes as he stares at me, his arms tightening around my body, holding me close to reassure himself that I'm okay. I shake my head as my thumb traces gently across the thin, raised scar that runs down the side of his face, wishing more than anything that my thumb were a magic eraser that could take away all of the marks those animals left behind on his skin and in his memories.

"Why were you on the floor? Did you fall off the cot?"

Even as I ask him this question, I know the answer. When I first walked into the room, the cot he was lying next to still had the folded squares of blankets and sheets with a pillow resting on top of the pile, right in the middle of it. The cot and extra bedding are kept in here for whenever we have a sick horse or one in labor and a stable hand needs to stay close by to keep an eye on things. A cot that Eli obviously never touched when he came in this room.

"I just…I don't sleep well in a bed. I'm not used to having a mattress and blankets and I know it sounds stupid, but it's easier to fall asleep on the hard ground," he explains, breaking my heart in two, thinking about the conditions he lived in for five years. "I couldn't get comfortable at my sister's house tonight and I couldn't sleep. I went for a drive and wound up here."

Gone is the urge to fight with him and the need to do whatever I can to push him away. All I want to do right now is soothe his pain, any way that I can. Replace all of his bad memories with good ones, and selfishly, let him do the same for me.

"I hate what they did to you," I murmur. "I hate that you have these memories and you can't get rid of them. I don't want you to hurt like this."

His arm suddenly slides out from behind my back and I wonder if I said something wrong. I wonder if he thinks I pity him or I feel sorry for him. I never want him to think that. I never want him to think he's anything less than a strong, amazing man who went through hell and back. Before I can get those words out, apologize for saying something stupid, I feel his palm slide across my hip and down my bare thigh. My eyes squeeze closed when I realize where his hand is going and I try to stifle a sob when I feel his palm run down the length of my left thigh.

"Don't," I warn him, my voice cracking with the words and my eyes stinging with tears. "Please, don't look at it."

His hand continues to move gently, up and down the scarred flesh, and I force myself to open my eyes even though I'd rather see anything right now than the disgusted look I know will be on his face.

I can't stop the sob that flies out of my mouth when he pushes his body slightly away from mine and I watch him look down at his hand still moving across my thigh. There's no disgust, there's no wince of revulsion, there's just Eli, staring softly down at my mangled leg like it's the most beautiful thing he's ever seen.

"I don't want you to hurt either, Shelby," he tells me softly as I feel a tear escape from my eye and drip down to my ear. "I don't want to talk about my shit or those stupid fucking dreams. Not right now. Right now, I just want to be here with you and forget about everything else."

His eyes come up to meet mine while his hand continues

to caress my thigh, sliding it behind my leg just enough to pull it up and hook it over his hip.

"I just want to forget," he whispers.

I should push him away. I should get out from underneath his body, come up with something to say to him to get him to walk away, get him to be angry with me and not want anything to do with me, but I can't. I'm completely powerless when he's touching me like this and looking at me like this and speaking to me so softly, begging me to help him forget the memories that haunt him while at the same time wanting him to take away my own nightmares.

I should push him away... but I can't. I won't. I would do anything for Eli, anything he asks, and that includes breaking myself wide open and letting him see all of my scars, inside and out.

Chapter 15

Eli

The nightmare still sits right at the edge of my mind. It reaches its claws out to try and pull me back in, make me angry, make me hurt, and make me lash out, but touching Shelby, looking down into her emerald green eyes, and having her soft, warm body underneath mine, pushes away the angry voices, the cut of a knife, the burn of a cigar, the smell of death, and the punch of a fist farther away until all that's left is *her*.

Her hands on my face.

Her breath on my lips.

Her voice in my ear.

Her sweet smell of peaches in my nose.

I bury my face into the side of her neck and breathe deep, forgetting about the smell of packed dirt, soiled clothes, grimy skin, and death.

My hand continues gently caressing Shelby's scarred thigh and I hear her sharp intake of breath and feel her swallow nervously against my lips as I press them to her throat.

"It's ugly," she whispers softly, her voice cracking with emotion.

Pulling my mouth away from her neck, I move my head back to stare down into her eyes, watching as silent tears fall out of them, trailing down her temples and off into her hair that's spread out on the floor behind her. I don't want her to cry any more than I want to remember that fucking dream. It pisses me off that someone has made her feel like any part of her isn't stunning. It hurts everything inside me to see that the strength I fell in love with all those years ago has been chipped away and left her feeling embarrassed and broken.

I want her to know she's the most beautiful woman I've ever met and I want her to see the same beautiful strength in her scars that I do. I know we have a lot to talk about and that should probably be the first priority, but I don't want to talk. I don't want to think...I just want to feel something other than scared and always on edge.

I move quickly, wrapping my arms around her body and pulling her with me as I get up to my knees and then twist my legs out under her until I'm sitting up with her straddling my thighs and her ankles locked together behind my lower back. With one arm wrapped tightly around her small waist, I press the palm of my free hand flat against her thigh once again and let my thumb trace gently over the scars.

"Nothing about you could ever be ugly, Shelby," I tell her softly, my hand moving up her thigh until my fingers skirt under the edge of her tiny little gray shorts.

Her breath hitches again as I slowly inch my fingers under the cotton material, the sound different than the one previously that was filled with sadness and fear. I'd know *this* sound anywhere. It's one I heard in my dreams for six years and one I would have died a thousand deaths to hear again. The tips of my fingers come in contact with bare flesh between her legs and I hear it again, the intake of breath coming from Shelby making my heart beat faster and my dick harden in my cargo shorts. This sound isn't full of anxiety or grief. It's a surprised gasp of want and need. I watch as her eyelids lazily drop and her lips part with a soft exhale of breath as my fingertips move with a featherlight touch over the lips of her sex.

Shelby's hands clasp together behind my head and I lean forward until our lips are almost touching, my fingers continuing to trace over her warm, wet flesh, teasing her until she starts to squirm against me.

"You have no idea how many times I've dreamed of this," I whisper against her mouth. "Touching you, feeling you, wanting you... it's the only thing that kept me going."

She moans softly when I speak, her hips jerking forward as my fingers continue to tease. I don't want to push her. I don't want anything to happen that she doesn't want or before she's ready. Even though I can feel her need against my fingers and can hear it in each gasp and whimper, I want her to say the words. I want her to tell me she needs this as much as I do.

"I missed you. I missed *this*," I mutter softly. "Tell me what you want, Shelby."

Holding my fingers still against her, I move my arm from around her waist and slide my palm up her spine and under the fall of her hair against her back. Clutching a handful of it at the nape of her neck, I tug gently until her eyes open to meet mine.

"I can't... this isn't... we shouldn't..."

Her protests are stuttering and weak, trailing off as she tightens her legs around my waist and shifts her hips forward again until I feel like I might go crazy by squeezing the muscles in my arms so tightly to keep myself from pushing inside her.

"I don't give a shit about *can't* or *shouldn't*," I whisper fiercely, tightening my hold on her hair before I do something stupid and plunge inside her without hearing the words just because I want it so much. "You make everything good again. Let me give you the same. Just one moment where we can forget about everything but *this*."

"Tell me what you want," I state again.

I hold my breath, moving my fingers the slightest bit to remind her what I can give her if she just says the words.

"You," Shelby finally breathes against my mouth. "I just want you, Eli."

She barely gets my name out before I move, pulling her mouth against mine and pushing my fingers inside her at the same time. Her lips immediately part with a gasp and I slide my tongue against hers as she rocks against my hand.

The taste of her, the feel of her...it's like coming home and I never want it to end. Everything about this moment is so familiar I can almost fool myself into believing I didn't spend six years without it. I can almost make myself believe I spent the last seventy-two months kissing her, touching her, making her moan and having the heat of her wrapped around my fingers instead of what actually happened. Pumping my fingers slowly in and out of her, brushing my thumb back and forth over her clit and swallowing her moans as she grinds herself against my hand, erases every thought from my mind but *her*.

Giving her pleasure.

Taking away her pain.

Healing her the same way she heals me just by whispering my name.

I forget about the time we spent apart. I forget about all the things left unsaid between us, all the uncertainty and hurt and apologies still needed, and focus only on this moment, right here. I never thought I would have this again. I thought I would die without ever touching her again and I'm not going to waste one second thinking about all the time we lost or letting anything ruin this perfect moment of having her back in my arms.

She pulls her lips from mine and sighs my name again, closing her eyes and letting her head tip back as she continues rocking her lower body in the same slow rhythm as the movement of my fingers in and out of her wet heat. I press my mouth to the soft skin right below her jaw and feel her pulse beating quickly under my lips. I slide my thumb faster against her, wanting nothing more than to feel her come apart and hear her lose control.

Her hips thrust harder, pushing my fingers as deep as they'll go, taking what she wants and racing toward what she needs. It's the hottest thing I've ever felt and I squeeze the fistful of her hair I'm still clutching until she brings her head back up so I can see her face.

"That's it, baby. Let me feel you," I mutter, watching the skin of her chest flush with need as she rocks her body faster, pants my name with each exhale of breath, and wraps her arms tightly around my shoulders, pulling me closer.

She throbs around my fingers and it feels like heaven. She whimpers as she gets closer to the edge and it's the most beautiful sound in the world. The weight of her on top of my thighs is something I've missed for far too long. I want to bottle up this moment and take it with me wherever I go. I want to spend the rest of my life giving her pleasure and taking away her pain.

"You're so fucking beautiful," I murmur, watching her

eyes flutter open, staring down into my own to see the truth of what I just said.

Letting go of the hold I have on her hair, I slide my palm back down her spine and wrap my arm around her body, holding her chest tightly to mine as I continue working my hand between her legs, touching her exactly how I know she likes.

I push deep and hold my fingers still inside her, curling them and pressing my thumb harder against her clit as she explodes, shouting my name and riding her release against my hand. I press my lips to hers and memorize everything about this moment until it's burned into my brain and stamped onto my heart.

She takes away my pain.

She erases all the bad memories.

She makes everything good again and I never want this feeling to end.

As her body jerks in my arms and the movement of her hips slows with the end of her orgasm, I realize that the speed in which she just came fills me with equal parts amazement, jealousy, and anger.

Amazement that she still craves me so much that she can't hold back and that I still know how to touch her to make her fall apart so quickly.

Jealousy that someone else had the privilege of touching her like this while I was gone.

Anger that he obviously doesn't appreciate the gift he has and doesn't know what the fuck he's doing since I made her get off in record time.

Which brings me right back to amazement. She's so perfect and beautiful when she lets go and trusts me to take care of her. After all this time, after all the hurt that lies between us...even if she wants to deny it, at least she still trusts me with this.

Shelby closes her eyes and rests her forehead against mine, trying to catch her breath and slow the rapid thump of her heart I can feel beating against my own. Even though I want to keep a piece of myself buried inside her for eternity, I move my hand from between her legs and wrap my arm around her body with the other one that still holds her tight.

Neither one of us says a word and she doesn't make a move to push me away or get off my lap. I silently wish the morning sun that begins to rise and the rays that start to shine through the window behind us would go away. I know as soon as the full light of day gets here, this moment will be broken and the reality of what just happened will come crashing back to Shelby, so I take what she's giving me now and enjoy it.

No matter what happens next, I will do all that I can to prove to her she can trust me with *everything* again, including her heart. I'll make her forget about the douche bag who hasn't taken care of her and doesn't deserve her and I'll make her remember that this is where she belongs and where she was always meant to be.

Chapter 16

Shelby

Will you stop pacing. You're making me dizzy," Meredith complains as I pause from taking another loop around my living room and glare at her.

I've done nothing but walk in circles, muttering to myself about how stupid I am, ever since I walked through the door of the guest house thirty minutes ago at the crack of dawn and found Meredith sitting on the couch with a cup of coffee in her hand, smirking at me.

"And for God's sake, stop mumbling and tell me why I caught you sneaking in here with a glow on your face, flushed skin, and sex hair," she finishes, taking a casual sip of her coffee and hiding her smile behind the lip of the mug.

We haven't spoken about anything of importance since she stormed away from me the other day, fed up with me and my unwillingness to confide in her. As much as I want to growl at her for the sex hair comment, I miss talking to my friend. Arguing with Eli, arguing with Meredith, quietly seething about Landry and our sham of a relationship and the...*whatever that was* that happened with Eli in the middle of the night has piled up on top of the wall I've built and brought it crashing down into rubble at my feet. I'm tired of not being strong. I'm tired of not standing up for myself, and losing myself in Eli just proves how weak I've become. As much as I wanted it, as much as I loved every minute of the way he instinctively knew how to touch me, I feel like an idiot for allowing it to happen.

"I was with Eli last night."

Meredith laughs, leaning forward to set her mug on the coffee table in front of her.

"Pretty sure I already got that memo. I guess it's a good thing you refilled your birth control prescription. How about you tell me why you seem to be pissed about it."

I sigh, walking around the table and flopping down on the couch next to her.

"You know why, Mer. I mean, I *just* broke things off with Landry. And even though she basically fired me and has been keeping her distance, my mother still has the power to ruin things. I can't afford to take that chance," I explain.

"Nice try. Tell me why you're *really* pissed."

With a huff, I turn my body to face her and cross my arms over my chest.

"That *is* why I'm really pissed. Do I need another reason?"

She shakes her head at me, mirroring my pose.

"First of all, fuck Landry. You said it yourself, you broke things off with him, so who cares? Second, your mother has been ruining things for you your entire life. You're pissed because Eli got under your skin and you think it makes you look weak," she informs me.

Just like always, she reads my mind and knows exactly what I'm thinking and the root of the problem.

"He hurt me and he broke my heart and he still hasn't explained why. A few minutes alone with him and I suddenly forget about all of that, and what's more, I didn't even care. As soon as he touched me, I didn't care that he left and I didn't care that the only explanation I got was some stupid lie about letters he wrote me," I tell her, throwing my hands up in the air in irritation. "I walked into that tack room and found him having a nightmare. It was horrible and I couldn't think about anything but taking away his pain and making him forget what he went through."

Meredith reaches over and grabs my hand, giving it a squeeze. "Tell me how you felt, when all of this was happening with him. Not how you feel now, after it's done, how you felt in that exact moment when you were together."

I don't even have to close my eyes to remember how good it felt to be in his arms again. How perfect it was to hear his voice, speaking so softly and lovingly. My body still tingles from the orgasm he gave me, and my heart beats faster thinking about how he still knew the exact way to touch me to give me pleasure, like he'd memorized it all those years ago and never let it slip from his mind.

"Flawless. Beautiful. Wanted," I whisper, answering Meredith's question.

My eyes fill with tears when I think about how many sleepless nights I spent thinking I'd never feel his arms around me again, how many times I screamed and cried, wishing for just one more moment with him to hold his face in my hands, stare into his eyes, and feel whole again. Feel loved again. Feel alive again. I've been dead inside for so long, and in just one night, he brought me back to life.

She smiles at me and gives my hand another squeeze before pushing herself up from the couch and holding one finger up in the air.

"Don't move. I'll be right back."

I watch her move quickly across the room and down the hall to the spare bedroom. Running the tips of my fingers over my lips while I wait for her, I realize they still feel swollen from Eli's kisses and it fills me with so many mixed emotions that I don't know how to handle them.

He touched my leg like it was the most beautiful thing he'd ever seen. He didn't cringe or look away, and when he told me *I* was beautiful, I could see it in his eyes that he meant every word. When the sun came up and filled the tack room with bright morning light, I scrambled off his lap and walked away from him without a word. I was embarrassed that I let myself get so carried away with him. That I let things go that far without making him talk to me. I waited all this time to finally hear the reasons why he left me and I threw them out the window as soon as he ran his hand without hesitation up my thigh, told me he needed me and that dreaming about me was the only thing that kept him going for all those years.

I've been so starved for how he used to make me feel back when we were together. I've tried so hard to replicate those feelings with Landry, but it's pointless. Landry doesn't make me feel flawless. He never makes me feel beautiful, and he certainly never makes me feel wanted. I'm his ticket to winning a seat in the state senate. I come from a family with money, power, influence, and everything he needs to attain his goals. He's using me to get what he wants, just like I'm using him to keep Eli and his family safe. Even though our relationship is one built on a foundation of lies, I still hoped I could someday feel something with him.

After being with Eli again, I know now that he's the only one who can make me feel alive. He's the only one who makes me want to be stronger and be the person I used to be. I just don't know how to do that, keep him protected and forgive him all at the same time without losing my sanity.

"I brought these with me just in case," Meredith says, pulling me from my thoughts as she rushes back into the room, cradling a shoe box in her hands. "And before you scream and curse at me, you should also know I looked at them already."

She tosses the shoe box on top of the coffee table, and it slides across the surface until I have to grab it before it topples to the floor at my feet.

"You brought me a pair of Louboutins? Um, thanks?" I question uncertainly, picking up the brown box with white cursive writing on top and resting it in my lap.

"Sadly, no," she tells me, wringing her hands together nervously in front of her as she looks back and forth between me and the box. "Just open it so we can get the screaming and cursing over with."

With a roll of my eyes at her dramatics, I lift the lid and look down inside the box, the smile immediately slipping from my face when I see what's inside. The lid drops from my fingers and my hand shakes as I slowly move it toward the stack of letters spilled all over the inside of the box. The first letter is addressed to me, in care of Meredith at her New York apartment, the return address in the upper-left-hand corner of the envelope from a military barracks post office box in the States. Quickly flipping through all the letters, dozens and dozens of them, I see they are all addressed the same way, with the first five coming from a barracks PO box and the rest coming from several different generic military PO boxes.

"Oh, my God," I whisper, swallowing past the lump in my throat and blinking rapidly to keep the tears from falling down my cheeks.

He was telling the truth. He wrote to me. And according to the postmark stamp on the letters, he started writing a few weeks after he left for deployment and continued doing so for months. Just like he said. Just like he tried to explain before I called him a liar and stormed away that day in the studio. I was so angry after I searched my mother's office, wanting to believe he was telling the truth and maybe she hid the letters from me. I was pissed when I came up empty-handed and assumed he had lied to me just to get me to easily forgive him and let him back into my life. I let that anger take over this morning when I walked away from him, still believing he had been lying and I'd just shown how weak I was by not forcing him to tell me the truth before I let him touch me.

I can't stop the tears from sliding down my cheeks as I grab the letter on top of the pile, pull out the folded piece of notebook paper from inside the already torn-open envelope, and read the three sentences written in the middle of the page in Eli's messy handwriting.

Everything I said in that note was a lie. I could never love anyone but you. I'm sorry, please forgive me and please, give me a chance to explain.

—Eli

My tears continue falling steadily down my face as I quickly pull out the letters in the next five envelopes, each one with phrasing similar to the first one, aside from each of them being written a week or so apart.

I will never forgive myself for writing you that letter. I love you more than anything in this world. Please forgive me and let me explain.

—Eli

I love you, Shelby. Only you. ALWAYS you. Please forgive me and write me back.

—Eli

It's killing me that I won't see you again for a year. Won't touch you again for 365 days. Won't be able to look into your green eyes and tell you how sorry I am in person. I love you, Shelby. Only you. ALWAYS you. I'm so sorry.

—Eli

We're being shipped out of the States tomorrow, but that's not going to stop me from begging you not to hate me. I'll be here, waiting for you to forgive me. Please, forgive me. I love you, Shelby. Only you. ALWAYS you. I'm so sorry.

—Eli

Crumpling the letters in my hands, I hug them to my chest and squeeze my eyes closed as I try to catch my breath through my sobs. He was telling the truth and it hurts so much more now that I know it. It breaks me in half seeing his handwriting, reading his words, and knowing that he really did try to fight for me. I don't even care why he left the way he did at this point. Knowing he hated himself for what he did and tried to reach me even while his life was on the line in a war zone makes me ache for him and how he must have felt when I never responded.

"Say something," Meredith says softly after my tears finally subside and I'm able to breathe again.

I open my eyes and look up at her, my best friend, the

only person in the world aside from Eli who knows me inside and out and saw what I went through when he left. Saw what his leaving did to me and what I allowed to happen to my life when he was no longer in it, hating everything about myself because I just couldn't stop loving him more than I hated him. I gave up my life to protect him and I'd do it all over again without question, but if I had seen these letters, if I had known what was going on in his mind after he left, I would have done all these things without losing everything of myself in the process. I would have done it in remembrance of his love for me and not out of some twisted sense of duty toward his honor and his family's good name.

"How could you keep these from me?" I mutter brokenly, the tears threatening to come back when I pull the letters from my chest and look back down at Eli's words. "How could you do this to me when you knew? You *knew* how much it killed me when he left. You've been sitting on these letters for six fucking years!"

Tossing the crumpled pieces of paper into the box and setting it down on the table in front of me, I shake my head at my best friend, questioning everything about our friendship. I wrap my arms around my waist, hunching over as I choke on a sob, never thinking in a million years my best friend would betray me and do something like this.

"Forget the last six years; you've been here for over a week. You've seen me wrestle back and forth with Eli being here and determined to get back in my life. Even though I didn't come right out and say it, you knew I'd given everything up for him and how hard it's been thinking I'd done all of this for a man who just threw me away and you STILL waited to give them to me. Why?"

Meredith's eyes fill with tears and I have to look away from her face before I do something stupid like give her a hug and forgive her immediately. She's the one who lied. She's the one who hid things from me and let me feel so twisted and confused.

"I'm sorry. I know that doesn't make up for anything, but I am. When the first letter came, you had just been in your accident and I was on my way out the door to the airport to get to you," she explains, swiping a tear from her cheek. "I didn't even open it, I just tossed it on my counter and left. When I got back to New York a few months later after spending time with you and seeing you so broken and hurting and losing everything you'd worked so hard for, and then finding a stack of more letters from him in my mailbox, it pissed me off. I thought he was going to hurt you again. I was afraid of what was inside of them and I didn't want you to hurt anymore."

She moves around the coffee table and squats down next to my legs, resting her hands on my knees.

"I didn't trust him, Shelby, and I just didn't want you to hurt anymore. I wanted you to heal and move on."

"Did you read them?" I whisper angrily.

Her eyes widen in shock before they quickly fill with hurt as she shakes her head.

"No, of course not."

I scoot away from her on the couch, her hands dropping from my knees as I move to stand up, putting as much distance between us as I can. I want to understand what she's telling me and try to put myself in her place if the situation were reversed, but I can't right now. It's too new, too raw, and hurts too much that she would do something like this to me. That she would keep these letters in a fancy shoe box in her closet all this time and never say one word to me about them. Never let me know that Eli wrote to me after he left, regardless if what was in those letters was just something else that would hurt me. I deserved to know that the man I loved, the man I grieved and the man I did everything for, tried to fight for me. I deserved to know he thought of me as much as I thought of him. I deserved to see those letters for myself and make up my own mind about my well-being. I don't know if I'd still be in the same place, living the same miserable life, if I had seen those letters years ago, but I deserved the chance to know the truth.

"Shelby—"

"Don't." I interrupt her, avoiding her eyes as I slam the lid on the shoe box and lift it into my arms. "I can't do this with you right now."

I see her nod her head out of the corner of my eye. I hug the box to me and walk out of the room and down the hall, slamming my bedroom door shut behind me and wondering why everyone in my life seems to think they know what's best for me and why they all think it's okay to make my decisions for me. Tossing the box onto the bed, I clutch my hands into fists, tip my head back, and scream at the top of my lungs. I let the anger, the betrayal, the hurt, and the disappointment come pouring out of me until my voice is hoarse, my knees give out, and I sink down to the floor, out of breath and out of giving a damn.

The walls have officially crumbled on this house of lies and I'm finished. I'm done being taken advantage of and used for everyone else's agendas. This is *my* life and it's about damn time I start living it again and making my own damn decisions.

Chapter 17

Eli

Tell me why we're doing this again? I had a lot of important things on my schedule today, like taking a nap," Rylan complains as I pull my new black Ford truck into the drive along the side of the stables.

"I didn't force you to come with me. You're the one who jumped in the truck without asking where I was going," I remind him, shutting off the engine and glancing around the property, hoping to catch a glimpse of Shelby.

I've been sneaking into the stables every night for the last week after the workers have gone home, hoping to talk to her, but she's been a no-show. I know she's avoiding me after what went down in the tack room the other night, and I knew it would happen, but I'm still pissed about it. I've had plenty of things to do that should have kept me too busy to think about her, but she's been the sole focus of my thoughts for six years. Now that I've touched her, tasted her, and held her in my arms, there's no way I can push her out of my mind, no matter what I have going on.

"I only got in your truck because I needed a break from being your bitch. I'm glad you finally rented your own place and I don't have to suffer through judgy looks from your sister anymore, but unpacking all your shit was exhausting," Rylan complains.

"You didn't unpack anything. You sat on your ass and told me where everything should go."

Rylan shrugs as I pocket my keys and get out of the truck, meeting him around the front of the vehicle. "And you can thank me anytime for making sure your place is now feng shui."

The best part about finding out I have a shit ton of money in the bank is being able to finally take control of my life instead of having to rely on my sister for everything. I bought my own truck so I didn't have to keep borrowing Kat's SUV, and I rented a townhouse in downtown Charleston so I didn't have to impose on her and Daniel any longer. She put up a good fight when I told her I was moving out, and I felt a little guilty about the worry that was written all over her face when I reassured her that I wouldn't be alone since Rylan was coming with me. I promised to keep going to see the military shrink and call her if I needed to talk, and spent the last few days moving in. Being able to pay a hefty deposit and a year's worth of rent up front in cash made the paperwork go through a lot faster than normal, and before I knew it, I had a place to call my own where I wouldn't have to worry about waking Kat up in the middle of the night if I had another fucking nightmare.

Not that I'd had any of those damn things since that night with Shelby, but I knew they were still in there, waiting to wreak havoc on my brain. My shrink wasn't too happy when

I told him I'd settled on the hobby of getting Shelby back, especially when I told him about her accident and how much she'd changed since the last time I saw her. He didn't think it was good for me to put all my focus on someone who might be just as damaged as I am. He wanted me to concentrate on fixing *myself*, not someone else, but I didn't give a fuck. Just because I'm required to talk to him every week, and he's the one with the fancy degree, doesn't mean he knows what's best for me and my fucked-up brain. The only thing that got him to shut up about how bad this all was for me was the fact that he was intrigued about the whole no nightmares or flashbacks since the night in the tack room.

"I can't believe you're making me see Paul. That guy hates me," Rylan complains again as we walk into the huge open door of the stables.

"It's been six years since we worked for him. I doubt he hates you anymore. And he only hated you because he always had to yell at you for not doing work."

Paul Walden has been the property and stable manager for the Eubanks Plantation for as long as I can remember. He's in his late sixties by now, and even though I haven't seen him around the few times I've snuck over here, he's the type of man who will never stop working. He told me on more than one occasion that they'd have to drag his dead carcass out of the stables before he'd even think about retiring. As gruff and old-school as he'd been, he was like a second father to me when I worked here. Scratch that. He was like an *only* father to me since mine never gave a shit about what I did.

Paul always took care of Kat and me in his stern, no-nonsense way. He let me borrow an extra car of his when mine took a shit and I needed to get Kat to school or doctors' appointments or make it in to work. When our parents were alive, he gave my sister and me a place to crash when we needed to get away from their excessive partying, and after they died, he had us over for dinner at least one night a week to make sure we were okay and slip money into Kat's hand when I wasn't looking, since he knew I was too proud to take a handout. He didn't hover and he didn't make me feel like I was too young or stupid to handle everything on my own. He stood back and let me take care of my own responsibilities, but he was always there to help, even when I was too pigheaded to ask for it.

"How could I possibly concentrate on shoveling horse shit when there were always hot chicks coming in and out of the stables?" Rylan questions as we continue moving down the long main hallway of the barn and I finally spot Paul talking to another worker at the end of the row of horse stalls. "You were too busy with your head up Shelby's ass to notice back then, but there were some fine specimens who boarded their horses here or stopped by for a look at one of them that was up for sale."

I ignore Rylan's rambling when Paul's head comes up as I get a few feet away from him and stop. I stand here quietly, listening to him give the worker a few orders before slapping him on the back and telling him to, "Get that shit done before I die of old age, boy."

The worker, not much older than I was when I first started working here, nods his head and runs away with wide, nervous eyes to do his duties.

"Still scaring the hired help, I see," I tell him with a smile as he walks up to me.

Even though it's been six years since I last saw Paul, he hasn't changed a bit. He still stands just as tall as me with just as many muscles hidden under layers of wrinkled and age-spotted skin from chucking hay bales. He still looks like

Clint Eastwood with his salt-and-pepper hair and tanned, weathered face from working outside in the sun all day, including the permanent scowl that's always in place.

"Scaring those young pups is the only way to get their asses moving so they don't stand around on their phones doing the Twitter and sending pictures of their privates to all of creation," Paul replies as I pull my hand out of the pocket of my jeans and reach it out to him.

He grabs it in a firm grip, shaking it once and giving me a nod.

"Good to see you again, son. Been watching what happened all over the TV since the news broke," he tells me in a low, gruff voice as he drops my hand. "Damn shame what happened to you boys over there, but I'm glad you made it home."

My heart starts thumping nervously in my chest and I have to take a couple of deep breaths to calm it before memories overwhelm me.

"What about me? Are you glad I'm home, too, old man?" Rylan jokes.

Both of us ignore him this time, and Paul takes a step back to lean his elbow on top of the wooden gate closing off the stall next to him. "You doin' okay, son?"

I copy his pose, resting my own elbow on top of the gate, swallowing back the vomit that's threatening to come right up into my mouth whenever someone brings up what happened.

"I'm getting there. Trying to do normal shit and forget about it, but the shrink they're making me talk to every week wants to keep dredging it up."

He takes one of the toothpicks he always keeps in the right front pocket of his flannel shirt and sticks it in the side of his mouth.

"I don't believe in all that therapy bullshit, but maybe if they'd had that for us when we came back from Nam instead of just throwing us back into civilization without so much as a how-do-you-do, more of us wouldn't have been so fucked in the head," he says, moving the toothpick around in his mouth as he speaks. "I don't know many men who could have made it through what you did. Lost a few of my own buddies in the war. Wasn't near as bad as what you went through, but if you ever get tired of the headshrinker and need to talk, my door's always open."

A few minutes of silence settle between us, and the bond we'd always shared strengthens with the knowledge that we both went off to war, saw some pretty bad shit, and came home to try and put the pieces of our life back together.

Paul pulls the toothpick out of his mouth and points it at me. "I know you didn't come here for a job, seein' as all people in this town can talk about is that fancy new truck you're drivin' and the big house you rented in town. And you sure as shit got better things to do than standin' around bullshittin' with me, so spit it out, son."

"Jesus, is nothing a secret in this town?" I ask with a shake of my head, irritated that no one has anything better to do around here than talk about me, and a little freaked out that Paul still knows me so well and knew I didn't come here just to shoot the shit with him.

"Only the things people *want* to keep a secret, you should know that by now. The missus was gettin' her hair done at the beauty parlor across from your house and all the gossips in Charleston were in there that day watchin' you move your stuff in. It's good you're settlin' in, doin' normal things normal people do. Folks'll stop talkin' about ya if you keep that up and don't do anything stupid to give them a reason to gossip."

I blow out a frustrated breath of air, knowing without a doubt that my reason for coming here is something stupid that the gossip mill would cut off their own arms to get a piece of. Even with that knowledge, I still have to try. I still need answers. Deciding to just get it over with, I do as Paul demanded and spit it out as fast as possible before losing my nerve.

"A week before I was deployed, someone anonymously sent a copy of the police report from my parents' accident to my apartment. Funny thing was, it wasn't the same report they gave me when it happened that I needed for the insurance company. In the report *they* gave me, it was a single car accident, my father was driving, and they both had blood alcohol levels well above the legal limit. In the one someone sent me, neither one of them had a trace of alcohol in their system, but the driver of the *second* car, who it claimed was at fault, sure as hell did."

I finally stop rambling and take a deep breath to calm my nerves. I'd never been intimidated by Paul, even when he was chewing my ass out in front of all the other workers for showing up to work a few minutes late when I'd been preoccupied with Shelby. As he stands here glaring at me silently, I'm scared as hell about what he'll say or do. This isn't just me being young and irresponsible. What I'm alluding to, and his possible connection to it, could ruin a lot of lives, and if what I believe is true, it would definitely cost him his job. I'm sure he's wondering why I didn't come to him with this when I first got the report, but I honestly never thought about him being the one who sent it until I had five years of nothing but time to think about it and dwell on it between beatings, and came to the conclusion that he was the only person in my life who could have done it.

"Why you telling me this, son?" he asks quietly.

"I think he might actually hate *you* now more than me," Rylan whispers from behind me. "I told you this was a bad idea."

Sliding my elbow off the gate, I cross my arms in front of me and stand tall. I spent too many years being kicked around and not being able to fight back or take a stand. As much as I love Paul and I appreciate everything he ever did for me, I can't let this go. That police report was the catalyst to everything that fucked up mine and Shelby's lives. It made me question everything I thought I knew about my parents. I *have* to know the truth.

"You know why I'm telling you this, Paul," I answer in a low voice. "And I think you already know what I'm asking. I know your son-in-law just graduated from the academy and had been hired in at the station a few weeks before my parents' accident. You knew the kind of life I had with them growing up. You saw how pissed I was and how much I hated them for doing something so stupid and leaving Kat and I to fend for ourselves."

Paul narrows his eyes at me, but I keep going, even as Rylan whispers in my ear, telling me to shut up before the old man takes a swing at me.

"You and Rylan were the only ones who knew about me and Shelby. That report I got in the mail had the license plate number of the other vehicle, but we both know it's not that hard to look something like that up and find out who the owner was," I finish.

The silence stretches out between us, much more uncomfortable than a few minutes before when we were bonding over war. Paul finally sticks the toothpick back in his mouth, shoving his hands in the front pockets of his jeans as he pushes away from the gate with his elbow.

"That was a long time ago, son. I'm thinkin' at this point,

after what you've been through, some things are best left alone," he states.

"I don't give a fuck if it was a hundred years ago!" I shout angrily. "People still refer to my parents as the town drunks who got what was coming to them. Kat and I were treated like the scum of the earth for YEARS because of that shit. That woman..."

I trail off and count to ten in my head to get my anger under control. At least I've gotten something useful out of all those fucking hours with the shrink.

"That woman," I continue, unclenching my fists and managing not to yell, "threatened me, my sister, and her own goddamn daughter when I confronted her. She got my deployment moved up an entire fucking *year* just to make sure I got the hell away from here and kept my mouth shut. Like I said, I don't give a shit how long ago it was. When you spend five years in hell, you've got nothing but time to think about this shit and it's about fucking time I get some answers and make the right person pay for all the damage she's done. Did you send me that report? Have you known all this time that my parents weren't responsible for that accident?"

Rylan whistles softly when I finally finish, and Paul starts rocking back and forth on the heels of his cowboy boots.

"I know you want answers, son, and I don't blame ya one bit. But you need to think about what this could do to the people you care about. The people you kept breathin' during those five years and the people you made it home to," he tells me softly. "I'm gonna say this one more time, some things are best left alone. I'm also gonna say, there's a woman livin' in the guest house a few hundred yards away who could use a little more happy in her life and a lot less livin' in the past that's filled with nothin' but heartache."

The traces of anger still flowing through my veins that

Paul sat on this information for all these years slowly fade away as soon as he brings up Shelby. I think about the kind of life she's been living the last few years, thinking I never loved her, getting into her accident and having all of her dreams ripped from her hands, on top of being stuck under her mother's thumb. As much as I want to know the truth, I know it won't set me free. It will only bring up a whole shitload of more problems, not just for me, but Shelby as well. I can't do that to her. Not now. Not after I've seen how broken she is and want nothing more than to take away all of her pain and make her happy again.

"I'm working on giving her a little more happy," I finally tell him with a sigh, realizing I'm not going to get the answers from Paul that I'm looking for.

"Well, work on it a little harder for shit's sake," Paul tells me, dropping the soft, concerned voice and going right back to being his crotchety old self. "I always liked that girl. She had so much sweet in her it's a wonder that pain in the ass mother of hers actually birthed her. Girl don't smile much anymore when I see her around the grounds. Don't laugh none either. It's not right, sweet girl like that with nothin' to smile about."

He raises his eyebrow pointedly.

"Now is when you should tell him how you made her smile when you diddled her a few feet away from where we're standing the other night," Rylan says under his breath with a laugh.

I growl at him and Paul lets out a long, suffering sigh as he jingles some things around in his pocket before pulling out a key attached to a rabbit's foot keychain. Grabbing it from him, I give him a questioning look. He takes the half-chewed toothpick out of his mouth and points it at me again.

"No sense in you picking that damn lock again. Maybe

with that thing, you can come up with a way to make her smile again."

"How did you—"

Paul lets out a gravelly laugh. "I've known about that room since the day her daddy had it built for her."

He takes a step toward me and lowers his voice.

"Ain't nothin' goin' on around here that I don't know about. I see everything and I hear everything. At my age, I've learned when to pick my battles and when to realize I might have jumped the gun about certain things in anger, without thinking about the repercussions. Life's too short to fight a war you can't win, son, no matter how wrong it is or how angry you are. Pick one you can win. She's one you can win if you do it right, and nothing else will matter after that."

Saying everything and nothing all at once, Paul gave me what I needed in a roundabout way. I give him a nod of understanding as he slaps me on the back, turns, and walks away, shouting at the top of his lungs for one of the stable hands to "Get your head out of your ass and feed the damn horses!"

Smiling to myself, I watch him go until he disappears around the corner.

"What the fuck did that even mean? I'm more confused now than I was when we got here," Rylan complains.

I stare down at the key in my hand, rubbing the rabbit's foot for good luck as I turn around and smile at my friend.

"Don't worry, I got what I came here for," I tell him, pocketing the key and heading back down the hallway to the barn door.

"So, what are you going to do now?" he asks, running to catch up with me.

"I'm going to make the pretty girl who lives in the guest house remember how to smile and laugh again."

Rylan throws his hands up in the air and shouts a "Hallelujah" to the sky when we get outside.

"What's the plan? Woo her with flowers, hire a hit man to take out her mother, tell her I'm single and available?" Rylan asks when we get inside my truck.

"No, no, and no. The first part of the plan is getting a new cell phone, then plugging in my old one and hoping all of my contact information is still in it," I inform him as I pull out of the drive and head toward town.

"That doesn't sound like anything that will end in smiles, or sex. I'm living vicariously through you, so I'm gonna need you to come up with another plan."

I give him the middle finger and turn on the radio. Raising the volume, I roll down the windows and take a deep breath of warm Southern air, knowing exactly what I need to do to get Shelby to smile again.

Chapter 18

Shelby

Sitting with my back against the headboard, I stare at the shoe box at the foot of my bed, my hands shaking with the need to open the lid and read the rest of the letters piled inside. As much as I want to read them, I've done nothing but sit here for five days and stare at the box, afraid to see what else Eli tried to tell me six years ago. Afraid to see his words, feel his pain, and understand how hard it was for him to have no idea if he'd ever see me or speak to me again.

I can remember exactly how it felt to have those same worries, my heart clenching in fear each time I thought of him being overseas and surrounded by danger. I couldn't imagine never hearing his low, gravelly voice whispering in my ear, feeling his rough hands running over my body, seeing the dimples in both of his cheeks when he smiled at me, or watching him run his fingers through his hair when he was frustrated. Even when my heart was broken and I believed the lies he'd told me. Even when my life was shattered and torn apart after the accident, and then again, when the news hit that he'd been killed, I still couldn't let go of the hold he had on me. I still couldn't move on, and I still couldn't believe I'd never hear him, feel him, or see him again.

I'm afraid to read the rest of his letters because I know there will be no turning back after I do. I won't be able to keep my distance if I open the lid on that box and see more of his heart, cracked and bleeding all over those pages that traveled thousands of miles to get to me. The tiny voice in the back of my mind that has reminded me time and time again to do whatever it takes to keep Eli safe will disappear as soon as I read those letters. I won't have that voice of reason keeping me focused and I won't even care as long as I'm with him. I knew from the moment I came home from college and he picked the lock on my studio for the first time that he would ruin me in the best possible way. I knew from the first second he kissed me that we'd be able to accomplish anything as long as we were together.

The *ding* of an incoming text sounds from my phone resting on the bed next to me. Glancing down, I don't even bother picking it up when I see it's from Landry. He's phoned and sent me text messages several times a day since he left. I haven't answered or responded. What in the hell would I even say to him at this point? I know I didn't give him any kind of an explanation as to why I ended things with him before he left, but I assumed my silence would at least show him that I meant it. I'm sure the longer I wait to reply, the sooner he'll go running to my mother and I'll have to hear about how I'm inconsiderate and rude and ruined everything.

I look down at the box at the foot of the bed, then back at my phone, then at the box again. Two more rapid-fire *dings* come from my phone and I don't even bother looking at it.

I quickly reach for the box and pull it onto my lap, settling back against the headboard as I lift the lid and toss it to the floor. Sifting through the first five letters I already read, I grab the next one going by date order and pull it out of the envelope.

October 23, 2010

Shelby,

Remember that day in your studio, the week after you'd gotten home from college? In case I forgot to tell you, that was the day I knew I was going to fall in love with you. I don't know if you'll ever read this and I'm not really good at this whole letter-writing thing, so I'm just going to tell you a story in these letters. I'm going to tell you the story of us, from my point of view, so you know exactly what I was thinking. I'm hoping it will be a better way for you to see that I meant everything I said in my first few letters. I love you, Shelby. Only you. Always you.

I'd never had as much fun in my life as I did the week after you came home from college. The highlight of my day was sneaking away from work, picking the lock on your studio, and seeing you dance for the first time. The highlight of my LIFE was watching the look on your face when I pissed you off and suggested you try dancing to some classic rock next time before I waltzed out the door like it was no big deal.

You had no idea how much strength it took for me not to stalk across the floor, pull you against me, and kiss you. You had no clue that the only reason I quickly turned and walked away was because I couldn't hide the massive hard-on I got just by watching you dance for a few minutes. I was afraid

I'd fucked up and just blew any chance I'd had of convincing you to spend time with me by being a sarcastic asshole.

My hands were shaking and sweaty when I snuck away from Paul the next day and picked the lock again. I felt like the biggest pussy in the world when I got butterflies in my damn stomach as soon as I pushed the door open and heard "Hotel California" blasting through the speakers down the hall.

I leaned against the wall at the back of the studio, holding my breath as I watched you lose yourself in the music until the song ended and you noticed me standing there. Just like the previous day, you put your hands on your hips and glared at me and it was the hottest fucking thing I'd ever seen. Since the whole sarcastic asshole thing worked the first time, I figured I might as well try it again.

"I dare you to try some rap tomorrow."

I winked at you like a douche bag, turned, and walked back out of the room. It killed me to walk away, especially when I heard you shout, "GO TO HELL, ELI JAMES!" when I got to the end of the hall. I laughed under my breath and it took everything in me not to turn around and run back into that room.

More than wanting to watch you dance again, I wanted to watch you get fired up and indignant, stomp your foot, and huff at me, because there was something underneath that attitude you tried throwing at me. SOMETHING that made you do what I suggested no matter how much it annoyed you. I wanted to know what you were trying so hard to hide from me with the rolls of your eyes and pretending like you didn't care if I came back or not. Instead of turning around, I went back to work and spent the rest of the day fucking everything up and listening to Paul yell at me about getting my head out of my ass because I couldn't stop wondering if you'd listen to my suggestion again.

The next day, I repeated the process of slinking through the stables when Paul wasn't looking, picked the lock, and couldn't stop the huge smile that spread across my damn face when I poked my head in the room. You usually danced in bare feet, but that day, you had on a pair of high-top Nikes.

With Eminem blasting from the speakers.

That day, you didn't move in your usual graceful way, but with a lot more hip action that brought up the same hard-on problem from the first day. At the end of your dance, you turned around and raised one eyebrow at me expectantly, not saying a word. Just waiting for me to give you another music choice, even though I could tell the very idea pissed you off.

God, I wanted to kiss you. Instead, I went with what was working for me and told you I wanted to hear some country. You might think I didn't know anything about you, or never paid attention to you in all the years I'd worked here, but you'd be wrong. It was all I could do NOT to follow you around like a puppy, even before you went off to college. It didn't take long for me to realize you were nothing like the spoiled princess I thought you were. I might not have said much to you all those years, but I listened to every damn word. And one thing I knew for sure, just because a girl grows up in the South, does not mean she likes country music. You hated country music when you were twelve and you still hated it when you went off to college. I wanted to see just how far you would take this thing that you didn't even realize was happening.

I'm not even ashamed that when I got home from work that night, I Googled all the dance shit I could and learned that what you were doing that day was called hip-hop. I watched a ton of videos and realized I'd also seen you dance ballet and contemporary. I also learned that none of the women in those videos came anywhere close to your talent, or had the same focus and love for what they were doing in their eyes.

When I grabbed on to the handle of the door the next day, I realized just how far you'd take it when I found it unlocked for the first time. It didn't even matter that what I heard piped through the sound system wasn't country. You wanted me in that room with you just as much as I wanted to be there.

The music was horrible and almost made my ears bleed, but just like every other day, I couldn't take my eyes off of you. Instead of waiting until the end of the song to confront me, your eyes met mine in the mirror as soon as I walked through the door. You turned around in the middle of the room, lifted your hand, and crooked your finger at me.

I smirked at you and shook my head, shoving my hands into the pockets of my jeans before I did something stupid like run to you as fast as I could and put them all over your body.

"What is this shit you're making me listen to?" I asked, deciding to try something new and actually have a conversation with you.

"It's Justin Bieber," you replied with a roll of your eyes.

"It's crap, is what it is."

Surprisingly, you didn't have a comeback. You took a few steps in my direction, pointed at me, and did that whole finger curl thing again, silently telling me to get my ass over to you.

"I don't dance, Legs."

It's a good thing I couldn't take my eyes off of you, otherwise I would have missed the little shiver that ran through your body when I called you "Legs."

You immediately stalked the rest of the way to me,

grabbed my forearms, and yanked my hands out of my pockets. Sliding your soft, warm palms against mine, you interlaced our fingers and tugged me towards you, walking backwards as I let you lead me.

"I said I don't dance, Legs. I leave it up to the professionals, like you," I informed you when we got to the center of the room.

You stopped walking, standing just a few inches away from me, and craned your neck to look up at me. I could feel the heat from your body and I wished I'd had the guts to mold myself to the front of you and wrap my arms around you.

"I've spent a week dancing my ass off with your stupid music requests. Now it's my turn," you informed me, giving me a taste of my own medicine with a sarcastic smile.

The beat of the music picked up, and with our hands still locked together, you started moving your hips to the rhythm of the song, dancing right in front of me. You used my hands to help you dance, lifting them up as you shook and twisted your body until I couldn't fight the smile I'd been holding back.

"You just need to feel the music, Cowboy," You spoke loudly over the thumping base and keyboard blasting through the speakers. "Feel the music and go with the flow."

You let go of one of my hands and held tightly to the other as you swung herself out and away from me with a flourish. Quickly twirling back towards me, my arm wrapped around your body as you spun until there was nowhere else for you to go and you slammed into my chest.

We stood there, chest-to-chest, me staring down into your gorgeous green eyes and you staring up into mine, both of us breathing a little too heavy. You felt so right against me. So good in my arms. I wanted to stand like this with you for the rest of the day, but I knew if I didn't do something fast, there'd be no hiding my hard-on that was two seconds away from poking you in the stomach.

I tightened my hold on our hands that were still linked together, gave your shoulder a little nudge, and spun you away, yanking you right back to me. As soon as your chest collided with mine again, I wrapped my free arm around your waist and held you tightly against me.

"Just feel the music, huh?" I asked with a wink.

"Um, yep. Sure," you muttered quickly, not making any move to push away from me.

I could tell by the look in your eyes and the way you pressed yourself even closer to me without realizing it that you felt the same thing I did. Not wanting to freak you out by professing my undying love for you before we'd shared more than a few sentences in the last week, I decided to do something that I hoped would put a smile on your face and maybe even shock you a little.

I started moving my hips and you moved right along with me, until your eyes widened when you realized we were dancing together. With our bodies flush from hip to chest and our eyes locked on each other, I started shuffling my feet, taking you with me in a dirty-dancing, ballroom-type move. I never thought the rare time my mother showed interest in me when I was younger and she forced me to take a ballroom dancing class that it would actually pay off someday.

With my arm still around your waist, our linked hands in perfect partner-dance formation up by our shoulders, you pressed your free palm to my chest. I hoped to God you'd think the rapid beat of my heart against your hand was because of the dancing and not because of you being close to me, or I'd never have the upper hand with you. I was beginning to realize it was going to take a lot of willpower to have any kind of advantage over you.

"I thought you couldn't dance?" you asked, as we expertly moved in sync around the room.

I immediately pushed against your hip, still clutching your hand as I pushed you away from me again and then pulled you right back. Your face lit up with a smile, and unguarded laughter flew out of your mouth when you slammed against my chest, staring up at me in awe.

"I said I DON'T dance, not that I couldn't. With the way you're lookin' at me right now, Legs, I'm pretty sure I'd agree to just about anything," I told you, before I spun you back out again, lifted our hands above your head, and twirled your body around and around in front of me.

Your laughter filled the room and it was the best fucking sound I'd ever heard in my life.

I take back what I said before I told you this story. I actually did fall in love with you that day... the first time I heard you laugh.

—Eli

When I get to the end of the letter, I want to scream through my tears. I want to curse and yell and smash everything breakable in this fucking house until I'm so exhausted I can't think anymore. My heart hurts so much that I don't know how to handle it. I drop the letter on top of the pile and press both hands to my chest as hard as I can to make it stop hurting.

I don't know what to do. I don't know what to feel and I just want the pain to go away. I need to be angry. I know how to handle anger and I know how to get rid of it when it overwhelms me. But I don't know how to stop hurting. I don't know how to stop wishing I could go back in time and stop him from leaving. Make him stay with me no matter why he felt he had to leave so we could have that moment in the studio back and have it be as perfect as it was that summer day six years ago. I don't even care if I can't dance anymore. I just want to go back and remember how good it felt to stop trying to hide how in love with him I was, back when I still had hope and I still had something left to give him.

My phone *dings* with yet another text message and I furiously swipe at the tears on my cheeks, pick the damn thing up, and lift my arm to hurl it against the wall. My eyes flicker to the screen and I slowly lower my arm and stare at the new text message from an unknown number

Hey, it's Eli. Would you look at that. It seems I still have all my old contacts. Now you can't ignore me. Five days is long enough, Beautiful. Meet me in the studio after the sun goes down. Don't worry. I have a key.

Chapter 19

Eli

"Oh, my God."

My head whips up and I quickly push away from the wall when I hear Shelby's quietly muttered words as she stops in the doorway of her studio.

My nerves have been shot to hell since I sent her a text message earlier and then spent the rest of the day in here. What if that wasn't her cell phone number anymore? What if she didn't show up? What if she hated it and hated *me*, thinking I was trying to force her back into the person she used to be?

Wiping my sweaty palms on the front of my jeans, I walk in her direction as she enters the room slowly, her eyes taking it in as mine take in her. Without any windows in this room, I couldn't see what was going on outside, but I heard a few cracks of thunder while I'd been working. Staring at Shelby as she spins slowly in a circle in bare feet, I realize it must have been pouring outside and I feel bad that I made her go out in the storm. I want to apologize, but my tongue is stuck to the roof of my mouth as I look at her.

Her long, strawberry blond hair is wet and stuck to her cheeks, shoulders, and down her back. She's wearing a teal-colored sleeveless dress that hugs her chest and falls to just above her knees, the wet material clinging to her thighs as she turns. With a small gold belt tied around her waist, thin gold straps over her shoulders matching a line of gold at the edge of the low scooped top of the dress, and the way the material lies on her body, she looks like a fucking Greek goddess. I think about all those days, months, and years I dreamed of her just to help me get through another night, and it takes me a minute to realize this isn't a dream. She really *is* standing right here in front of me, close enough to touch.

"Did you do all this?" she asks softly when she finally finishes looking around.

"You're stunning," I blurt out, unable to think about anything else but how beautiful she is and how thankful I am to be alive and here with her right now.

She pulls the wet skirt of the dress away from her thighs and shakes it a little, then runs her fingers through her long, wet hair.

"I'm a mess. I didn't realize how hard it was coming down until I got outside," she tells me with a nervous laugh.

Moving slowly, I walk toward her and stop when I'm a few inches away. The rain has amplified the peach smell of her skin and surrounds me like a piece of heaven.

"I'm sorry. I didn't know it was that bad out there. Why didn't you just drive over?"

The corners of her mouth tipped up in a small smile quickly fall and she drops her head, avoiding my eyes.

"I can't...I don't like to drive when it rains," she whispers.

My heart drops right down into my stomach and I move, sliding my hands around her waist and pulling her against me.

"Shit. I'm such an asshole. I'm sorry, Shelby," I mutter as I press my lips to the side of her head.

I close my eyes and sigh when her hands slide through my arms and wrap around me, her palms flattening against my back.

"It's okay. I'm fine. Now, can you please answer my question. Did you do all of this?" she asks again.

I can hear the smile in her voice, and when she presses her cheek to my chest, I forget what the hell she just asked, what day it is, and my own name. She's so warm and soft and I don't know how in the hell I lived without having her right here where she belongs, holding me so tight.

She pulls her head away from my chest and looks up at me, the smile coming back to her face, letting me know the plan I came up with after talking to Paul was a good one and she doesn't hate me.

"It's not that big of a deal. I just cleaned it up a little," I tell her with a shrug, tightening my arms around her.

"Eli, this place was a dirty mess. There was so much dust on the mirrors and the floor you could have built a sandcastle with all of it," she replies.

I'm definitely downplaying how much work it took to get her studio back to looking like an actual studio and not like something out of a horror film. It took three bottles of Windex to get all the layers of dirt and film off the floor-to-ceiling mirrors that line the entire back wall. I wound up having to rent a commercial floor buffer and sander after I swept the wood dance floor and saw what condition it was in. After a few coats of wax, replacing all the lightbulbs in the ceiling, and setting up her table by the door with fresh towels and bottled water, it took a lot longer than I thought it would.

Seeing the smile on her face makes it all worth it.

"But wait, there's more!" I tell her in my best infomercial voice as I let go of her with one arm, reaching into my back pocket.

Pulling out the small black remote, I aim it in the direction of the new sound system I set up in the corner of the room and hit Play. As soon as the first few notes of the pop song blast out into the room, it happens.

Shelby's head tips back and she laughs. Her entire body shakes in my arms and I have the sudden urge to drop down to my knees and cry like a fucking baby when I hear the sound that haunted my dreams for six years.

"I don't see what's so funny. I've heard this is a really popular song," I tell her, deciding to go with doing whatever I can to keep that smile on her face before I turn into a pussy right at her feet.

"It's popular all right. It's also very Biebery," she tells me with another laugh.

"I seem to recall you liking this Bieber guy at one time."

Her smile is so bright I shouldn't have bothered replacing the lightbulbs. She could light up this entire room with that thing.

"And *I* seem to recall that he made your ears bleed."

I shrug, sliding the remote back into my pocket and wrapping my arm back around her, slowly starting to rock us from side to side. "Eh, he's kind of growing on me. And anyway, the lyrics aren't half bad."

She shakes her head at me and lets out another small laugh.

"Do I even want to ask how you know what the lyrics are, or that this is a popular song?" she asks, swaying with me to the music, not even realizing she's doing it.

"One of the things my shrink suggested to me when I first got home and couldn't sleep for more than a couple of minutes at a time was to do stupid, mindless shit like catch up on current events," I explain. "Stuff like read about celebrity gossip, look up the *Billboard* charts for the last few years, and listen to the new songs and watch reality TV. Anything that didn't require much brain power so I could settle my thoughts and just fucking relax."

Her smile softens and she cocks her head as she looks up at me.

"I'm sorry. I shouldn't have asked you that. You don't have to talk about that stuff if you don't want to."

With our bodies still gently moving to the music, I slide one hand from around her waist and bring it up between us, smoothing off a few pieces of hair that are still stuck to her cheek and tucking the strands behind her ear.

"I'll tell you anything you want to know, Shelby. All you have to do is ask. I'm okay talking about it. It's easier with you," I tell her with a reassuring smile, unable to stop myself from running the tips of my fingers down her cheek.

The chorus of the song picks up and the Biebs starts singing about being sorry, knowing he let his girl down and wondering if it's too late to *say* he's sorry. The kid might be a punk, but he says the words I want Shelby to hear and feel and *know*.

Moving my fingertips down until they slide off her jaw, I reach my arm behind me, grab one of her hands, and pull it around up by her shoulder. Lacing my fingers through hers, I take the swaying one step further and start to move my feet, my hold on her body forcing her to move with me.

She licks her lips nervously and lets out a shaky breath.

"Eli, I can't dance," she mumbles so softly that I barely hear her over the music.

Leaning down without stopping the movement of our bodies, I press my lips to her ear and speak just above a whisper. "Close your eyes."

I pull back just enough to watch her do as I said, her eyelids slowly lowering until her long, black lashes are resting against the skin of her upper cheekbones.

Kissing the tip of her nose, I slide my lips across her cheek and place another kiss right in the middle of it before pressing our cheeks together and speaking again.

"You just need to feel the music, Beautiful. Close your eyes and just feel the music."

I push her a little further, my palm against her back sliding down and around to her hip. With my hand splayed against the side of her body, I start swaying and rocking my own hips to the beat of the music, pushing my palm against her just enough to guide her movements to match mine.

"I can't do this. I'm scared," she tells me quietly.

Her hips are moving perfectly with mine, all on their own, just as fluid and natural as always.

"Does your leg hurt?"

She pulls her cheek away from mine to look up at me, shaking her head no.

"It doesn't hurt, it just feels... bruised. It always feels like this when it rains."

The song ends and the silence in the room only lasts long enough for a loud crack of thunder to be heard from outside before the next song I put on the playlist starts right up. As fate would have it, the next song is called "Barefoot and Bruised."

When I added the song to the playlist for tonight, I had no idea Shelby would show up here, so beautiful and perfect in her wet sundress and bare feet, with her leg feeling bruised. I added it because the words to this song were a thousand times better than the stupid Bieber one.

"If your leg starts to hurt, you tell me, okay? I'm right here beside you," I remind her, echoing the words of the song.

She nods her head and takes a deep breath as we once again start swaying to the music in perfect sync.

"You saved me, Shelby," I whisper, pressing my forehead against hers. "For five years, you saved me, and you didn't even know it. Now it's my turn to save *you*."

I feel her breath against my face when she lets out a shaky sigh.

"Close your eyes, Shelby. Just close your eyes and feel the music."

When her eyes close once again, I push my lips forward and press them against hers.

Chapter 20

Shelby

November 4, 2010

Shelby,

Do you know what I miss the most? What I think about more than anything else when I'm alone in my bunk at night, it's pitch black, and all I can hear is the distant sound of gunfire and bombs exploding? That little sound you'd make when I kissed you. Even with all the noise going on around me, I can still hear that little gasp you'd make as soon as our lips touched. Even when it wasn't a surprise and you watched me lean in, you still made that sound. Goddammit I miss that sound. I miss you. I love you, Shelby. Only you. Always you.

Remember that day we first kissed?

The muscles in my arms screamed in protest as I grabbed

another bale of hay and chucked it into the next stall. After eight hours of Marine conditioning all day and Paul putting me on grunt work tonight as punishment when he found out I was a half hour late coming back from my dinner break two days ago, all I wanted to do was take a shower and fall face-first into bed.

Even with all the extra shit work I was given and how sore and exhausted I was, I couldn't help but smile, knowing that extra half hour I'd gotten with you and the reason for my lateness was worth it. I'd chipped away a little bit of your attitude, got to hold you close and dance with you, and even made you laugh.

It was definitely worth feeding all the horses without any help.

Bending over, I grabbed a bale and paused before lifting it when I heard a strangled sigh come from behind me. I quickly looked over my shoulder and found you staring right at my ass.

"Enjoying the view, Legs?" I asked with a smirk.

You rolled your eyes and pushed off of the wooden post you'd been leaning against, crossing your arms in front of you.

"Why are you so annoying?" you asked.

Lifting the hay bale, I threw it into the stall and tossed the hooks to the ground.

"Why are you so beautiful?" I countered, pulling my work gloves off and shoving them in the back pocket of my jeans as I stalked over to you.

You took a quick step back as I advanced, but forgot all about the post behind you and smacked right into it, halting your attempt to get away from me.

I kept moving until we were toe-to-toe. Leaning into your body, I brought one hand up and rested it on the post above your head.

"You really need to stop looking at me like that," I told you quietly, staring down at your face.

You nervously licked your lips and my eyes darted to your mouth. I knew from experience you had the softest lips I'd ever tasted and it was getting harder and harder not to kiss you, but I knew you needed to warm up to this thing happening between us before I went there. As much as it killed me.

"Looking at you like what?" you whispered, your voice coming out small and shaky, so unlike the fire that blazes from it when you usually speak to me.

And so fucking hot.

I chuckled under my breath, giving you a sweet smile instead of a cocky one so you knew without a doubt I wasn't making fun of you.

"Looking at me like you want me inside you...you're killing me, Legs," I admitted, looking back up into your eyes.

Your mouth dropped open and I could tell you were struggling not to roll your eyes and give me attitude.

"I'm not going to kiss you again," you muttered, lifting your chin indignantly. "I tried that once and you were a jerk."

Bringing my hand that dangled down by my thigh up between us, I brushed my thumb gently across your bottom lip, suddenly realizing what the deal was with all the attitude you had been giving me. I hurt you when you left for college, and you weren't about to let it go that easily without making me work for it.

"Maybe I wanna kiss you this time."

My thumb continued to stroke your full bottom lip and your mouth parted with a sharp intake of breath, your chest rising and falling much more rapidly now. I honestly didn't have a clue how I managed to continue standing here up against you so casually when all I wanted to do was lift you up so your long legs could wrap around my waist and shove myself between them.

"I was an idiot four years ago. I said a lot of stupid shit I didn't mean. That kiss...Jesus Christ, Legs. I haven't been able to get that kiss out of my fucking head for four years. I haven't been able to get you out of my head for four years," I muttered, giving you as much honesty as I could so you'd start to trust me. "Wondering if your lips are still as soft, wondering if you'd taste the same, wondering if you'd gasp into my mouth again and make me hard as a rock with just that one little sound."

Your cheeks flushed and you swallowed nervously a few times, lighting a fire inside of me that I knew would never go out.

"I know you're not going to kiss me again, and I deserve that after the shit I said to you. But just so you know, I'm going to fight for you, Legs. I'm not giving up and I'm not going anywhere."

With one last swipe of my thumb across your bottom lip, I couldn't hold back any longer and I said "to hell" with warming you up to the idea of the two of us together. I dipped my head down and tasted those soft, gorgeous lips. You gasped right when my mouth touched yours and it sounded just as good as it did four years ago.

Every kiss I've ever given you is burned into my brain, Shelby, but that first one...that one is my favorite.

—Eli

His kiss consumed me the moment his lips touched mine. I was already so twisted with emotion from the words he'd said to me and how easily he got me to dance without even realizing it, that I wouldn't have known how to push myself away from him right now even if I wanted to.

My mouth parts for him immediately, wanting nothing more than to taste him again and let him heal every part of me that's been broken. As soon as our tongues touch, he bends his knees and tightens his hold around my waist, lifting me up against him. My legs immediately wrap around his waist and my hands fist into his hair as he turns and walks us out of the room.

I don't know where he's taking me and I don't care. I'll go anywhere with him as long as he keeps kissing me like he can't get enough of me.

His boots pound against the floor as he picks up the pace, with his legs and with his mouth. His tongue pushes deeper and the kiss grows harder and more frantic when I hear the snorts and whinnies of horses before they're quickly muffled by the slamming of a door.

The flash of lightning illuminates the room when my eyes open as he pulls his mouth away from mine, his breath coming out fast and heavy.

"I wanted to take you to my new place. Buy you some flowers and cook you dinner, but it's twenty minutes away and I've waited six years for this," he tells me, his eyes staring deep into mine as more lightning strikes and brightens up the tack room he brought us into.

"I don't need dinner and flowers, I just need you," I whisper as he turns us and leans down, pressing me into the cot in the corner of the room and covering his body over mine.

He settles between my legs, resting on one elbow to hold himself above me, his hand running down my side and over the material of my dress. His warm palm presses against my scarred thigh, slowly sliding back up and under my skirt.

I've never been touched like this since the accident, so surely and without hesitation that the emotions overwhelm me and I can't stop my eyes from welling with tears. I quickly blink them away before Eli can see them and think something is wrong. Nothing could be more right with this moment.

"You deserve to be in a bed, not in a cot in a horse barn," he mutters, looking down into my eyes as his hand moves up and down my thigh, sliding behind it to lift it up and hook it over his hip.

Bringing my hands to his cheeks, I cup his face in my palms and lean up, pressing my mouth gently to his before pulling back.

"I already told you, I don't need anything but you, Eli."

He sighs, resting his forehead against mine.

"Say my name again," he tells me softly.

I smile, craning my neck so I can press my lips to his ear.

"Eli, Eli, Eli," I whisper.

With a low, muttered curse, he turns his head and takes my lips again. My body ignites when our tongues touch and I move my hands from his face to slide them down his sides, yanking and tugging at his shirt. He breaks the kiss long enough to lean back and pull his T-shirt off and I press my palms to his muscled chest, an ache building inside my heart when I feel lines of scars under my fingers.

I look up into his face to see him watching me with apprehension. An ache builds inside my chest, thinking about what he went through and I don't want him to believe for even one second that he's anything less than an amazing, strong, beautiful man.

"We both have scars," I remind him.

"Yes," he says with a strangled whisper that threatens to crack my heart open.

"Does mine make me look weak?" I ask.

"Fuck no," he immediately replies as I continue running my fingers over his chest.

"Neither do yours."

He groans quietly when I dip my head forward and press my lips against each mark I can feel. One of his hands immediately comes up and he slides it through the hair at the back of my head, holding me against him as I kiss each painful memory away. When I finish, his fingers tighten in my hair and he pulls my head back and reclaims my mouth.

We move in a blur of hands and arms and shifting around on the small cot, removing each other's clothes as fast as we can, pausing to kiss in between each article that's removed. When I'm naked and lying completely bare and open beneath him, he slides his body down the length of mine, stopping with his head above my thigh.

Pushing myself up on my elbows, I watch as he takes *his* turn, kissing every inch of my scarred leg so softly and with so much care that I know this moment will be burned in my mind forever, making me feel cherished and beautiful. I let the people closest to me make me feel ugly and ashamed for too long.

Eli moves back up my body, pushing himself between my thighs as he goes. Locking my ankles behind his back, I hold his face in my hands once more as he rocks his hips, sliding himself against me, over and over, until I can feel my wetness coating him. His mouth hovers above mine, our lips barely touching as I pant and gasp while he continues to tease me.

It's been so long since I've wanted something this much, craved someone this immeasurably, and as he pulls his hips back and pushes slowly inside me, I know I'll only ever feel this way with him.

"Only you, always you," I whisper against his lips with a

groan as he slides fully inside me, saying the words he wrote to me all those years ago in his letters.

My name floats from his mouth on a whisper and the sound is filled with such awe and wonder that it takes my breath away as I push my hips up to bring him deeper.

"Say it again," I murmur against his mouth as he begins slowly rocking in and out of me.

His mouth leaves a trail of kisses down my cheek until he gets to my ear.

"Shelby, Shelby, Shelby…mine."

His hands grab on to mine and he takes them away from his face, lacing our fingers together as he pulls my arms above my head and presses them into the cot.

I groan his name and my head tilts back as he continues moving slowly in and out of my body.

His mouth finds mine again and his tongue pushes past my lips, sliding against mine in the same rhythm as his cock moving inside me, over and over. My body feels alive for the first time in six years, pleasure tingling up my spine and pulsing between my legs. I don't have to be ashamed of what I want and what I need when I'm with Eli and I've missed this part of myself. I want to let go, be wild, and have this man who heals me take everything I have to give.

I break the kiss, keeping my lips against his when I speak with another groan as he pushes deep and grinds himself against me.

"Harder," I whisper against his mouth.

A strangled, desperate sound flies past his lips, one of need and barely concealed control.

"Six years, baby," he pants as he starts moving a little faster and I tighten my thighs around his hips. "I'm barely holding on. Don't wanna hurt you."

He's still holding my arms above my head, and I squeeze

his hands tightly, wishing for the hundredth time that I could go back and never let him leave me. Never have one second of missing out on *this*.

"I'm not going to break. Please," I beg, pushing my hips up to meet him.

He growls low in his throat and immediately pulls his hips back and slams inside me, hard, just like I wanted. I shout his name and every thought flies from my mind. Suddenly there's nothing but Eli—the feel of him taking me, the sound of his body slapping against mine, and the curses he mutters as he moves above me. The legs of the cot scrape against the wooden floor, inching closer to the wall as he drives into me with such force that I can barely breathe from how good it feels.

He fucks me like he can't get deep enough, can't move fast enough, can't get close enough. He claims me with each slam of his hips against mine and I know I'll never be the same again after this moment. Our sweat-slicked bodies slide against each other as we give and take, and still, it's not enough.

I'm dying.

I'm alive.

I can't breathe.

I'm whole.

My release doesn't creep up on me slowly, starting at my toes and moving up my legs. The built-up pressure explodes out of me all at once like a million fireworks, my back arching as Eli slams his mouth to mine, swallowing my cries as the waves of pleasure pulse between my legs.

I tug my hands out of Eli's and yank my arms down, my palms smacking against his back and my fingers digging into his skin as his hips move impossibly faster and harder. He wrenches his mouth from mine and buries his face in the side of my neck to muffle his moans as his orgasm hits him as hard as mine, his hips jerking and shuttering through his release. With one last hard thrust, he collapses on top of me. I wrap my arms around him, holding him to me as tightly as possible so I can feel the rapid beat of his heart against my chest.

Chapter 21

Eli

Are you planning on living with me forever, or do you have a plan? Do you need an intervention?"

Rylan laughs at me as I finish putting away the box of plates, cups, and silverware that Kat gave me as a housewarming gift when she stopped by yesterday to see how I was doing. I can tell she still isn't fully on board with me moving out of her house, going by the way she hovered over me, asked me a hundred times if I needed anything, and reminded me to call my shrink if I needed someone to talk to. At least she didn't try to tell me again that I could come back to her place at any time, but that might have had something to do with Daniel giving her shoulder a squeeze each time she even thought about saying it. At least she liked the place and she was impressed with how quickly I'd unpacked and settled in.

"Is this your subtle way of telling me I'm cramping your style?" Rylan asks as I close the cabinet door and turn around to find him lounging on my couch with his hands behind his head.

"Not right at this moment, but you're going to need to find something else to do when Shelby gets here in a little bit," I remind him.

It's been a week since the day I cleaned out Shelby's studio and we spent the night together in the tack room, and we'd spent every night since then doing it again and again. We never made plans to meet, we just kept showing up at the same time, long after the workers had all gone home. Sometimes I'd get there first and have the music playing when she got there, and sometimes she got there first and I was able to spend a few minutes standing in the back of the room, silently watching her stretch out her muscles. When she'd catch my eyes in the mirror, she'd apologize for not giving me much to look at like she did six years ago, and I'd reassure her it didn't matter. Just knowing she was trying and actually looked happy doing it was all that mattered to me. I didn't know much about her injury other than what Meredith had told me the night she took me to the high school and I didn't want to upset Shelby by asking about it before she was ready. The only thing that kept echoing through my mind was the night she broke down right in that studio, so lost and hurting when she told me she couldn't hear the music anymore. I just wanted to give that back to her, any way I could. I wanted her to remember what it was like to have hope and know she could do anything she put her mind to.

Every night for a week, we'd dance together in that studio until the temptation of holding each other and touching each other became too much and we'd wordlessly move to the tack room and spend the night making up for all the time we lost. We could have come back here, we could have gone to her guest house, and we could have gone a hundred different places to be alone, but always wound up back in that damn tack room. There was something familiar about being there, like we were reliving the past, and I don't think either of us wanted to break the spell just yet and join the real world. Waking up each morning with Shelby in my arms, the two of us laughing while we scrambled around for our clothes so we could sneak out of the barn without anyone seeing us, felt just like old times. I know it should make me happy that we'd so easily fallen back into our old habits, but it didn't. We weren't the same people we'd been six years ago and we couldn't turn back time and make everything that had happened during that time disappear. There was nothing better than touching her again, being inside her again, and kissing her again when I'd done nothing but dream of those things for so long, but we couldn't keep doing this forever. We needed to talk. I needed to know what she wanted and I needed to make damn sure she knew where I stood and what *I* wanted.

I couldn't keep ignoring the fact that every night we were together, her cell phone would *ping* with several incoming texts and she'd shrug them off and tell me they were nothing important. I saw who they were from when she'd glance at her phone before quickly shoving it away. I knew she had someone else in her life, and I knew we needed to talk about it, as pissed off as that made me.

"So, you're finally going to bring her here instead of slinking out every night to meet her at the stables?" Rylan asks, giving me a knowing look when I glare at him. "I see all and I know all. Also, you're not the quietest guy in the world when you're trying to sneak out of the house late at night."

He laughs with a cocky smile as he pushes himself up from the couch and walks into the kitchen.

"You need a job. Or a hobby," I tell him irritably as he flops down on one of the bar stools lining the island in the middle of the kitchen.

"Why do I need a job when I have you for a sugar daddy? he asks with a wink. "And my hobby is watching you try not to fuck this shit up with Shelby. Again. It brings me great joy to see you bumbling around like an idiot without a plan."

"I have a plan," I tell him through clenched teeth.

"You had *one* plan—to clean up her studio and get her to dance again. Mission accomplished and it got you laid. Repeatedly. Nice work, by the way, but I think you're going to have to work a little harder than that to get what you want. You might have to, dare I say, *talk* to each other. About important shit," he reminds me.

"Which is exactly why she's coming here tonight instead of us meeting at the studio, where it's too easy for us to fall back into old habits," I inform him, even though I don't know why I continue confiding in him when he takes entirely too much joy out of making fun of me and riding my ass.

"And you're seriously letting all that shit go about your parents' accident? You're okay with forgetting about what happened and not getting the truth after all these years?" he questions.

I shrug as I grab my keys from the bowl on the counter.

"Paul was right. It was a long time ago. As much as I want justice and as much as it kills me knowing someone else was responsible and will never pay the price, some things are better left alone and some things are worth more than retaliation," I explain to him as I head to the front door, Rylan sliding off the bar stool to follow behind me. "The only good thing that came from the hell we lived through is that I know we're not always guaranteed to live another day.

I'm not going to waste the time I was given back focusing on something that isn't worth it. Being pissed all the time and hating someone for what they did to my family…it's not worth it. It's not going to make me happy and it sure as hell isn't going to make Shelby happy. She deserves to finally be happy again and I'm not going to fuck that up by ruining her life a second time."

With my hand on the doorknob, I glance at Rylan over my shoulder. "I sound like a pussy, don't I?"

He laughs, leaning his shoulder against the wall and crossing his arms in front of him.

"Of course you sound like a pussy, but it's better than you sounding like a selfish asshole. You can't say talking to a shrink isn't working for you. You're like the poster child for *Therapy worked for me and it can work for you, too!*" he cheers, throwing a fist up in the air.

"Seriously, when are you going to get a job and move out?" I grumble as I open the door and head outside to run to the grocery store so I can grab what I need to make dinner for Shelby.

"I'll leave when you don't need me anymore!" he shouts with a laugh.

Chapter 22

Shelby

December 12, 2010

Shelby,

I know you think one of my favorite things was to watch you dance, but actually, one of my favorite things to do was just be with you. Any way I could. I miss being able to talk to you. About anything. About everything. I even miss how whenever one of us wanted to talk about something heavy and deep, we could easily make it lighter, easily distract each other so the time we spent together wasn't wasted with worries and what-ifs. And even though I know we have a lot of heavy and deep things to talk about when I get home, I still can't wait to be distracted by you again. I love you, Shelby. Only you. Always you.

You and I had been inseparable for weeks. Whatever free

time either of us had, we spent it together and I didn't even care how much sleep I was losing or how exhausted I was every day at my two jobs. You finally realized I wasn't going anywhere and you finally stopped fighting me every step of the way, opening up to me and letting me see the strong, amazing woman you'd become.

"If you could go anywhere in the world, where would you go?" you asked, quickly switching to a new topic.

I tried to hide the scowl on my face when you told me about some douche bag your mother had been trying to set you up with for years. I did my best to not let my jealousy show when you told me your mother invited him over for dinner that night and demanded you be there, but obviously I hadn't done a great job.

We were lying in the grass a few acres away from the stables, me on my back and you on your stomach by my side, your chin resting on top of your hands as you looked over at me.

"Wherever you are," I told you with a smile.

You laughed and shook your head at me.

"I'm being serious."

"So am I," I told you with an easy shrug.

"We barely know each other," you countered.

I rolled to my side to face you, tucking a strand of hair behind your ear.

"I know you're the strongest person I've ever met. I know you don't give a shit what anyone else thinks. I know you work your ass off in that studio every day to make your dreams come true. What else do I need to know?" I asked.

We'd spent a lot of time talking the last few weeks and it made me laugh that you still thought we didn't know each other. You didn't even realize how much you'd opened up to me and how much you'd let me see, and you had no idea that the stuff I'd shared with you weren't things I went around announcing to everyone I knew.

I'd told you about my life growing up, my parents and their accident, joining the Marines, and continuing to work at the stables so I could put my sister through college.

You'd told me about your father and how he'd had the studio built for you, and how it was your little secret between just the two of you, that you both kept from your mother.

You had no idea how good it felt knowing that you trusted me enough to let me in on the secret you'd only ever shared with your father and Meredith. Whenever I had any doubts about not being good enough for you, not having enough money, not having anything to offer you other than myself, you'd erase all of those uncertainties just by being honest and not being afraid to tell me anything.

"What are we doing?" you whispered as you stared into my eyes and I slid my hand down your side and wrapped it around your waist. "I'm probably moving to New York in a few months and you're a Marine who could get stationed anywhere in the world. This is crazy."

It was crazy when you put it that way, but I didn't care. I also didn't tell you that I'd already asked about a possible transfer to New York. I had no idea where this thing was going between us, but I knew where I wanted it to go. I knew when I kissed you a few weeks ago in the stables that there would be no turning back. You'd gotten under my skin and into my heart and I knew I would do anything to keep it that way. After years of denying my attraction to you and refusing to allow myself to have you, I would stop at nothing to make sure I never lost you.

"Don't worry about what happens tomorrow, or next week, or months from now. All I care about is being with you, right here, right now, just like this," I told you as you wrapped your arms around my shoulders and smiled.

"You make it sound so easy."

I returned your smile, tightening my arms around your waist.

"Because it is easy. Especially now that you've stopped trying to pretend like you hate me," I joked, which earned me a smack on the chest. "The only thing that's hard is knowing you're having a fancy dinner tonight with some schmuck your mother adores who could give you everything I can't."

I wanted to kick myself in the ass for saying something a little too honest and deep when I watched the smile fall from your face. I opened my mouth to apologize, but you quickly leaned forward and kissed me, sliding your hands through my hair and making me forget what I'd just been thinking when you slid closer and pressed your body right up against mine.

You pulled your mouth away before I was ready and gave me that smile again.

"Fine, I won't worry about tomorrow as long as you won't worry about tonight," you told me with a shrug. "Since you avoided my first question, now you get three. Favorite color, favorite movie, and favorite food?"

You quickly moved your hand between our mouths when I tried to lean in for another kiss.

"You're killing me," I muttered against your hand, groaning when you tortured me even further by sliding one of your legs over my hip.

"First you answer the questions, then we get to the good stuff," you laughed, letting out a surprised squeal when I quickly rolled us until you were beneath me.

"Green, Shawshank Redemption, Peanut Butter Captain

Crunch," I spoke rapidly, your laughter immediately dying with a soft moan when I pushed between your thighs and kissed you before you could ask me anything else.

You made it easy to forget about my worries and insecurities, and I could only hope as I slid my hand under your shirt, that I did the same thing for you.

Fuck, I miss the sound of your voice. I miss the smell of your skin. I miss your smile. I miss your laugh, I miss your kiss.

—Eli

There's a knock on my bedroom door, and I look up from the letter I just finished reading when Meredith opens the door and peeks her head in.

She gives me a sad smile when she sees the letters strewn all over my bed, and I feel a moment of remorse that I've completely ignored her in the last week by either locking myself in this room to read the words Eli wrote to me all those years ago, or to race off to meet him.

"I know you're still mad at me and that's okay," Meredith tells me as she opens the door wide and moves farther into the room. "I did something really shitty, thinking I was protecting you, and I'm sorry. I just want you to be happy, Shelby."

I open my mouth to tell her that I *am* happy, but she holds up her hand to stop me.

"I know he can do that for you. I see it on your face every time you come back from being with him, but just be careful. He's been through a lot, and so have you. You guys can't stay locked up in that barn forever. You're going to have to come out and face the world someday, and you can't do that if you don't talk to each other."

I'm still hurt and angry by what she did, but it's hard to stay mad at her. If the shoe were on the other foot, I might have done the exact same thing. I'd do anything to protect Meredith and keep her safe, and as misguided as her attempt was, I know she didn't do it to intentionally hurt me.

"I forgive you," I whisper.

Her chin quivers with emotion and her eyes fill with tears. She quickly clears her throat and smiles at me as she moves to the side of the bed, leaning down and giving me a quick hug before pulling back and straightening her shirt.

"Enough of this emotional shit. My car is waiting out front to take me to the airport. I'll call you later when I land?"

I nod my head and return her smile, knowing we're going to be okay as I watch her walk out of my bedroom and hear the front door close. I close my eyes and rest my head back against the headboard with a smile, knowing that no matter what, Meredith will always have my back and be there for me.

* * *

I took a few deep breaths to calm my nerves as I walked up the steps to Eli's new place, but it didn't work. We'd spent the last week doing nothing but ripping each other's clothes off almost as soon as we saw each other, and even though each time was more amazing than the last and it's all I wanted and all I thought about when we weren't together, I knew we couldn't keep going like this. We couldn't close ourselves off in the tack room night after night, staying in our safe little cocoon and avoiding the world around us.

As easy as it was to fall back together, as natural as it was just to *be* together, Meredith was right, there were things we needed to talk about that I'd been avoiding. I kept convincing myself to keep it easy and keep it light because he didn't need anything hard in his life right now. I told myself he'd been through too much and shouldn't have to deal with the added pressure of my drama and bullshit on top of that, but I couldn't do it anymore. Not after reading his letters and not after seeing just how strong he was after the years of hell he'd lived through. The more time I spent with him, the more amazed I was at how easily he'd been able to come home and adjust back into his life. He'd mentioned a few times that he'd been talking to a therapist since he came home, but a part of me couldn't believe that's all it took to make him forget and move on and remember how to live again. Especially after the nightmare I witnessed him having in the stables and the scars those people left behind.

I shouldn't have been so surprised. He used to always tell me I was the strongest person he ever knew, but he had no idea just how strong *he* was. After the horrors he'd seen and been forced to endure, he still put my needs first. He still worried more about me than he did himself and I refused to take that for granted or let him down. I stopped being the weak and pathetic woman who wouldn't stand up for herself because of *him* and he needed to know that. I saw the look on his face the few times I got a text from Landry when we were together and I tried to pretend like it wasn't anything important, and it kills me that I wasn't honest with him right in that moment. He's here, he's alive, he's fighting for me, and I need him to know that I'm fighting right back, even if it might take some time.

When he called and invited me over for dinner tonight, saying he wanted to show me his place and that we needed to talk, it felt good to know we were thinking the same thing. Until I got in my car and headed over here and thought about everything we needed to discuss. Like why he lied to me in that first note when he left for deployment, if he really *is* doing okay, if he's told his sister about us, if he's sure I'm still what he wants, and if so, *what exactly* does he want. Not to mention the elephant in the room who keeps texting and calling, the one I used to try and move on from Eli, the one I'd hoped would help me forget him. I have to tell Eli that I let another man touch me and try to take his place, even though it's obvious now that no man could ever replace him, could ever be more than him or better than him. I have to tell him I allowed another man into my bed and into my life while he was being tortured and abused and clinging to thoughts of me and my love for him just to keep him alive. I have to tell him the other man is still in my life because I've been too much of a coward to break it off and too distracted being with Eli again to even care, and I'm scared to death Eli's going to hate me for it.

My mother is another story. Even though she's been strangely absent lately and she hasn't made any more threats since she reminded me of how she could still have Eli investigated for treason if I didn't hold up my end of the deal by staying away from him, I know when she finds out about all of this, there will be hell to pay, and Eli needs to be prepared. I need to be the strong woman Eli came home for, stand on my own two feet, make my own decisions, and take back my life. I won't risk his security or that of his family by telling him everything she's done and everything she's threatened until I talk to her first, but don't want him to spend one more day thinking I gave up or that I chose this life. I just want him to be safe. I just want him to be happy, and I just want to find a way to make him understand without putting him at risk.

As I lift my hand to knock, the door is flung open before my fist can even make contact with the wood. Just like every time I see him again, it feels like the first time. Butterflies flap around in my stomach and my heart beats faster when I see Eli standing in the doorway with a smile on his face, wearing a T-shirt and jeans and his hair still damp from a shower.

Before I can say anything, his arm is around my waist and he's pulling me against him and into the house, slamming the door behind me and pushing me up against it. His body presses into mine and his hand goes to the back of my head, his mouth slamming into mine before I can even take a breath or look around the foyer. I lose myself in his kiss and his taste and his touch, and the pep talk I gave myself while I was standing out front completely flies from my mind.

I can't think about anything else when he's this close and I don't care about anything else when he's kissing me. His tongue swirls around mine and his leg pushes between my thighs and all I care about is never wanting this feeling to end. Never wanting him to stop touching me or kissing me or wanting me. I've had too many days, months, and years of feeling so empty and feeling *nothing* that I don't know how to stop craving it or how to stop needing it like I need air to breathe.

I know I should pull back, slow this down, and do all the talking I convinced myself on the way over needed to happen, but it's physically impossible when the heat from his body warms everything cold inside me and the smell of his skin surrounds me.

Eli suddenly stops the kiss and pulls his head back, both of us breathing heavily and staring at each other.

"I invited you here because I thought it would be less distracting than the stables, so we could talk," he pants.

"Yes...talk," I mumble distractedly as my eyes move down to stare at his lips.

He presses his thigh up between my legs and I whimper, my hands fisting into the material of his T-shirt by his chest as his head dips down to the side of my neck.

"Fuck, you taste so good," he whispers, biting down gently and then tracing the tip of his tongue over the same spot.

I groan as he continues kissing my neck until my head thumps back against the door behind me, the sound bringing me somewhat back to my senses.

Moving my hands to the back of his head, I clutch on to his short hair and pull him away from my neck so I can see his face.

"Talking is important," I remind him, my eyes fluttering closed when he starts sliding his thigh back and forth between my legs.

"Very important," he confirms in a low voice, his hands moving slowly over my breasts and down my sides until he gets to my hips and clutches the material of my skirt in his fists.

As he leans in to kiss me again, I press my hand to his mouth to stop him and he growls against my palm. Dropping my hand down to flatten it against his chest so I can feel his heart beating against my skin, I raise one eyebrow and wait.

"Fine," he sighs loudly. "You're right. Favorite smell, favorite time of day, favorite memory?"

He fires off the questions rapidly and all I can think about is the letter I just read this morning, how some things never change no matter how much time we spend apart, and how I suddenly don't want to do anything else right now than let him distract me.

"Whatever soap you use, whatever time it is now, this one right here," I tell him quickly, cutting off his satisfied chuckle by yanking him back to me and attacking his lips.

I stand on my tiptoes, pushing away from the door to

mold my body to the front of him and wrap my arms around his shoulders. I think about all the time we lost and how many times I wished for just one more moment with him. I've been given that second chance to touch him whenever I want, and I don't want to waste it.

When his hands slide up my thighs and under my skirt to grab my ass and lift me up against him, I immediately wrap my legs around his hips and tell myself, *Just a few more seconds and then I'll make us stop.*

When one of his hands moves from my ass, slides under my tank top and up my rib cage, moving my bra aside as he goes, I think, *I just need a little bit more, then I'll make us stop.*

When his rough palm cups my breast and his thumb slides over my nipple as he walks us through his new house that I'm not even seeing, I tell myself, *I deserve a few more minutes of feeling like this.*

When he sits us down on the edge of the bed with my legs straddling his thighs, rolling my nipple between his thumb and his finger, my hands scramble between us, unzipping his jeans and pulling his cock out. When he moans into my mouth as I squeeze him and run my palm up and down his thick, hard length, I think, *He deserves a few more minutes of feeling like this, too.*

When his hands fly to my hips and he lifts my body just enough for me to slide my lacy underwear to the side and guide him where I need him, when he doesn't hesitate to thrust himself inside me hard and deep, I stop thinking about putting a halt to this.

When his fingers dig into the skin of my ass as I grind myself against him and when he sucks my tongue into his mouth, I stop thinking about anything else we should be doing right now.

When his hands clutching my ass help move me, slamming me down on his cock over and over, when he pulls his mouth away from mine and begs me to fuck him harder, fuck him faster, when he tells me how good I feel, when he tells me he still can't believe I'm real, when he tells me he can't live without this, can't live without *me*, I stop thinking about anything but how good it feels to be so consumed and so filled by this man that I've never stopped loving.

When I come so quickly it takes my breath away, when I ride him harder and faster until he shouts my name, when I can feel his cock pulsing with his release, when he reaches between us and his fingers find my clit, I stop thinking about all the things I need to say.

When he holds himself still inside me as his orgasm subsides, when his fingertips circle and slide and move faster, when he makes me come again and I moan his name with a sigh, when he tells me he loves me, tells me nothing else matters, begs me to stay…I stop thinking altogether.

Chapter 23

Eli

So much for talking.

Staring down at Shelby's hair spread out on my pillow with her face soft and relaxed in sleep, I forget what was so important that we needed to talk about last night. I forget everything but how good it feels to open my eyes and see her lying next to me, feel her body curled up against mine, and listen to her breathe. Nothing is more important than this moment, right here. Being happy and content and not having any worries other than what I'm going to feed her for breakfast when she wakes up.

After I opened the door to her last night and saw her standing there in a casual white tank top and blue and white patterned short skirt with her long, gorgeous legs on display, I forgot all about my concerns and just wanted to kiss her, hold her in my arms, and finally believe she's here with me and it wasn't all a dream. Every time she leaves me, I have moments of panic that none of this is real. So many minutes wasted during each day where I have to stop and remember how to breathe and push back the images of filth and pain, and screaming and death, that flash through my mind. I never feel like myself again until she walks back into the room and I can touch her, feel the heat from her skin, the silk of her hair, and listen to the sound of her voice, erasing all my doubts and fears.

Shelby sighs in her sleep and the *ping* of her phone goes off on the nightstand next to her. I watch her eyes flutter open at the sound and she turns her body away from me, grabbing the phone and bringing it close to her. I stay silent as she quickly presses a button to blacken the screen, setting the phone back on the nightstand before rolling back to me.

Her face lights up with a smile and she lifts one hand up and presses it to the side of my face.

"Good morning."

Her voice is raspy and still full of sleep and I'm instantly hard for her, but I don't move to pull her close. The peaceful moment from just a few seconds ago has been interrupted, and no matter how much I want to ignore it and lose myself in her, I can't do that now.

"It's okay if you need to take that," I tell her, nodding in the direction of her phone.

She rubs her thumb back and forth over my cheek and shakes her head.

"Nope, it can wait."

Her body starts to slide closer and I press my hand against her chest to stop her, hating the look of confusion on her face.

"Shelby, it's fine. I'll go take a shower and give you some privacy," I reassure her, even though all I want to do is slide between her thighs and push inside her, reminding her she's *mine*.

I move to roll away and get out of bed, but her hand grabs my arm and tugs me back to her.

"Please, don't go," she begs softly as I flop down onto my back and stare at the ceiling.

"I get it, okay? I understand and I'm not mad. I hurt you and I was dead for five years. It's selfish of me to think you would have been alone all that time."

She sighs, closing the distance between us to rest her arms on my chest and slide one of her legs between mine. Both of her hands grab my face and gently turn it toward her.

"It's not what you think, Eli. It isn't...he isn't—"

"I told you, it's okay," I remind her, cutting her off as she flounders for the right words. "You don't have to explain. I thought I needed you to, but I don't. I'm not mad, I just don't want to know. I don't want to have this image in my head of you with someone else. I just...don't want to know. You let go and you moved on and that's *okay*. I get it. Just let me get out of the room so you can handle whatever it is."

I try to move away from her again, but her thigh tightens around mine and her arms wrap around my waist, holding me against her. I can see she wants to talk about this, and I don't know what else to say or do to make her understand I can't do it. I can be tolerant and supportive, but I can't lie here next to her and listen to her tell me about the man she had in her life while I was gone. The man who got to touch her and kiss her and hold her when I was thousands of miles away fighting to stay alive. I had a moment of weakness the other night and Googled him. That was all the information I needed to make me feel small and weak and like I wasn't good enough for her. I don't need that shit swirling around in my brain if I want this to work between us. I want her to be happy and I want her in my life, however I can have her. Even if that means I have to share her, as much as it would kill me. I'd do it and I'd suck it up as long as it meant she'd continue to come back to me.

"I need to get something. Will you stay here, right where you are, and not move?" she asks softly.

She waits for me to nod before she quickly scrambles out of bed and covers up her naked body with my T-shirt that was tossed on the floor last night. I listen to her bare feet pad across the floor, down the hall, and out into the living room. I continue staring up at the ceiling until I hear her walk back into the room. Turning my head, I watch her walk toward the bed, my shirt hanging off one shoulder and stopping mid-thigh. She crawls back into the bed, clutching something in her hands in front of her. Crisscrossing her legs next to me, I keep my eyes glued to her face as she stares down at whatever she's holding in her hands.

"First of all, that was a text from my mother, not him," she starts. "I ended things with him before he left to go out of town. Before our night together in the stables."

Her eyes meet mine and she gives me a small smile, cocking her head to the side.

"And second, I never let you go. Ever."

She holds her arm out toward me and opens her palm. Pushing myself up, I scoot to the headboard, leaning my back against it before I look away from her eyes and down into the hand she's holding out to me.

My heart stutters in my chest and my mouth drops open as I reach out with a shaking hand and pull my dog tags out of her open palm. I trace my fingers over the stamped letters and numbers that spell out my name, rank, and company number.

"Did you know your sister had a funeral for you?" she asks quietly.

I nod my head as I continue staring down at the tags,

trying to block out the images of the day they were ripped from my neck and tossed to the ground. My sister told me they had a small service at the cemetery, not telling me too much about it other than how pissed she was that because of the suspicion still clouding what happened at the time, she couldn't get the Marines to agree to a full military burial or get them to issue a military headstone.

"I overheard people talking about it at one of the charity events I was attending," Shelby continues. "I went a few hours after it was over, when I knew your family would be long gone."

She clears her throat and I look up to see her eyes fill with tears as she stares unblinking at the tags, lost in her memories. My heart breaks all over again knowing what I did to her, how I left, and feeling ashamed that I never told Kat about us. Never explained to my family how much this woman meant to me and she was forced to sneak into the damn cemetery like a stranger.

"When I got there," she speaks again, "I saw your tags lying over the top of the headstone. I knew it was wrong and I knew I shouldn't take them, but I couldn't stop myself."

A tear falls down her cheek and her mouth trembles as she keeps going, each word she speaks breaking me in two. I slide my hand around to the back of her neck, pulling her toward me until our foreheads are touching. I close my eyes and listen to each shaky breath she exhales, wishing I could take away all of her pain as she relives this moment.

"I picked them up and held them in my hands and all I could remember was the last time I saw you wearing them. It was the day I left for my audition and we'd taken a blanket out into one of the old pastures, do you remember?" she asks, pulling her head back and her eyes finally meeting mine.

I nod my head silently, remembering that day all too well. We spent the morning naked and wrapped up in each other under the shade of Shelby's favorite magnolia tree, making plans for our future after she nailed the audition. Then we said good-bye so she could pack and head to the airport, I came home to find the police report someone had sent me, and I made the stupid decision to confront her mother without talking to her first.

"Your body was on top of mine and your tags hung down between us, sliding against my chest every time you moved," she says softly, only remembering and knowing about the good part of that day. "When I got to the cemetery and saw them there, held them in my hands, and closed my eyes, all I could remember was the feel of them against my skin every time we made love. I held onto them and I could almost imagine they were still warm from your body and I could almost pretend like you were still alive and I'd see you again."

"Shelby..."

I say her name and it comes out in a cracked voice, my throat clogged and tight with so much emotion I can barely handle it.

"I was so angry and so hurt, but it didn't even matter. Nothing mattered but having a piece of you I could keep with me. I took the tags and I kept them in a drawer in my jewelry box," she admits.

I drop the tags into my lap and lean toward her, cupping her face in my hands and wiping her tears away with my thumbs, each one that falls down her cheeks feeling like a knife to my heart.

"I never let you go, Eli," she whispers. "Never. Every time I questioned my life, every time I felt sorry for myself, I opened the drawer to my jewelry box and ran my fingers over them, remembering what it was like to be happy and loved, and it helped me get through another day."

I press my forehead to hers and let out a shuddering breath, wishing there was something I could do to take away her pain, cursing myself for being jealous and angry.

"I can't take back the choices I made. I can't erase the things I did no matter how much I wish I could, but you need to know I never let go. I tried to move on, but it didn't work. He could never replace you, he could never make me feel the way you did, no matter how hard I tried," she tells me through her tears. "It was always you, only you."

Tipping her head up, I kiss the tears from her cheeks, telling her I love her and that I'm sorry in between each press of my mouth against her warm, wet skin. When I'm finished, she pulls her head back and runs her hand softly down the side of my face.

"There's things I need to do, stuff I need to take care of, and it might take some time—"

I interrupt her words with another quick kiss, pressing my forehead to hers once again.

"It doesn't matter. I'm here and I'm not going anywhere," I tell her. "I'm all in, Shelby. I was all in the minute I knew I wasn't going to die in that prison. I was all in the first time I saw you again and knew I wasn't dreaming. I'll wait for you, as long as it takes."

She cuts *me* off this time, slamming her mouth against mine as I wrap my arms around her and push her back to the bed, yanking the T-shirt up and off her body in my hurry to get her naked and feel her skin against mine.

Her legs come around my hips and I push my boxer briefs down just enough to free myself and quickly push inside her, needing her more than I ever thought possible. With each thrust, each slide of my cock through her hot wet heat, and each chant of my name that falls from her lips, I feel myself letting go of doubts and insecurities and I finally feel like I'm home, where I belong.

There are still so many things I need to tell her, something important that tries to claw its way to the front of my mind, something I know will change everything and try to ruin the happiness we've finally found, but I push it back because it doesn't matter. Nothing else matters right now but this moment and finally having everything I've ever wanted. I forget about everything but the feel of Shelby wrapped around me, the sound of her voice in my ear, and the smell of peaches that always makes everything better.

She makes the bad things all go away...

Chapter 24

Shelby

All right, I have one really important question that needs to be answered," Eli tells me seriously, pushing himself up on one elbow on the blanket next to me.

Following our night together at his house two weeks ago when I showed him his dog tags, we've spent as much time together as possible, knowing that everything will change as soon as I figure out how to stand up to my mother.

After spending all of our time with each other in the tack room and then not changing it up much by locking ourselves in Eli's bedroom for a few days, we finally managed to get out of bed so Eli could give me a tour of his new house and actually do something normal for a change, with our clothes on. I've had a hundred different opportunities to tell him about the things my mother threatened me with over the years to keep Eli protected, but each time I open my mouth to give him the last of my secrets, he laughs or he smiles and I stop myself. I'm not ready to watch the happiness leave his face and I'm not ready to be the one to bring more pain and guilt into his life. Not now. Not yet. Maybe not ever.

I feel horrible that I'm keeping such a big secret from the man I love, but I just want to enjoy these peaceful moments with him and pretend like the rest of the world doesn't exist, is that too much to ask after all we've been through? Does he really need to know about the sacrifices I made to keep him safe? All it will do is pile up guilt onto his already heavy shoulders and I don't want to do that to him. I don't want to be the one to bring him any more pain after what he's gone through.

When we woke up this morning, Eli packed us a lunch, grabbed a blanket from his hall closet, and drove us out to the plantation, pulling up to the stables and giving me a wink when I asked him what we were doing. As soon as we got inside the barn, we found Paul standing beside two horses all saddled up and ready for a ride—Ariel, and Belle's foal, Tiana. I'd broken the news to Eli a few days ago that his favorite horse, Belle, had died giving birth to Tiana. He was sad that he didn't get to say good-bye to his favorite mare, but more than happy to shower Tiana with the same love and attention he did her mother.

Eli helped me up onto Ariel before getting into the saddle of Tiana, and we rode out side by side into the back acres of the property until we were as far away from the stables as possible while still being on Eubanks land. We tied up the horses to a tree, spread out the blanket in the grass, and curled up next to each other just like we used to do that summer long ago. We talked about everything and we talked about nothing and it was perfect. I knew we were living in the past, trying to re-create a moment in time that was long gone, but I didn't care. It felt good and it felt right lying here next to him under the shade of a big oak tree. It was like we were getting to know each other and falling in love all over again, just like we did six years ago.

"Go ahead, ask your important question," I tell him, turning on my side to face him.

"I have to know. After all this time, you have to tell me..." He speaks softly, dragging out his question. "How in the hell do you always smell like peaches?"

It definitely isn't the question I thought he would ask, figuring he knew it was time to come back down to reality and talk about something serious, but his silly question makes me throw my head back and laugh.

"Why are you laughing? This is a serious question that has plagued me for years. You bathe in the juice of fresh peaches every night, don't you?" he asks, just making me laugh harder when he dips his head down to my neck, runs his nose along my throat, and takes a deep breath.

Knowing this "getting to know each other again" moment will be cut short if he continues breathing against my neck and sliding his lips across my skin, I press my hands to his chest and gently push him away.

"I use peach-scented body wash, shampoo, and lotion," I tell him, laughing again as his face falls when he finds out I don't take baths in peach juice like he imagined. "My dad used to give me that stuff every year for my birthday, and after he died, I kept buying it because it reminded me of him."

Eli presses a kiss to my forehead and holds his lips there comfortingly for a few seconds, still knowing after all this time that memories of my father are like a double-edged sword. I love talking about him and remembering him, but at the same time, thoughts of the only parent I had who actually loved me unconditionally make me sad and wish he were still here with me.

"Well, I'll always be grateful to that man for giving you

something that smells so delicious and kept me going for five years when I would dream about that damn smell," he tells me, smiling to lighten his words.

Even though our "normal" outings of horseback riding, driving a few towns over to go to dinner and catch a movie, and the other handful of things we've done the last few weeks have included a lot of talking, Eli has never once spoken about what he went through with anything other than nonchalance or downplaying the little pieces he let slip. Each time he does it, I worry and I fear for the things that still haunt him, wondering if he's holding himself back or he's afraid to go into detail because it will upset me. I don't need him to tell me everything, but I need him to know I'm here for him, whenever he needs me or whenever he's ready to open up more.

"Are you doing okay? You haven't said much about your appointment with the therapist the other day," I say gently, trying my best not to push him, but still needing him to know he can talk to me about anything.

"I'm fine, and there's not much to say," he tells me with an easy smile and a shrug, sliding his arm around my waist and pulling me closer to him on the blanket. "It's pretty much the same thing every week, like I told you. He asks me about the nightmares and I tell him you take them all away and remind him that spending an hour with him when I could be with *you* is a waste of time and a detriment to my recovery."

Just like always, he brushes off my concern and makes a joke. I try not to let it bother me that Eli never wants to confide in me about what he went through and I remind myself that I have no experience with this kind of thing and have no idea if his behavior is normal or not. He seems fine, he seems happy, and he doesn't act like what happened to him still plagues him. I don't want to keep bringing it up and pushing it to the forefront of his mind when he's doing so well and he's figured out how to move on and let go.

"You know you can always talk to me, right? About anything?" I remind him, just like I've done every time I've tried to get him to talk recently.

With his elbow still holding him up on his side, he rests his cheek on his hand and smiles at me.

"I know. Don't worry about me, okay? Everything is fine as long as you're here with me."

His words should make me happy, knowing I'm the reason he's fine, but they don't. For the first time, lying here next to him with the warm Southern air floating over us and the sun shining bright in the sky above us, his words fill me with fear and dread. About what he *isn't* saying and about what will happen when it all becomes too much for him and he can't keep it bottled up inside any longer. It's the same apprehension that has kept me from telling him about the threats my mother held over my head and the tattoo on the inside of my wrist, hidden under the watchband or my fears about what will happen when Landry comes home.

Eli pushes himself up from the blanket and starts spreading out the lunch items he packed for us, changing the subject to tell me about his niece and the funny things she says now that she's learned how to speak in complete sentences. Just like always, his easy smile and the sweet sound of his laughter distract me from my worries. I refuse to ruin our time together worrying about what Landry and my mother will do when I can no longer keep mine and Eli's relationship in the safe little bubble we've been in the last few weeks.

Staring at the dimples in his cheeks and listening to the happiness in his voice, I run my thumb over my watchband, realizing some secrets are better left buried. Some truths aren't worth the pain they'll bring and I will do anything I can to make sure Eli never has to feel one minute of pain again because of me.

As we sit side by side on the blanket and enjoy our lunch and easy conversation, I can only hope that when the time comes for Eli to tell me about his years in captivity, I'll know what to do and I'll be able to give him the strength that he selflessly hands over to me, every day I'm with him.

Chapter 25

Eli

"Why don't you ever take *me* out to dinner or take *me* horseback riding? It's like you don't even care," Rylan complains with an overexaggerated sigh while he leans against the doorway of my bathroom and watches me shave.

I feel a little guilty that I haven't been spending as much time with him lately, but right now, being with Shelby is the only thing that matters. Even though he continually busts my balls and makes jokes, I know he understands. He just likes to annoy the hell out of me by complaining all the time.

"Shelby's got some work to do tomorrow, so how about you and I catch up on shitty reality television and order pizza?" I ask, looking up at his reflection in the mirror in front of me.

"Fine. Whatever. I guess I'll always be your second choice," he mutters, pushing away from the wall to stand right behind me. "Have you guys talked?"

I roll my eyes, rinsing off the blade in the pool of water in the sink before bringing it back up to my cheek.

"Yes, we've talked, Dr. Phil."

Rylan sighs and shakes his head at me.

"I mean, have you talked about important stuff, dumbass. I know you haven't told her everything or you wouldn't be standing here all casual while you try and pretty up that ugly mug of yours."

My head starts to pound right behind my eyes and I squeeze them closed, pressing my hands against the edge of the sink and taking a few deep breaths to make the pain go away. Rylan's words make my gut churn with an unknown fear and I have no idea why. Shelby and I have done nothing *but* talk the last few weeks.

We talked about the summer we fell in love and we talked about how she's been trying to ease her way back into dancing again. She told me about Meredith's writing career and about how mind-numbing her job is working for her mother. I told her about Kat and Daniel's life together and about my niece, Lilly. We did regular things like a regular couple and it felt good to do stuff like that and feel . . . normal.

"Of course we've talked about important stuff," I scoff, opening my eyes to glare at him through the mirror.

"Right. Sure you have. Why don't I believe you? Why do I feel like there's still something huge you haven't told her yet?"

The pain slices through my head and I wince, wishing he would just stop talking.

"We're getting to know each other again, all right? It's good. It's better than good, so just leave it alone," I warn him.

I hate being short with my best friend, but I don't like the way his words make me feel—confused and anything *but* normal.

"You need to tell her about what happened over there, Eli. You can't keep all of this to yourself or it's going to eat away at you and you're going to lose her," Rylan tells me softly.

"Shut up! Just, shut up," I finally growl, tossing the razor into the sink and grabbing my head with both hands to try and stop the headache that just won't quit. "Everything is fine and I don't need you telling me what to do or what to talk about with Shelby. We're *fine*."

We stare at each other silently through the mirror until Rylan finally takes the hint, delivering one last annoying reminder.

"You need to tell Shelby what happened over there and let go. Just...let go."

I don't reply to him as he turns away from me and walks out of the bathroom. As soon as he's gone, my headache starts to ebb and I tip my head from side to side to stretch out the kinks in my neck from clenching my muscles so tightly.

He's wrong. I don't need to tell her what happened over there and I don't need to even *think* about what happened over there. She knows it was bad and that's all she needs to know. Telling her all the gory details won't do anything but screw up the progress we've made. I don't need her looking at me with pity, not now. I just need to be with her and everything will be fine. We'll talk about the letters I wrote her, and soon we'll have to talk about her mother's involvement in my life and what she's done to hurt me and my family, but that's where the sharing will end. I refuse to make the rocky ground we're standing on as we get to know each other again crumble at our feet. I know I'd never lose her over something like accusing her mother of trying to ruin me, but I also know it won't be pleasant. It will kill her knowing her flesh and blood was responsible for what happened to me. She'll feel guilty and she'll hate herself, thinking there might have been some way for her to prevent any of it from happening.

She makes the bad all go away, and that's exactly where it needs to stay.

Chapter 26

Georgia

This has gone far enough. I've done everything you've demanded of me for years and it has to stop. You got what you wanted. Why can't that be enough?" I plead as I stare at the man standing across the room, casually picking up a framed photo of Shelby as a teenager.

I want to scream at him not to look at her, not to touch her, but I keep my anger and fear in check, knowing it will only enrage him.

"You know why it's not enough, Georgia. You were supposed to get rid of him for good, and now he's back, threatening to screw everything up," he informs me, placing the photo back on the shelf as he turns to face me.

"I never had *any* intentions of getting rid of him. That was *your* doing. I got him away from Shelby, like you asked. I'm sure he has enough problems to deal with after what you had done to him, that coming back for Shelby is the least of his concerns," I reply, hoping, wishing, and praying that what I'm saying is true.

If Eli James comes anywhere near my daughter again, bad things will happen to everyone. This man has proven that he will stop at nothing to get what he wants, and what he wants is Shelby. The idea that I've fostered his needs, even encouraged them, makes me sick to my stomach, but there is nothing else I can do, short of turning myself in. I made the selfish choice. One I will live with for the rest of my life. Someone is bound to get hurt no matter what I do.

I've never been very good at being a mother. I had bigger and better things in my sights than being stuck at home with a child, and when I found out I was pregnant, it was too late to do anything about it. I never could figure out how to stop blaming my daughter for ending all my dreams. I knew Shelby hated me for the way I treated her, the way I stifled her, and the way I tried to turn her into something she wasn't. I can only hope that Shelby will see that all the things I've done recently were to protect her and the man she cares about, in my own twisted way. To make up for never being a very good mother. For allowing this man to blackmail me so I could keep my reputation intact. I knew that shouldn't have been my one and only concern at the time, but my status in this town is all I have. The only thing that makes me stand out and makes people notice me. A way to relive my glory days, back before I had a child, when all eyes were on me and everything I ever wanted was in the palm of my hand.

I'm a coward and I'm a fool, and if this man weren't standing right in front of me, I would crumple to the floor, the pain of what I've done to my daughter so acute that it almost takes my breath away.

I had no way of knowing that each time I succumbed to his threats, Shelby would pay the price and I wished more than anything that I could go back and make a different decision. Tell the truth instead of covering it up. Deal with the consequences instead of worrying about my reputation.

I hoped that he would lose interest when he saw that Shelby never returned his feelings, but it only made him angrier, more aggressive, more vicious with his warnings and his extortions.

"You better hope that's true, Georgia," he says in a low voice with a raise of one eyebrow as he stalks across the room to stand right in front of me. "You better hope he stays far away from Shelby or there will be consequences. I'd hate to have to let this town know all of the things you've done with their money, right under their noses. I'd hate for anything to happen to Mr. James and his family... or Shelby."

I want to scream and shout at him that *he's* the one using charity money for evil instead of good. *He's* the one fooling everyone. *He's* the one forcing my arm, threatening me to do corrupt things because he knows I'll do anything to make sure no one else loses their life, but you can't reason with someone who is crazy. Someone who will stop at nothing to get what he wants. And he wants my daughter, even if he threatens her life in the same breath.

I made the mistake of trusting him to fix a problem for me years ago, and I never lived it down. I could only hope that Shelby was strong enough to stand up to him when the time came, no matter what I'd done to keep her down all these years.

"Shelby has always known what's at stake. She knows that with one phone call the rumor of Eli being a traitor can be brought to light again and Eli's sister and brother-in-law's businesses can be shut down," I remind him, hating the words as they came out of my mouth and the part I played in all of it.

Hating *everything* I had to threaten Shelby with just so

she didn't stray from the path. So she didn't do anything to anger this man and give him another reason to make threats. This man claimed to love Shelby and would stop at nothing to have her, but he had no idea what love was.

I wish I learned what it meant to love something so much you would do anything to protect it before it was too late. Before I'd fallen so far down this deceptive hole that there was no way of finding my way out without good people being hurt. Without my daughter being caught in the crossfire.

I can't take it anymore. I can't take the lying and the deceit. I can't take one more second of letting this man bully me. I've done enough damage and it's time to pay for my mistakes.

"But it doesn't matter anymore, because I'm done. With all of this. I'm finished with your threats and I'm finished with you hurting my family just to get what you want. I'm turning myself in and I'M DONE!"

He laughs cynically then immediately wipes the smile from his face and stares at me with so much anger that it chills me to the bone.

"You're done when I say you are."

As he walks out of the office, whistling to himself like he doesn't have a care in the world, I hope and I wish and I pray that Shelby will find the strength I know she possesses to see through this man and what he's done.

And to someday forgive me for the part I played in all of this.

Chapter 27

Shelby

December 30, 2010

Shelby,

It kills me that I haven't heard from you. I have no idea if you're reading these letters and hating me even more, or just throwing them away without looking at them. I don't want to bother you anymore, so this is the last one I'm going to write. The hardest one I'm going to write, which is why I kept it for last. I'm sorry. I'm so sorry. I should have been a stronger man and I'll always regret that I wasn't. I love you, Shelby. Only you. Always you.

I'd been on edge since you left for the airport for your audition. I knew you'd only be gone overnight and I'd see you again tomorrow, but I still couldn't shake the uneasy feeling I had when we said good-bye and I watched you walk away.

That nervous feeling became full-blown fear, anger, and panic, settling like a rock in the pit of my stomach when I got back to my apartment and opened up an envelope that had arrived in the mail with no name or return address.

I acted without thinking. I scanned it and e-mailed it to your mother with a threat for her to come clean before I went to the authorities, and quietly seethed in my living room until I got a reply, a few hours after I'd sent it.

Twenty minutes later I was walking into your mother's office at the plantation, being led through the sprawling home by a staff member, stepping foot over the threshold of a house I was more than welcome to work at, but never good enough to enter.

She dismissed the staff member with a terse nod, walked out from behind her desk and across the room towards me. I held my ground and crossed my arms over my chest, feeling confident that I had the upper hand with this woman who'd ruined my life, my sister's life, and had done everything she could to make you miserable and afraid of her.

Your mother didn't speak until she'd slammed the door of the office closed and turned to face me.

"How dare you threaten me," she seethed.

"How dare I?" I fired back, dropping my arms and taking a step towards her. "How dare YOU. Tell me, just how many dicks did you have to suck to make it all go away?"

Her hand cracked against my cheek before I'd barely gotten the last word out. I'd never wanted to hurt a woman before, but it took everything in me not to wrap my hands around her neck and choke the life out of her for what she'd done to my family. For the pain she'd caused and the hours and weeks and years we'd spent hating the wrong people.

She stared at my face with an open mouth and wide eyes, and for one second, I could almost imagine I saw guilt and shame in her green eyes, the same color as yours, but completely void of your same light and hope and happiness.

"You have no idea what you've done by sending that e-mail. No idea what problems you've caused by not leaving this alone," she threatened.

She stalked away from me and went back behind the comfort of her desk, putting distance between us like she instinctively knew my hands were clenched into fists at my sides because it was the only thing that stopped me from hitting her back.

"Your unit's deployment has been bumped up. You'll be leaving tonight, as soon as you pack your things and get your affairs in order."

The blood drains from my face when she speaks in a monotone voice, so cold and uncaring, like she's reciting the facts to a math problem instead of ruining my life all over again.

"Bullshit," I muttered.

I knew it was only a matter of time before our unit's turn to go to war, but we'd been briefed countless times and reassured we had at least a year before that could be a possibility. Plenty of time for you and I to get settled in New York, for me to put a ring on your finger and officially make you mine before I had to leave you temporarily. There's no way in hell Georgia Eubanks, no matter how much money she had, could make something like that happen so quickly. No fucking way.

"Go ahead and check your e-mail, Mr. James. You'll find a message from the military confirming what I just told you."

With shaking hands, I pulled my phone out of my back pocket and opened the e-mail app. Nausea filled my mouth with spit and made me break out in a cold sweat when I saw the e-mail with my orders.

"You need to get out of my daughter's life and you need to get out now. If you want Shelby to have her silly dreams of being a dancer and your sister to finish college and have a secure future, you will leave and never look back."

My head whips up from my phone, the sickness rushing through me immediately exchanged for anger once again.

"Are you seriously threatening me right now? Threatening your own fucking daughter? MY SISTER?" I shouted.

"You won't call Shelby, you won't text Shelby, and you won't see her again," she orders, like I hadn't even spoken. "You will leave her a note, saying whatever you have to to get her to let go of you and move on and you will forget about everything you saw in that report you so foolishly e-mailed to me. If you don't, everything I said will become a reality, and I know you don't want that for anyone. Make the right choice, Mr. James. I tried…my hands are tied…you have no idea what you've done…"

With those final words, she sat down in her chair, lifted up the receiver of her phone, pressed a few buttons, and turned her back on me.

I'd come in here so angry and so sure of the outcome, and in just a few minutes Georgia Eubanks had slid the rug right out from under me.

Feeling like I had no other options, not if I wanted to protect everyone I loved, I made the only choice I could, not even realizing it would be the worst decision I'd ever made.

In one final act of defiance, I grabbed a large, expensive-looking vase from a side table by the door, turned, and hurled it across the room. The only satisfaction I got from that was the wide, scared look on your mother's face when she whipped her chair around as soon as it shattered against the wall by her head.

I'm sorry, Shelby. I'm so sorry. I wish all of these words

weren't true. I wish I could take them back and make it so none of this ever happened, so that I was a stronger man and never walked away from you, but I can't. I'm sorry.

—Eli

With my hands clutching tightly to the ballet barre attached to the mirrors that ran the length of the studio wall, I bowed my head and tried not to scream.

When I left Eli earlier today, after another laid-back, easy afternoon of riding horses and reminiscing about the summer we first fell in love, I ran home to finally read the last letter and almost wished I hadn't. I wanted nothing more than to pretend like I hadn't seen those words, didn't know what my mother had done, didn't have the proof of it back in my bedroom or the realization that I'd probably always instinctively known she had something to do with the way Eli left and chosen to ignore it.

I'd also ignored the text my mother sent me a few weeks ago the morning I was in bed with Eli, simply stating that we needed to talk. After reading that letter, I wanted nothing more than to turn my back on her and never speak to her again. She never cared about me, she never cared about my happiness, she only cared about herself. The pain in my chest is so acute that I can't stop the sob that flies from my mouth when I think about the words Eli wrote and remember everything she stole from me.

The only reason I finally agreed to meet with her, the only reason I'm here right now, is because I want to understand. I want to know how it's possible for a mother to hate her daughter so much. I want to know what was in the e-mail Eli sent to her that day and I want to know why he didn't tell me about it, but I'm scared to death to finally have all the answers.

I thought coming here to the studio to stretch and listen to music before I met her up at the house would calm my nerves, but the longer I stay here and avoid the inevitable, the worse I feel.

"I was always jealous of you two."

My head flies up and I quickly whirl around when I hear her voice. My heart flutters nervously, wondering how she found me here, how she knows about this room, and why she doesn't look at all shocked to be standing in the doorway.

"You and your father," she continues quietly, assuming the surprised look on my face has something to do with the statement she made. "I was always jealous of the connection the two of you had."

She steps farther into the room, her heels clicking against the wood floor and I take a moment to really look at her. Gone is the demanding, haughty look on her face, perfectly pressed business suit, and every hair flawlessly in place. She looks like she's aged twenty years as I continue to stare at her when she stops in the middle of the room, twisting her hands together nervously in front of her. Her black pants suit is full of wrinkles and her usual tight, slicked-back French twist has started to come loose, strands of hair falling against her face and around her shoulders. She looks so vulnerable and small and it makes me sad. It should make me happy that she finally looks as miserable as she's made me feel most of my life, but it doesn't. I don't know how to deal with the emotions I'm feeling for her right now. I've spent so much of my time resenting her and she made it easy with her nose up in the air, looking down on me all these years. It's hard to hate someone who is standing in front of you, cutting herself open and bleeding all of her emotions out into a puddle at your feet.

"I never wanted to be a mother, but I still hated how close

the two of you were," she goes on. "Going off together all the time, sharing secrets and laughs and a bond that I could never understand. I never wanted a child, but I still hated that the two of you had something like that and I didn't."

I want to speak, ask her a thousand questions, shout a million insults, and scream at her until my voice is hoarse, but I can't make the words come. I can do nothing but stand here, tightly clutching onto the barre behind me, letting her finally tell me what I'd always wanted to know. Everything finally makes sense, but it's not a relief to hear her say these words to me. I stopped giving her the power to hurt me a long time ago, but it doesn't stop the pain from spreading through my heart hearing her admit she never wanted me.

"I always knew about this studio, too. I followed the two of you one day when you snuck off, thinking I wasn't paying attention," she explains quietly. "I watched you dance and... it hurt everything inside of me. It made me angry and it made me hate you even more. I knew it was horrible and I knew it was wrong for a mother to feel like that when she discovered her daughter had so much talent, but I couldn't help it. I couldn't stop it."

She pauses to run her hand nervously against the side of her head, trying to control the wayward pieces of hair that have fallen out of her updo, but she gives up after a few seconds when they won't conform.

"Why?" I finally whisper.

With a deep breath, she closes the distance between us, reaching into the front pocket of her suit jacket and pulling something out. I look away from her eyes at the item she holds out to me when she gets right in front of me, letting go of the barre with one hand to take the picture from her.

Staring down at it, I can hardly believe what I'm looking at. The photo is worn around the edges, a crease lining the center of it from the number of times it must have been folded and unfolded over the years, but there's no mistaking what it is or who it is. It's a picture of my mother, probably not much older than nineteen or twenty, wearing a black leotard, a sheer black chiffon ballet skirt, pink tights, and pink pointe shoes, with her leg extended gracefully up by her head and her arms in perfect first position. Her face is so serene and peaceful and *happy* that I almost wonder if my eyes are playing tricks on me. I've never seen her look anything but hard and disappointed.

"What is this?" I mutter, even though I know what it is, but I'm so confused that I feel like my head is spinning.

"I was one of the best premier dancers for the New York City Ballet," she tells me quietly, staring down at the photo I clutch tightly in my hand. "Dancing was the only thing I'd ever known. The only thing that made me happy and the only thing I wanted to do for the rest of my life."

I don't know whether to scream at her, or drop down to the floor and cry. All these years, we had so much in common and I never knew it. She never *let* me know it, and for some reason, she hated me because of it.

"I know you don't understand, Shelby, and I wish I could change the way I felt when you were younger and the way I treated you, but I can't," she goes on. "I never thought I'd want anything more than ballet, until one day, when I was twenty, a man came to the ballet. He acquired access backstage when it was over and he handed me the largest, most beautiful bouquet of pink roses I'd ever seen."

A sad, wistful expression comes over her face and it takes my breath away.

"He asked me out on a date, and I accepted. I didn't come from money, my parents were blue-collar workers who could barely pay the bills. He took me to fancy restaurants, he showered me with expensive gifts, and he loved me more than I ever thought someone would," she tells me softly. "I fell for him hard, and in a few months, I got pregnant with you."

All of the pieces start falling together. Why she hated me, why she hated it when she found out I could dance...it all makes sense now.

She blamed me for taking away her dream.

"As I'm sure you know, my schedule was grueling and exhausting. I ignored the nausea, pushed through the fatigue, and never gained weight. I didn't find out until it was too late to...well, until it was too late."

I toss the photo to the ground angrily and cross my arms in front of me. The silence in the room is deafening, and I want to smack her across the face for how little she cared about me from the moment she found out she was pregnant. Something most women would think was a blessing, she thought was a curse and hated the idea of it. Hated *me*.

"Too late to get rid of the problem, that's what you meant to say, right?"

She swallows nervously and gives me a terse nod of agreement.

"Your father was over the moon with happiness when I told him. He always wanted a family and was finally getting what he wanted. He had no idea that it wasn't what *I* wanted. No idea that it would ruin everything I'd worked my entire life for. I figured I'd have you, hire nannies, and work twice as hard to get back to the only thing I ever cared about, but it didn't work that way. By the time I'd given birth to you and recovered, it was already too late to go back. The ballet world moves quickly and there's always someone else waiting in the wings to take your place, someone better, younger, stronger, and with no attachments."

I can do nothing but shake my head at her, holding back the tears that are pooling in my eyes.

"I didn't know how to be a mother and I didn't want that life, but I still hated it that you went to your father for everything. I hated that the two of you were so close and I felt like a third wheel around you. Then, when I found out you could dance and that you were a hundred times better than I'd ever hoped to be, I hated that you were going to get the dream I'd always wanted. The one I gave up to have you and the one I still wanted more than anything else in the world, so much that it consumed me and I couldn't stop myself from being so jealous and angry," she admits.

I finally have the answer to the question that plagued me my entire life. The reason why my mother never hugged me, never smiled at me, never encouraged me, and never treated me like anything but a thorn in her side. I should feel relief finally knowing the truth, but I don't. Everything inside me feels bruised and battered, knowing there's nothing I could have done to change things. Nothing I could have done to make her love me. She hated my very existence. But it still doesn't explain everything.

"Why did you send Eli away?" I demand. "I can try to understand why you treated me the way you did, why you hated me so much and made my life miserable, but I can't understand why you'd do that to *him*. Why you'd hurt him and threaten him and take him away from me? As much as you loved dance, as much as it consumed you and made you happy and you couldn't imagine your life without it, that's *exactly* how I felt about Eli and you took him from me. If you hated me that much, why didn't you just let me go? Send me away and let me live my life and never speak to me again? Why did you have to hurt him? WHY?"

I can't hold the sobs in any longer and my voice rises in

a shout, so hurt and so angry by her actions and her choices and how easily she could ruin so many lives because she couldn't let go of the past and couldn't find her own happiness.

"Tell her. She deserves to know the truth."

My mother's head drops and mine whips toward the sound of Eli's voice to find him lounging against the door frame. I want to run to him, wrap my arms around him. and let him take away all of this hurt and pain that engulfs me, but I can't move. My knees are locked and my feet are rooted in place as my body shakes in fear, already preparing myself for the final blow I'm waiting for my mother to deliver.

"I tried," she whispers, so softly that I have to crane my neck forward to hear her better over the loud thumping of my heart pounding through my ears. "I know it was too late, I know I couldn't make up for what I'd done, but I tried. I did whatever I could to protect you, but I had no other choice."

For a minute, I'm confused all over again thinking she's still speaking to me, until she finally lifts her head and looks back at Eli.

"I'm sorry. I'm so sorry," she tells him, tears clogging her voice.

"So, you admit it? After all these years, after everything you've done, you finally admit it?" he asks.

She nods her head silently and I watch the pain wash over Eli's face, tightening his features as he closes his eyes and runs his palm down his face.

"Shelby's father had made a lot of careless choices with our money over the years. Things I knew nothing about until he died and it was too late to figure out how to fix them." She speaks rapidly, looking back and forth between me and Eli. "I didn't know what to do. We were going to lose the house, we were going to be bankrupt and left with nothing. I had a bad night, too much to drink, and I went for a drive, just wanting to clear my head and forget about things for a little while. It was dark and I was upset and it all happened so fast."

My hand flies to my mouth and my body bends in half at the waist. I shake my head back and forth, not wanting her to keep going, not wanting to hear the next words out of her mouth. I hear myself chanting softly as I cry, telling her to stop.

Stop, stop, stop, please don't say what I know you're going to say. Please don't let this be true, please, please, please.

"I lost control when I went around a curve and it happened so fast," she says again. "I didn't know what to do. I knew it was bad but I didn't know what to do, so I called Landry."

My hand drops from my mouth and I whimper when she says his name, still shaking my head back and forth trying to shake this knowledge and this truth from my head before the weight of it crushes me.

"So he's the one who covered it up. Made it look like the accident was all my parents' fault and took you completely out of the equation. Why? Why in the hell would he ever do something like that for you?" Eli asks angrily

I can barely understand the words he's saying and the questions he's asking; all I can think about is that my mother killed Eli's parents. My mother is the one who tore apart their family, left Eli and his sister alone and forced him to work himself to exhaustion for years just to keep a roof over their head. I don't understand how he doesn't hate me. I don't understand how he could even look at me without being sick and disgusted, always assuming but never knowing for sure until now.

"Don't clam up now, you're on a roll," Eli tells her angrily when she doesn't immediately answer his questions. "Why in the hell would Landry do that for you?"

My mother looks back at him and then slowly turns to look at me.

"I'm not clamming up. I know you don't care how I feel, and I know I deserve that, but this is hard for me. You have no idea how difficult it is reliving all of the selfish choices you made and thinking about the people you hurt along the way, but I know I need to do this. You need to hear all of this from me, and not from someone who will twist the truth to suit his needs," she whispers brokenly.

My mother takes a deep breath and my world crumbles around me into a pile of ash as she continues.

"He fixed everything. He covered it up and he paid off all of the debt because he knew," she whispers. "He knew I was desperate. He knew I would have done anything to protect myself and to keep the life I had. He knew and I let him use me. I let him do whatever he wanted because I was weak and selfish. I let him continue holding it over my head for years, I let him threaten me and I let him take advantage of everything just to keep it quiet. I never wanted anyone to know. I never wanted anyone to find out what I'd done and the person I'd become."

I take a few steps away from her until my back hits the ballet barre, wanting to be as far away from this woman as possible. I'm ashamed of her for being so weak and only caring about her reputation and her money after what she'd done.

"Why did he do it? What did he want so badly that he would do all of this for you?" I ask angrily, already knowing, already *realizing* what she's going to say and feeling like a fool for never seeing it before now.

"You," she sobs softly.

My knees unlock as soon as she says that one word. The one I knew was coming but wouldn't allow myself to truly believe until she says it. My knees give out and my legs buckle, the weight of all these truths at once finally becoming too much and it takes me down.

Chapter 28

Eli

I'm across the room in a flash as soon as I see Shelby's legs give out, my arms going around her right before she hits the floor. I should have gone to her sooner, should have held on to her as soon as I walked in the door and heard Georgia telling her how much she hated her.

When I received a phone call from Paul a few hours after Shelby left me, all he said was that I needed to get myself over to the stables immediately. That Shelby was "in her room" and her mother was heading that way.

I knew her mother wanted to talk to her and I knew Shelby was nervous, but I had no idea Georgia would say the things to her that she did. I can't even imagine how it must feel to have your own mother tell you she never liked you, never wanted you, and was always jealous of you. My parents might not have been around much, weren't very good at taking care of anyone but themselves, but they never hated us.

My heart breaks for her more than it does for myself. I couldn't stand the way Shelby's worried, tear-filled eyes looked at me when her mother admitted to killing my parents. I want her to know I wasn't shocked, that I'd known all along. My shock only came from Georgia finally admitting the truth, but I don't have time to do anything more than cradle Shelby in my arms and rock her back and forth as her mother continues.

"I'm sorry, Shelby. You have no idea how sorry I am," Georgia tells her.

She wraps her arms around her own body to comfort herself, staring at her daughter as she clings to me, pressing her face into my chest.

"I spoke to Landry earlier and told him I was finished playing his games. As soon as we're finished here, I'm turning myself in to the police for what I did to your parents, Eli."

Running my hand soothingly down the back of Shelby's head, she finally pulls her face away from my chest and stares at her mother. The tears are all dried up and she looks at her with absolutely no emotion.

"I think we're finished here," Shelby whispers.

Georgia takes a step toward us and lifts her arm to touch Shelby, but quickly thinks better of it, dropping it back down to her side when I tighten my arms around her and Shelby presses her cheek back to my chest.

"I tried. I know it was too late, but I tried," Georgia tells us again.

I want to ask her what the hell she's talking about, how she tried to do anything but ruin us, but I don't want to hear anything else out of her mouth. I don't want her to say anything else that will crush Shelby.

When Shelby doesn't say anything to her, Georgia nods,

lifting her eyes to mine. When she realizes I'm not going to give her anything either, she finally turns and walks from the room, Shelby and I standing together quietly, watching her go.

We stay like this silently for a long time, Shelby's arms locked tightly around my waist and me continuing to rock her back and forth gently. After a while, she finally looks up at me, resting her chin on my chest.

"Tell me what you need," I whisper down to her, hating the sorrow I see etched on her face.

"Just you," she replies. "And maybe some music. I don't want to think about anything right now, I just want to dance with you."

I smile at her, running my hand down the side of her face before I pull away and quickly walk over to the sound system. Powering it up, I set it to a jazz station, walk back to Shelby, and pull her into my arms again. Neither of us says a word as I take her hand and begin to lead her. We dance in silence and I let her feel the music, knowing I'll stay here and dance with her forever, or at least until the shock wears off and she's ready to talk.

I should have known the peacefulness of our quiet dancing wouldn't last long. I should have taken the time to really process Georgia's words when she told us she'd called Landry and told him she was done. So many things I should have done, but especially the most important one—allowing that thing clawing at the back of my mind to finally be set free on my own, in my own way, in the comfort of Shelby's arms so it didn't wreck us both.

* * *

"Well, isn't this just the sweetest thing I've ever seen."

Shelby's eyes dart to the door and I sigh when I hear his

sarcastic voice. I thought we might have a little more time alone before this had to happen, but I should have known when Georgia said she spoke to him that he wouldn't be smart enough to realize it was over. That *he* was over.

Gently moving Shelby out of my arms, I turn to face Landry, pushing her behind me to keep her safe. He looks like absolute shit. His normally slicked-back hair is standing on end as if he'd held it in his fists and tried to yank it out by the roots. His face is flushed, his white dress shirt is dotted with sweat stains, and his tie is loose and hanging all askew.

"No, really, don't stop dancing on my account. Or would you rather fuck him right in front of me, Shelby, since you've obviously had no trouble doing it behind my back?" he asks angrily, tilting his head to look behind me.

"Go to hell, Landry," Shelby fires back. "My mother has already gone to the police. It's only a matter of time before they find you and arrest your ass as well."

He tips his head back and laughs.

"No one can touch me—haven't you figured that out yet, Shelby? God, it was so pathetic watching you scramble around for all these years, doing whatever Mommy Dearest asked. I mean, obviously it benefited me since I finally got to fuck you after all those years I spent wanting you, but still. Pathetic."

He laughs again when Shelby darts out from around me. The only thing stopping me from punching him in the face is wrapping my arms around Shelby and holding her back from doing the same.

"He's not worth it, Shelby," I say quietly in her ear as she squirms and tries to fight my hold on her.

"I have to give that woman credit, though," Landry muses, shoving his hands in his front pockets. "As weak as she was, she sure turned into quite the firecracker. I wanted to kill you and get you out of the picture permanently, but she convinced me sending you on deployment was a better idea. And it worked, too, until your deployment was almost up and I knew you'd come running back home to her. A few phone calls to the right people and voilà! Your unit heads off into the most dangerous, IED-infested area there is. Boom. No more Eli. You couldn't just stay dead, could you?"

It's Shelby's turn to clutch at my arms and try to hold me in place, but it's no use. As soon as he says those words, as soon as he mentions the explosion that killed my brothers, I'm charging across the room.

Somewhere in the back of my mind I can hear Shelby shouting my name, but all I can hear are the sounds of explosions and screams, all I can see is red, and all I can feel is rage. My hand wraps around his neck and I slam him into the wall at his back, getting right in his face.

"You killed my men," I growl. "Did you have me taken hostage, too? Was my five years in hell the result of another phone call to the right people, you *sick* son of a bitch?"

I tighten my fingers around his neck and he reaches up to claw at my hand, choking out his words with a cocky smile on his face.

"That was just luck. But I did make sure to send them a nice hefty bonus to finish the job I started."

Yanking him toward me, I shove as hard as I can and slam his back into the wall once more. I feel Shelby's hands clutching to the back of my shirt, trying to pull me away, but I ignore her as I squeeze and squeeze and squeeze. The memories slowly start to flash through my mind—the scorching heat from the blast, the shrapnel and pieces of my brothers raining down on me, the ringing in my ears, the punches to the face, being dragged across the sand, blindfolded, kicked... the sounds, the smells, the pain, it surrounds me until it's all I can do not to kill this man for being the one responsible for everything.

"Eli! He's not worth it, Eli. Please, he's not worth it."

Shelby's voice finally penetrates, repeating the words I'd said to her just a few seconds ago, and I slowly start to loosen my hold around Landry's neck, his red face and bulging eyes still holding an air of satisfaction and arrogance even as he coughs and sputters and tries to drag in breaths.

"*I'm* not worth it?" he croaks, his hands rubbing the skin of his throat when I finally let go. "What about *him?* You're actually going to choose *him* over me? A man who couldn't even keep his best friend alive?"

Blood rushes through my ears and pain explodes behind my eyes. Images try to push their way to the front of my mind but I won't let them. Not here. Not now. I'm not ready for this.

"He couldn't even save his *brother* and you think he's going to save *you?*" Landry shouts at Shelby, his eyes narrowing as he leans toward me. "Tell me, did Sergeant Edwards beg for you to help him right before they put a bullet in his brain?"

I stumble backward, shaking my head frantically back and forth. It sounds like Shelby is screaming from somewhere down a tunnel. I want to go to her, I need her to make this all better, but I can't get to her. I can't move. I can't stop his words from penetrating and I can't stop everything from hitting me all at once.

Rylan joking with Kat, but her never acknowledging him.

Kat asking me if I'd taken my meds anytime I spoke to him.

Rylan asking Paul a question and Paul not even looking in his direction.

Kat looking like she wanted to cry when I told her Rylan was moving in with me.

Rylan aiming the remote at the TV but never getting it to turn on.

Rylan with the same shaggy hair and beard.

Rylan never changing, never finding anything to do, never moving on.

"You need to tell Shelby what happened over there and let go. Just...let go."

"I'll leave when you don't need me anymore."

I squeeze my head in my hands and close my eyes, trying to make it go away. Go away, go away, go away. I'm not ready.

Shouting, the pounding of footsteps and gunfire sound from outside the room and I wonder just how many people they need to bring in here to kill two weak men who can barely move.

My hands are quickly shackled to a wall above my head right next to Rylan, my broken body groaning in protest. No matter what happens next, I will not give in. I was born a Marine and I will die a Marine.

"Ooh Rah," we both whisper to each other, not breaking eye contact as a loud explosion shakes the walls, rattles our chests, and rains dirt and rocks down on us from the ceiling.

How much can a man take before he breaks?

I see one of our captors rush over to stand in front of Rylan, lifting his arm and aiming the gun right at his head.

I hear myself screaming, screaming, screaming, tugging as hard as I can on the chains, kicking my legs, doing whatever I can to make this asshole point his gun at me instead.

Rylan's eyes never leave mine. He tells me it's okay. He makes a joke that we all have to die sometime. He tells me never to stop fighting. He tells me to get my girl back and live a good life for both of us.

He stops telling me anything else when the gun explodes.

I can't breathe. I try to scream, I try to fight, I try to kick and claw away from the nightmare that I don't want to believe is real. I drop to the floor and curl into a ball, trying to make it all go away. It's not real, it can't be real.

I didn't save him.

I *couldn't* save him.

I can't do this. I can't handle this. I just want it all to go away.

Closing my eyes even tighter, I do what I can to make it all go away, but it's no use.

I finally know how much a man can take before he breaks.

Chapter 29

Shelby

It's been a week since the day in the studio when everything came crashing down. Seven days of crying, of worrying, of pacing the halls of the hospital, sleeping in a chair next to Eli's bed and begging him to come back to me.

The doctors called it PTSD with a side of a psychotic break. I call it misery and guilt and a pain so deep that I don't know how to fix it. For Eli or for myself. I didn't know what to do when Landry said those words to Eli. I couldn't stop screaming when he dropped to the ground, holding his head in his hands, whispering and chanting to himself under his breath.

I didn't pay attention when Paul came running into the room, with the police right on his heels. I know he told me he called them when he heard all of the commotion, but I didn't care. I didn't get any satisfaction out of watching Landry shout and curse and being led out of the room in handcuffs. I didn't care about anything but the broken man I knelt down next to on the floor, held in my arms, and tried to soothe with soft words and apologies.

Nothing made sense when the ambulance got there and strapped him to a gurney. Nothing made sense when he wouldn't open his eyes at all during the ride to the hospital and just kept muttering to himself, "*It's not real, it's not real, it's not real.*" I didn't understand. I thought he was just in shock, reliving his nightmare all over again, but that was far from the truth. So far from it that I hate myself and I blame myself for not realizing it sooner, for not pushing him to talk more, for not wondering why we never talked about something so important.

Being distracted with each other always helped us . . . until it didn't.

Nothing made sense, I didn't understand, and there was nothing I could do but sit by his side and wait for him to wake up and finally talk to me about what we should have talked about weeks ago.

Kat was a little shocked to see me at the hospital when she arrived with her husband, but the shock quickly switched to worry for her brother when after a few days, he still hadn't opened his eyes. The two of us kept a quiet vigil next to his bed, telling him we loved him, telling him we were sorry, and saying whatever we could to bring him back, but nothing worked. I blamed the doctors for doing nothing but pumping him full of drugs, but I had no idea what else they could do for him in a situation like this. They said we needed to give his mind time to rest and heal. I just wanted him to wake up and smile at me and tell me everything would be okay. That *he* would be okay. I couldn't stand sitting by his bed day after day, seeing him so still and small when he'd always been larger than life to me. I wanted to curl up into a ball and cry for him, but I knew that wasn't what he needed. He needed me to be strong and to fight for him when he couldn't do it himself.

"Shelby, can I talk to you for a minute?" Kat asks softly, nodding her head in the direction of the door, indicating that she wants to leave the room.

I nod, standing up from my chair to lean over Eli and kiss his cheek.

"I love you. I'm not going anywhere," I whisper into his ear, smoothing his hair off his forehead before I join Kat in the doorway.

We walk silently through the halls to the elevator and down to the first floor to the cafeteria. We both get coffee and she leads us to a table over by the window. Kat and I had just spent seven days and nights together, but we'd never said more than a few words to each other when one of us would leave to grab food, something to drink, or go to the bathroom. She'd sent her husband out to my place to grab extra clothes when I refused to leave Eli's side. She introduced me to the doctors when they'd come in to talk to her, but we'd never discussed my reasons for being there. I fell in love with her immediately when she never questioned me or asked me to leave, quietly accepting that it would require a force of nature to take me away from Eli now.

"He never told me about the two of you," she starts, wrapping her hands around the cardboard cup to warm them. "He never told me about a lot of things, I guess."

She looks down at her coffee sadly and I reach across the table and grab one of her hands, giving it a soft squeeze.

"The two of us...it's a long story. One that started six years ago. You were away at college then, and now...it just happened so fast."

She nods her head in understanding, squeezing my hand right back.

"You love him."

It's a statement, not a question.

"Yes," I whisper. "Always."

She nods again and sighs.

"I should have pushed him more to talk to me. Every time I tried, he'd smile and tell me he was fine. I knew he wasn't fine. I knew every time he talked to Rylan like he was sitting right next to him, or made plans to move him into his new place, that he wasn't fine, but I thought he just needed time. I thought he would eventually realize what he was doing."

She looks up at me when I say nothing and sees the confused, questioning look on my face.

"Did he ever mention Rylan when he was with you?"

I think about all the time we spent together, doing everything but talk about important things. He spoke to me about meeting with a therapist and he briefly discussed the five years he was held captive, but he never mentioned Rylan. Never once talked about the best friend he went to war with, that he watched die right in front of him.

"Never," I tell her. "I knew he'd died when they were over there, it was all over the news when Eli was first rescued. I guess I just thought it was too painful for him to talk about, and like you, I thought he just needed time."

I watch as Kat's eyes fill with tears, and my own vision gets cloudy.

"The first day he was back in Charleston and we brought him home to live with us, I was making dinner and I heard him tell someone to get their feet off the coffee table and stop being such a slob," Kat tells me. "Daniel had run out to the store and took our daughter with him, and when I asked Eli who he was talking to, he said it so quickly, so naturally, and so easily, "*I'm talking to Rylan, obviously.*"

Kat laughs sadly through her tears and shakes her head.

"I thought he was kidding at first and it shocked me speechless. Until he did it again. And again, and again. Every day, he'd talk to Rylan or talk *about* him like he was standing right there next to him. Rylan was like a brother to me, too, and I missed him, but I didn't go through the things with him that Eli did. I didn't know what he needed to do to cope and grieve so I let it go. I shouldn't have let it go."

I move my hand from Kat's to wipe away the tears that started to fall down my cheeks when she spoke. He was so broken, so hurting, and I had no idea. Why didn't he ever do any of these things when he was with me? Was he so busy dealing with my drama and trying to put me back together that he didn't have time to process anything, didn't have time to heal or grieve or let go of the best friend he was forced to watch die right next to him?

How could I have been so selfish? When I looked at him, all I saw was strength and determination and I wanted that so much for myself that I let him give it to me. I let him build me up when, all along, he was crumbling inside. He gave me everything he had and left nothing for himself.

"Whenever he spoke to Rylan, I would quietly ask him if he'd taken his medication," Kat continues. "The doctors had him on all kinds of things for depression and anxiety and I just thought maybe he wasn't taking them or he'd skipped a dose. I was just so happy to have him back that I didn't want to upset him. I didn't want to hurt him."

Her reasoning is the same one I gave myself. I didn't want to force him to talk if he wasn't ready. He'd been through so much and I just wanted him to be happy.

"I recognized you when I first got to the hospital," she suddenly says, giving me a small smile. "From the night he was deployed. I was home on break and you stopped by the apartment, do you remember?"

I want to laugh and cry all at the same time. I'm strangely happy that she remembered me and it was probably the initial reason she didn't immediately kick me out of Eli's room, but I hate thinking about that night.

"Yes," I reply softly. "You gave me a letter from him."

She nods, her smile getting wider.

"I'm such an idiot. When you told me your last name, I knew it was from the stables he worked at and I thought it was a resignation letter or something," she laughs. "It was a love letter, wasn't it? I had a mushy love letter from my brother in my hand and I didn't even read it."

I can't help but laugh right along with her even though the memories of that night, reading his words, losing control of the car, losing my dreams... it all tries to overwhelm me. There's something about her laugh, though, so kind and genuine that I can do nothing but join in.

"Not exactly," I admit. "He was kind of a jerk in that letter."

She purses her lips and shakes her head.

"Yep, that sounds more like my brother."

We laugh together again and I try not to feel guilty that I'm sitting here laughing and smiling when Eli is upstairs fighting with his grief and his fractured mind. Kat makes it easy to relax for a little while and let go of the worry.

"You'll be happy to know that he more than made up for being a jerk. I have a whole shoe box filled with mushy love letters."

She claps her hands together like a toddler and I laugh louder.

"Mushy love letters that you will absolutely let me read one of these days so I can tease him, right?" she asks.

"I don't know, how horrible was he to you when you were growing up?" I barter, taking a sip of my coffee.

"Are you kidding me? He was the worst. Anytime a guy

came to pick me up for a date, Eli would sit right next to him on the couch, put his arm around the guy, and tell him he knew fifty different ways to kill a man and hide the dead body," she tells me with a roll of her eyes. "And don't even get me started on Rylan."

Kat falters when she says his name, but I can tell it feels good for her to talk about him and remember him. She spent all this time worrying about Eli and not being able to grieve for Rylan on her own and I know she needs this.

"Did you know he lived with us?" she asks.

I nod my head, remembering when I came home from college and spent the first few days flirting with Rylan just to make Eli jealous. We only spoke a handful of times, but he was definitely a talker. I knew his entire life story five seconds after meeting him. After Eli and I got together that summer, he confirmed what Rylan had told me, and even though he was pissed about the whole flirting thing, I could see every time he talked about his friend how much he cared about him.

"So, imagine being a teenager and having not one, but *two* overprotective brothers trying to scare away your dates," Kat says with a roll of her eyes. "It was like good-cop, bad-cop, but they forgot who should be which and they both decided to be the bad cop. My prom date senior year dropped me off five blocks from our apartment because he was sure Eli and Rylan were waiting up with shotguns in their hands."

We share another laugh, both of us pausing to drink more of our coffee. I'm jealous of what she had growing up and I want to cry at the unfairness of it all. She had two men in her life, and they all cared so much about each other. I can't imagine how much she must be hurting right now losing one of them, and not knowing if the other will ever be okay.

"I wish I'd had something like that."

She cocks her head as she looks at me.

"You don't have any brothers or sisters?"

I shake my head. "Nope, just me. My father died when I was a teenager and I recently found out my mother never wanted children and has always hated the sight of me."

Kat's smile falls and I quickly let out a small laugh to reassure her.

"It's fine. It's something I've sort of always known. Eli was there when it happened. He made it better. He always makes everything better for me."

My voice cracks with emotion and Kat reaches over to place her hand on top of mine.

"I want to help him, but I don't know how," I whisper, trying to hold back the tears.

"I have a question, and it might seem a little weird. When exactly did you two get back together after he came home? Like, the exact day?"

Pausing for a minute, going back through the time we've spent together, I'm shocked to realize it hasn't been as long as I thought it was. Being with Eli always makes me lose track of time, makes me feel like I'm moving twice as fast as the rest of the world.

"Well, we saw each other again for the first time soon after he got back to Charleston. But it was a little complicated and difficult. So, technically, three weeks ago. Three weeks ago today, actually," I admit, feeling my cheeks heat with embarrassment that I sort of just told Eli's sister the day we first had sex again.

She ignores my discomfort and smiles the biggest smile I've seen yet.

"I think you already did help him," she tells me.

I shake my head in confusion and she continues.

"Three weeks ago today, is when he stopped waking up

with nightmares every night," she tells me softly. "I remember because it was the same day my daughter was cutting a tooth and I was up in the middle of the night anyway. And he never woke up. He'd been waking up screaming every night since he came home, and that night, he never woke up once. Or any night after that until he moved out and I wasn't keeping track of his sleeping habits anymore, but I'm pretty confident he wasn't having them at his new place either."

I close my eyes and take a deep breath, hoping that what she's saying is true.

"You already helped him, Shelby, without even knowing it. I'm sure you'll be able to do it again."

"Kat!"

I open my eyes and we both look up when we hear the shout, seeing Daniel jogging across the cafeteria to us with a worried look on his face.

"I've been looking for you, I tried calling your cell," he tells her when he gets to our table.

"Sorry, I must have left it back in the room. What's going on? What happened?"

He looks back and forth between us before squatting down next to his wife and grabbing both of her hands.

"Eli's gone."

I gasp and Kat's head jerks back in shock.

"What do you mean he's gone? Where is he?" I ask, pushing my chair back and standing up from the table.

"I don't know. I went up there and he wasn't in the room. I asked the nurses and they never saw him leave. They've called security, but his hospital gown was lying on the floor and his clothes and shoes he came in with are gone, too."

Daniel helps Kat up from her chair and we all move quickly out of the cafeteria. When we get back upstairs and speak to the nurses, he still hasn't been located.

Running into his empty room, I grab my purse from the floor and snatch my keys out of it.

"We'll go to our house and then stop by his," Daniel tells me.

"I'll drive to my place and a few others," I confirm, promising to call them if I find him and making them do the same as I rush to the elevator.

I have to find him. I have to give him back his strength. He needs it now more than me and I will do anything to bring him back and let him know I'm not going anywhere. I will help him get through this, no matter what it takes. I'm going to believe what Kat told me and hope to God I can help him again.

Chapter 30

Eli

"This is really depressing, man. Couldn't we have gone to a bar or something?"

I continue staring at the headstone in front of me, trying to block out the man speaking next to me that I know isn't really there.

"I mean, drinking away your troubles sounds like a much better idea than staring at this thing."

He kicks the toe of his boot against the side of the cement marker with his name on it and I squeeze my eyes closed.

"This isn't real, this isn't real, this isn't real."

When I hear nothing but the sound of cicadas chirping in the nearby trees, I slowly open my eyes and let out a low, irritated growl.

"Sorry, still here," Rylan says with a smile, waving at me like an asshole. "I told you, I'm not going anywhere until you don't need me anymore."

I quickly look away from his face with the full beard and his hair pulled back into that stupid man-bun, rereading the words etched into the stone, trying to make it real, trying to make it hurt, trying to do anything to make this madness go away.

"I don't need you anymore," I whisper, choking with the lie as I say the words.

I hear a car door slam from somewhere behind me and the slide of shoes through the grass as they get closer.

"I have a feeling that isn't true," Rylan replies. "Buckle up. And don't be an asshole."

The light breeze in the air floats the smell of peaches around me before she finally gets to me. I feel her hand press lightly against my back, and for the first time since I met Shelby, I want to move away from her touch.

I clench my hands into fists at my sides while she rubs slow, soft circles against my spine until it's too much, I can't take it anymore and I jerk away from her hand. She moves around in front of me and I try to turn, try to keep my back to her, but she's not having it. She grabs my upper arms and squeezes, using all of her strength to hold me in place and not turn away from her.

"What do you need? Tell me what you need," she asks softly.

I finally lift my head when she speaks and I wish I hadn't. I look into her beautiful green eyes and I just want to let her wrap her arms around me and make everything better, like she's done since I got home. But I can't do that anymore. I can't pretend anymore. Nothing will be better again and I can't fool myself into thinking it will.

"I need you to leave," I tell her in a low voice.

"Didn't I *just* tell you not to be an asshole?" Rylan grumbles from next to me.

"Shut up, shut up, shut up," I whisper, squeezing my eyes closed.

"Eli, please. Just talk to me. I want to help you but I don't know what to do," Shelby pleads sadly, moving forward and pressing her body against mine.

It hurts so much I can barely breathe. She feels so soft and perfect against me and I just want to take whatever she wants to give me. I want to take it all and never give it back. I want to lose myself in her but I can't. It's not right. She doesn't deserve this. She's been through too much and I can't let her take on this burden as well.

I step away and turn my back on her again, immediately missing the heat from her body, and I want to scream and cry and blame someone else for this mess, but there's no one else to blame. There's no one else to point a finger at and I need to take responsibility.

"There's nothing to say and you need to go. You can't help me. You can't fix me, so just go."

She whispers my name and it tears me in half.

"I'm not leaving you. I love you, I need you, just stay with me."

Her words are like a knife to the chest, and instead of crying, instead of feeling sorry for myself, I go with another emotion. I whirl around to face her and let the anger take control.

"You don't need me, I can't save you, I can't give you what you need so JUST GO!" I scream.

"I don't need you to save me, I just need you to stay with me!" she shouts back.

Shelby takes a couple of deep breaths before taking a tentative step toward me.

"Just stay with me, please," she whispers. "We'll figure this out together. I'm not leaving you."

I shake my head and try to give her a sarcastic laugh, but all that comes out is a strangled whimper.

"You saved my life and I ruined yours," I tell her.

She shakes her head in disagreement, reaching for me, her face filling with pain when I move back before she can put her hands on me.

"I was too weak to talk to you before I was deployed. I was too weak to do anything but lie to you in a fucking note," I remind her. "*I'm* the reason you got into your accident, *I'm* the reason you can't dance, *I'm* the reason you let those people break you down, *I'm* the reason your life went to shit. There's no fucking way I'm going to let you take on anything else, especially not someone as fucked up as I am."

I take another step back from her when she tries coming at me again.

I want her.

I need her.

I can't have her.

"Don't you dare put all of that blame on yourself," she argues. "I'm just as much at fault and I made just as many mistakes. I never danced again because I never tried. Not until you made me. You helped me. You *healed* me. You're not fucked up, you went through something horrible, and you just need time."

I close my eyes and do everything I can to block out her voice, her smell that still floats in the air, and the urge to give in and let her heal me. All I do by blocking out her goodness is allow the bad parts to get through, and before I know it, the sounds of the birds chirping and the breeze rustling through the trees are replaced with gunfire and screaming.

We were almost free.

Thirty more seconds and the Navy SEALs were pouring into the room.

Thirty more seconds and we would have been free.

But he pointed the gun.

My arms were still shackled and I couldn't move.

But he pointed the gun.

I kicked and I screamed and I pleaded.

Oh, God, he pointed the fucking gun and he pulled the trigger.

I gasp loudly and my eyes fly open to find Shelby still standing here in front of me with a sad, worried look on her face and it kills me. It kills everything inside me until there's nothing left.

"Can you really stand here and tell me you're healed? That everything is better and everything is fine after what your mother said to you? After what she did to you? After what that asshole you let into your life did to you?" I ask, hating myself even more when I see her flinch, but unable to stop myself.

I shake my head at her and keep talking before she can argue with me again.

"Two broken pieces don't make a whole. They just make a bigger fucking mess for someone to clean up. You don't need any more messes in your life and all the time in the world isn't going to fix mine."

Without another word, I turn and walk away from her. I ignore her when I hear her shout my name and I keep walking, putting as much distance between us as I can before I show her just how weak I really am by giving her this burden.

"You're really starting to piss me off," Rylan mutters, running to catch up with me.

Chapter 31

Shelby

In another life, like the one I was living before Eli came back to me, I would have let everything he said to me at the cemetery crush me, break my heart, and fill my head with doubts and insecurities. I would have run away, locked myself in my room, and cried myself to sleep every night, playing what he said to me on a loop until I believed every word he spoke and convinced myself he was right—this could never work. We were both too broken to ever be one whole, united piece.

I didn't lock myself away, I didn't cry myself to sleep every night, and I didn't replay his words in my head over and over until I had no choice but to believe them. I refused to believe them. I refused to walk away. I refused to think he was right. I didn't know how to fix his mind and it killed me. I've spent so many years protecting him and trying to save him, and now, when he needed me the most, I didn't know what to do. I didn't know how to help him say good-bye to Rylan, to grieve for the friend he lost and to stop feeling like it was all his fault, but I wasn't about to give up. Eli never gave up on me. Not through a year of deployment, not through five years of hell, and not when he came back and thought I'd let him go and moved on.

I don't know how to heal his mind, but I know I can heal his heart. I know how to make those broken pieces fit back together again and I won't give up, I won't leave, and I won't stop until he comes back to me.

"Are you sure you don't want something to eat?"

I look up at Kat and smile, fluffing the pillow behind my back that I leaned up against the door.

"I'm good. I'll grab something if I get hungry," I tell her, getting comfortable in the makeshift bed I put on the floor right outside Eli's room.

After he walked away from me in the cemetery, I gave him a few hours to cool off before I went to his house. He had locked himself in his room and refused to come out or answer me, no matter how many times I knocked. After Kat and Daniel both tried to get him to come out, we waited twenty-four hours before calling his therapist. When he couldn't get Eli to answer his knocks or talk, he told us to just give him time. He assured us that he didn't believe Eli would harm himself and that he just needed to be alone to heal. Since we could hear him shuffling around in there every so often, and could hear the muffled sound of his voice talking to himself, or most likely Rylan, we let him be. For the most part.

Kat and Daniel had a daughter to take care of and couldn't be here around the clock. I had nowhere to be and nowhere else I'd *rather* be, so I sat down in front of his door and hadn't moved in ten days other than to stretch, go to the bathroom, or take a quick shower. I always leave food for

Eli outside his door, and it's always gone when I come back from those sporadic, few minutes I'm gone. Knowing he's eating what I've left out for him, even if he doesn't open the door when I'm sitting right there waiting for him, gives me a little comfort at least.

Both Kat and Daniel rotated shifts, stopping by as much as they could, checking in on me, sitting with me to keep me company or forcing me to eat. They stopped telling me to go home and get some rest after the first two days when they realized I was adamant about not leaving.

"I just cleaned out the fridge and filled it with fresh stuff from the store. If I don't see at least an apple or some of that lunchmeat gone by the time I come back, I will hold you down and force-feed you," Kat threatens.

I laugh quietly, picking up the shoe box and resting it on my lap.

"Thanks for asking Daniel to grab this for me," I tell her, lifting the lid and setting it down on the floor.

"Are you kidding me? This has been the highlight of my life. YOU HEAR THAT, ELI? THE HIGHLIGHT OF MY LIFE. YOU WILL NEVER LIVE THIS DOWN!" she shouts at Eli's closed door.

She can joke all she wants, but I heard her sniffling from the living room when I first started doing this, and I saw her red and blotchy face from crying when she hurried past me to go to the bathroom. Having her roll her eyes at me and yell that she had something in her eye has been the only thing keeping me from falling to pieces each time I did this.

Kat leans down and kisses the top of my head before turning and heading back out into the main part of the house. Shifting the pillow behind my back a little higher, I reach into the box and grab one of the envelopes, pulling the letter out and unfolding it.

"'Shelby, remember that day in your studio, the week after you'd gotten home from college?'" I read aloud, forcing my voice to remain strong and level when reading Eli's words all over again make me want to curl into a ball and cry for him.

"'In case I forgot to tell you, that was the day I knew I was going to fall in love with you. I don't know if you'll ever read this and I'm not really good at this whole letter-writing thing, so I'm just going to tell you a story in these letters. I'm going to tell you the story of us, from my point of view, so you know exactly what I was thinking. I'm hoping it will be a better way for you to see that I meant everything I said in my first few letters. I love you, Shelby. Only you. Always you...'"

I pause when I hear a sniffle from the living room and smile to myself in spite of my sadness. Resting my head against the door, I lift the letter up higher and raise my voice a little louder as I continue to read Eli's story to me.

I want him to listen, I want him to *hear* and remember. Remember what it was like when two broken people could heal each other. Remember what it was like when he loved me so much that he lived through five years of hell to come back to me. Remember what it was like when two people from opposite worlds found everything they'd ever needed in each other, and never let it go. Not through war, not through death, not through pain, not through people trying to tear them apart, and certainly not through this.

We would make it through this as well, I had to believe that.

As I read Eli's words, I imagine him leaning up against his side of the door, right behind me. I continue reading as I shift to my side, holding the letter in one hand and lifting the other over my arm to press my palm against the door. Resting my head right next to my hand, I keep right on reading, imagining him holding his hand up against mine through the door. It becomes so real that I can almost imagine I feel the heat from his hand against mine through the thick wood.

I keep reading until my voice gets hoarse. I keep reading until I have to struggle to keep my eyes open. I keep trying to get through to him the only way I know how, and I refuse to stop fighting.

I won't give up, I won't leave, and I won't stop until he comes back to me.

Chapter 32

Eli

"You're an asshole, have I mentioned that lately?"

I try to ignore the voice that never fucking shuts up, but it's impossible. He's been locked in this room with me for ten days, and no matter what I do, he won't go away. I've sat here with my back pressed to the door, listening to Shelby read those letters I wrote, refusing to go away, refusing to stop trying, and I just can't make that fucking voice shut up.

Every time I'm tempted to open that door, crawl across the floor and into her arms, he says something else and it reminds me how screwed up I am.

My hand has been pressed against the door since Shelby first started reading and I still kept it pressed there long after she quieted and I assumed she fell asleep. As much as I hated hearing her on the other side of the door and knowing I couldn't go to her, her voice is the only thing that quiets the one in my head. When she's reading those letters, when I close my eyes and just listen to the soft cadence of her voice,

Rylan disappears. He doesn't speak, he doesn't flop down on my bed, he doesn't bitch at me, he just goes away. As soon as Shelby stops talking, he's right back in this room again, dragging me through hell and splitting my mind in two.

"Will you just open the fucking door already?" he shouts in frustration and I hear the bed creak.

My hand slides down the wood and I keep my head pressed against the door, refusing to look across the room. Part of me wants to look and see him standing there, so real and so alive because then it wouldn't hurt so much. But then I remember he's not real or alive, and if I'm still seeing him in this room, I'm still fucked.

"You're not real, you're not real, you're not real," I chant quietly to myself with my eyes still closed.

"No shit, Sherlock!" Rylan shouts. "I'm not real, so let me fucking go!"

With a growl, I scramble to my feet and stomp across the room, so fed up with this bullshit and feeling like I'm going crazy and just wanting it to stop.

"Don't you think I'm trying?" I argue back. "I don't want you in my head! I don't want to see you standing here when I know it's not real!"

He scoffs at me and rolls his eyes. "You're not trying. You're giving up. Everything you need is on the other side of that door and you refuse to open it."

I shake my head and take a step back from him.

"I can't do that to her. I can't hurt her or put her through this. She has enough problems in her life right now, she doesn't need another one."

Rylan advances on me and gets right in my face.

"You think this isn't already hurting her? You think pushing her away and not giving her a chance to help you doesn't kill her?" Rylan fires back angrily. "She went through hell for *you.* She gave up her entire life for *you.* She let people dictate her every move for fucking *years* to keep you safe. After everything she sacrificed, you're just going to let her go? She gave up her life and her happiness to save you, and she doesn't even get *you* in the end? What kind of bullshit is that?"

I don't understand what he's saying, none of it makes sense, and I wonder if it's possible to go even crazier than I already am.

"She's been sleeping on the fucking floor *for you.* Reading those letters *for you.* She deserves a fucking light at the end of that tunnel, man, and for whatever reason, you're that light for her. You're going to deny her that after everything she's done for you, after everything she was *forced* to do for you, just because you can't wake the fuck up?" he yells angrily.

"What the hell are you talking about?" I whisper in disbelief.

"Don't tick me off by pissing away the second chance you were given."

He pokes his finger into my chest, getting in my face again.

"Just let. Me. Go."

"I DON'T KNOW HOW!" I roar at him, wrapping my arms around my waist and dropping to my knees. "It was my fault, all my fault. I should have protected you, I should have stopped them. I tried to stop them but I couldn't do it. I couldn't save you. Oh, God, I couldn't save you!"

I rock myself back and forth, choking on my tears and the pain that threatens to rip my chest wide open.

Rylan squats down in front of me and pats me on the back.

"You couldn't save me and I never expected you to,

brother. It wasn't your job to save me," he tells me in a low voice. "We were thirty seconds away from *both* of us dying in that shithole, but it didn't work out that way. You couldn't save me, but you can still save *her*. She gave everything up to protect you. Just let me go."

I force myself to look at him, clenching my teeth and lifting my head.

"What are you talking about? What does that mean?"

He smirks at me and shakes his head. "I'm not gonna give you all the answers. Tell her to take off that watch she's always wearing."

I open my mouth to start losing my shit on him all over again, quickly snapping it closed when I realize he's not just talking nonsense to make me crazy.

The only reason I even noticed the watch that Shelby always wears is because of the number of times I'd seen her run her fingers over the inside band. It was like a nervous tic whenever she was upset or scared or nervous. She did it the night we first saw each other again in the stables, she did it a bunch of times the night of the charity dinner, she did it when she first let me have it in her studio that same night, the first time I touched her leg, when she told me she kept my dog tags, and the entire time her mother unloaded all of that bullshit on her.

I think about all the times I've kissed her, all the times I've touched her, all the times I've held her in my arms, all the times I was chained to a wall and had nothing but memories of all those times to keep me going. I remember how it felt to see her again when I never thought I would get the chance. I remember how good it felt when she let down her walls and let me back in. I remember how good it felt to build her back up again, make her stronger, make her a fighter, remind her what it was like to be happy and loved.

I remember how good it felt to let her heal me, let her distract me, and let me remember how to live again. All of it was good, every single second, every single moment, it was all good because of her. Because she was there making it all better. It was always Shelby. Only Shelby.

"It wasn't your fault. Just let me go," Rylan tells me again.

"I don't know how," I whisper back.

"Yes you do. She's right on the other side of that door. Tell her to take off the watch. Just let me go."

My head drops as I close my eyes.

I think about her laugh, I think about her smell, I think about dancing with her in the studio. I think about how fucking afraid I am that I'm not good enough for her. That my screwed-up head will ruin everything.

"Just let me go."

Rolling over onto my hands and knees, I push myself up and reach for the door, knowing I have to stop living in fear. Knowing I have to do this if I want any chance at a future with her.

I think about her smile, I think about that little gasp she makes when I kiss her, I think about the silky feel of her hair when I run my fingers through it, and I think about how nothing in my life makes sense when I'm *not* thinking about her.

"You don't need me anymore."

My hand wraps around the doorknob and I reach my other hand up to turn the lock, knowing he's right. Knowing Shelby is all I need.

"I don't need you anymore," I whisper back to him.

"Just let me go, just let me go, just let me go..."

His voice trails off until there's nothing but silence in the room as I open the door and step out into the hallway.

Chapter 33

Shelby

I rush up the steps to Eli's house, feeling guilty that I left, even if it was just for fifteen minutes. At three o'clock in the morning, something jerked me awake from my bed on the floor outside his room. I could have sworn I'd heard Eli shout, but after sitting perfectly still and listening quietly for a few seconds and not hearing another sound, I realized I must have been dreaming.

With my butt feeling numb and a stiff neck from falling asleep in such a bad position, still sitting up with my head pressed against the door, I had been too on edge and too sore to go back to sleep. I quietly slipped on my shoes and let myself out of the house to take a walk around the block.

Letting myself back into the house, I turn and close the door as gently as possible, closing my eyes and leaning my forehead against it after I engage the deadbolt. I breathe slow and deep, trying to calm my thoughts and come up with a new plan. Reading the letters obviously didn't work. I got through every last one of them before I passed out. Reading them again, out loud, made me feel every emotion I did the first time I read them. Sad that we'd been torn apart and heartbroken that it took so long for me to finally have them in my hands and know what he'd been feeling. But most of all, and more important than anything else—loved. So incredibly loved and cared for, even when he was thousands of miles away and had no idea if I was reading his words or would ever forgive him. That love swallowed up the feelings of sadness and hurt, it made butterflies flap in my stomach, it made me happy, and it made me smile.

I just wanted him to feel the same. I wanted him to hear those words he wrote to me so many years ago and feel the love. Remember it and let it consume his own sadness and heartbreak, but it didn't. I'm out of my element and I don't know what I'm doing. I have no other plan and I have no other ideas short of kicking down the door and dragging him out of that room.

With a defeated sigh, I pull my head back from the door and slowly turn. A short, terrified scream rips from my throat when I get all the way around and see Eli standing silently a foot away from me.

"Oh, my God. You scared the hell out of me," I tell him in between rapid breaths, pressing my hand against my chest to slow my heart down.

Even while I'm trying to calm myself down from the surprise of seeing someone standing behind me and the shock that it's Eli and he's out of his room, I can't stop looking at him. I haven't seen his face in ten days and it's the most beautiful sight I've ever seen. His eyes are red-rimmed and bloodshot, his cheeks and jaw are covered in stubble, and he's still wearing the same clothes from when he left the hospital, but he's still the best thing I've ever laid eyes on.

It's impossible to believe I made it through six years without looking at his face when after only ten days I was climbing the walls and ready to kick down his door.

"Are you hungry?"

It's the dumbest question in the world but the only thing I can come up with to say to him right now. I've told him I was sorry, I've asked him what he needed and what I could do, I've begged him to stay with me and pleaded with him to let me help him. I've already said everything I could that was important. All that's left is something stupid and trivial.

"Take off your watch," he tells me softly.

I'm momentarily thrown from hearing the sound of his voice again, so deep and raspy and like music to my ears, that I didn't even hear the words he said.

"Huh?"

His eyes hold mine for a few minutes until he looks away and down.

"Take off your watch," he repeats, just as softly.

I finally process what he's saying and realize he's looking down at my hand, which I hold pressed against my stomach to calm my nerves. I swallow nervously, the fingers of my right hand automatically going to my inside left wrist.

"What?" I ask again lamely, pretending like I didn't hear him just to buy myself some time.

With his eyes still down at my wrist, he closes the distance between us until we're toe to toe. I can feel the heat from his body and I shiver, realizing just how cold I've been lately without it.

I stare up at his face in a daze until I feel his hand wrap around my fingers. He pulls them away and I realize I was just toying with my watchband without being aware that I was doing it.

I continue looking up at his face when he gives up waiting

for me to do what he said, pulls my hand away from my stomach, and flips it over until my palm is facing up. My eyes fill with tears when he gently presses his thumb and forefinger against the clasp and the band loosens. My hand shakes when he slowly slides the watch dangling from my wrist down over my hand, shoving it into the front pocket of his jeans.

He lets out a shaky breath and a soft groan, his fingers tracing over the tattoo on the inside of my wrist. Even though I pissed off the tattoo artist by asking for it to be done the wrong way, facing me instead of facing out, it's still obvious what it says even if he's reading it upside down.

"'For Eli,'" he whispers quietly, saying the words as his fingers continue running over the cursive lettering.

He finally brings his head up and I have to bite down on my lower lip to stop it from quivering, but nothing can stop the tears from spilling out of my eyes when I see the softness and love in his when he looks at me.

"You tattooed my name on your wrist," he states.

"Yes."

He pulls my arm toward him, resting my hand against his chest and flattening my palm over his heart by pressing his hand on top of mine and holding it there.

"Why?" he asks, sliding his thumb back and forth over the top of my hand.

"To remind me," I whisper.

The corner of his mouth tips up into a half smile and I can see one of his dimples, even through the stubble on his cheeks. I want to reach up and run my hand over his face, trace the tips of my fingers over his lips just to make sure he really is smiling at me and I'm not imagining it.

"I'm gonna need more than that," he tells me, the other corner of his mouth tipping up to match the first side.

I know it's way past time for me to tell him about this and I know he deserves to know everything, but I'm so afraid of taking that smile off his face and making him feel guilty again. I just got him back, I just got him out of his room, talking to me and touching me, and I don't want him to disappear again. I don't want to do anything to upset him, but I can't keep this from him any longer.

I sigh and force myself to look away from his face so I don't have to witness the loss of his smile, staring at his hand still pressing against the top of mine instead. I focus on the feel of his heart beating against my palm instead of the words that come out of my mouth and what they might do to him.

"To remind myself that everything I did was for you. So that every time I had to agree to something I hated, every time I had to say yes to another request that chipped away at another piece of me, I could look down at those words and know I was doing it for a reason. To know none of it mattered as long as you were okay."

His chest rises and falls with a deep breath under our hands and I still refuse to look up at him.

"When the news hit that we'd been killed, they speculated that I was a traitor and responsible for it. But that theory was squashed not long after it came out. You?" he asks.

"I agreed to go out with Landry," I admit in the smallest voice possible.

"My sister almost lost her business and Daniel almost lost his job because of some tax fraud bullshit, but that went away within a few days and they were told it was a mistake. You?" he questions.

"I agreed to stay in Charleston and work for my mother," I whisper, squeezing my eyes closed.

"And when I was first rescued, they tried to pin that shit

on me again, but it went away quickly. Too quickly. You?" he asks.

"I agreed to get more serious with Landry and take on more job duties for my mother," I confess.

Silence fills the room and all I can hear is the ticking of the clock above the fireplace mantle. Eli is quiet for so long that I'm afraid he's taking this time to fill himself with anger and guilt and I brace myself for him to drop his hand still holding mine next to his heart, walk away, and lock himself back inside his room.

"Shelby, look at me. Please," he begs gently.

I slowly open my eyes and lift my chin, holding my breath until his free hand comes up and cups my cheek.

"You saved my life, and I ruined yours," he whispers, repeating the words he said to me at the cemetery.

"Never," I reply back, leaning forward until I'm pressed against him, trapping our hands against his chest between us. "I would do it all over again in a minute. I would make all those same choices again as long as I knew it was for you and that you'd come back to me."

He leans his head down and presses his forehead against mine and I continue before he can even think about moving away or believing the words he just said.

"You saved me, too. I gave up and I was lost. You gave me back the music, you gave me back my strength, you gave me back my hope... you put all the pieces back together, and you made me whole again."

Eli lifts his chin and presses his lips to my forehead, holding them there and sliding his hand out from between us to cup my other cheek.

"I don't know if I'll ever be able to really dance again, but you made me want to try. You brought me back to life. I don't care if we're a couple of broken pieces and we're making a huge fucking mess," I tell him, throwing his words back at him as gently as I can, but firm enough so he knows I'm serious and I truly believe what I'm saying. "I'd rather be a complete mess with you than spend another day shattered all over the floor alone."

Pulling my head back so I can see his face, I move my hand from his chest and slide both of my arms around his waist.

"Please, don't leave me. Let me help you. Let me fix this," I beg.

The smile finally comes back to his face and he wraps his arms around me, pulling me tightly against him. I turn my head to the side and rest my cheek against his heart so I can hear it thumping in my ear.

"You already did," he finally says quietly, resting his chin on top of my head. "You already did."

Epilogue

Eli

Six months later...

Flipping the quarter around in my fingers, I lean down and place it on top of the stone, resting my palm over it for a few seconds before moving back to stare down at the headstone.

"I'm not being an asshole anymore, I hope you're proud of yourself," I say to the cement marker.

"That wasn't exactly what I had in mind when I suggested we come pay our respects," Shelby informs me, moving around me to set a shiny penny down next to my quarter.

"It's okay, he'd appreciate it," I tell her when she gets back to my side and wraps both of her arms around my waist.

I drape my arm around her shoulders and pull her against my side.

"Tell me again what the coins mean," she requests.

Sliding my free hand into the front pocket of my jeans, I continue staring down at Rylan's grave. This is the first time I've been back here since the day I snuck out of the hospital and everything went to shit. I'd been putting it off for months, but after listening to my therapist nag me about it every time I met with him, and Shelby not so subtly reminding me every couple of weeks that she'd be more than happy to go with me when I was ready, I knew it was time.

I tossed and turned all last night after I'd finally told her I was ready. I came close to throwing up the pancakes she made for me this morning. I made her drive us here because my hands were shaking too badly for me to hold on to the steering wheel, but now that we're here, a strange calm has settled over me and I wish I would have come sooner.

"You leave a penny for someone you might not have known very well, but you still considered a friend," I tell her. "You leave a quarter if you were with the soldier when he died."

The coin thing dates back to at least the Roman Empire and I first learned about it during boot camp. Rylan used to joke with me that if he died first, I damn well better show up at his grave with nothing less than a handful of fifty-dollar bills, because he was worth much more than a quarter.

I can almost hear him calling me an asshole and giving me the finger.

Almost, but not really, thank God.

I stopped hearing his voice and seeing his face when I finally learned how to let him go. He told me he would leave when I stopped needing him, but I think he knew that would never happen. I would always need my best friend. I would always miss him and wish I could have saved him. Not a day goes by that I don't have to stop myself from picking up the phone to call him about something.

I don't know if I'll ever be able to fully get rid of the guilt that he died and I lived, and I'll never understand why him and not me, but I'm learning to do as he asked and not waste the second chance I was given.

I'm not fully healed and I'm not sure I'll ever be, but every day gets a little bit easier. Shelby makes sure I never miss a meeting with my therapist, she hands me my pills and a glass of water every night before bed, and she always lets me know she's not going anywhere, no matter how hard it gets or how many times I retreat into myself or pull away. She's always there, pulling me right back out of the darkness, filling me up with more good than I ever deserved. She makes everything better just by being in the same room with me, making sure I'm okay without hovering and making me talk even when I don't want to.

Shelby also convinced me to finally reach out to the two other men in our unit who were captured along with Rylan and me and lived through the same hell we did for five years. I didn't want to face them when we were first rescued, because I knew seeing them and speaking to them would force me to accept the truth that Rylan wasn't here. Talking to them now, sharing the same fear and pain and nightmares, knowing there are two other men out there who experienced the same things I did and having people who fully understand the struggles I'm dealing with has helped more than anything else.

Even through all the bullshit going on with her mother's confession and the back and forth with lawyers for months, forgoing a trial when she immediately agreed to jail time. Through all the phone calls from the media wanting a statement from Shelby and practically the entire town showing up at the plantation at one point or another to either give their support or try and get a piece of gossip, Shelby has held her head up high and pushed it all aside to make sure I'm okay.

She amazes me every day. I'm in awe of her strength every time I look at her and realize how lucky I am that she has stuck by my side, never wavering in her determination to heal me and fix all of our broken pieces. She always reassures me that she got the better end of the deal. During my breakdown, my stay in the hospital, and the ten days I kept myself locked in my room, Shelby and Kat formed a bond that will never be broken. After every time we have my sister and her family over for dinner, after every time we stop by their house so Shelby can cuddle my niece, and after every time she hangs up the phone after speaking to Kat or Daniel, she gives me a hug and thanks me for giving her a family. One who loves her unconditionally, stands by her side, and supports her no matter what she does.

Shelby also gives me credit for helping her heal the rift between her and Meredith. I wanted to be just as pissed when I found out Meredith had been the one to keep all those letters I'd written to Shelby because she thought she was protecting her, but if I'd learned anything in the last few months, it was to let things go and move on. After a few phone calls back and forth to Meredith and coming up with a plan, a package arrived for Shelby a month ago that made her immediately dissolve into tears, call her best friend, and make amends. I'd secretly photocopied all the letters and e-mailed them to Meredith, who took them all and turned them into a book. Nothing she would sell to a publisher or release on her own, a book just for Shelby and me called, *The Story of Us*. She'd taken the letters and I'd filled in the blanks with present-day information and she'd turned it into an amazing story that I still couldn't believe was ours. I still couldn't believe we'd been through all of that and come out on the other side. We keep the book on the mantle in the living room, where we can always look at it, or read a few pages if we ever need a reminder of how much stronger we are when we're together.

"You doing okay?" Shelby asks, tipping her head back to look up at me.

I smile down at her and nod.

"I'm doing okay," I confirm.

With Shelby's arms still around my waist and mine still draped over her shoulder, we turn and walk away. Glancing over my shoulder one last time, I keep my eyes on Rylan's name as we walk until it gets too small to see.

"I won't piss it away, I promise," I whisper under my breath, turning my head back around as I grab my second chance by the hand and walk to the car.

Two years later…

The sound of shitty pop music echoes from the studio when I push open the door and walk down the hall. Pausing in the doorway, I smile when I see her in the middle of the room with her back to me, moving her feet from side to side and shouting directions so she can be heard above the song.

I watch her lift her arm above her head and the thirty or so kids in the room copy what she does. Her eyes meet mine in the reflection of the mirror and she smiles back at me before turning around, lifting her hand in the air, and crooking her finger at me. When all thirty kids turn around and mimic what she's doing, I throw my head back and laugh.

When Georgia went to jail, she signed the entire Eubanks Plantation over to Shelby. It was hers to keep and do with as she wished. It didn't make up for everything she'd done, but at least it was something, and Shelby knew exactly what she wanted to do with it as soon as she'd received the papers in the mail from her mother's lawyer. Her mother hasn't tried to contact her since then, and I worry that someday Shelby will regret not making amends with her, but I'm not going to push it. If that day ever comes, I'll be right here by her side, giving her the strength she's always given me.

Eighteen months ago, the Eubanks Plantation became the Rylan Edwards Camp for Children of Veterans and Deployed Soldiers. Since opening day, we'd had full registration for every session. We'd kept on all of the original staff that worked at the house, the grounds, and the stables, and we hired a few therapists to talk to any families who needed it. The house was turned into sleeping quarters for the kids, I split my time between helping out with group therapy and giving horse riding lessons, and Shelby provided dance lessons in between throwing charity functions to help raise money to fund the camp. I initially protested when she first told me she was going to organize one, not wanting her to do something that had made her so miserable in the past, but it was a wasted effort. Nothing about this camp or helping these children could ever make Shelby miserable.

As Shelby finally gets the kids turned around and back to practicing the moves she'd already taught them, she tries once again to lift her hand and crook her finger at me. Pushing away from the doorframe, I walk through the middle of the room, avoiding flailing arms and kicking feet as I go.

When I get to her, I look down, and just like every time, I'm filled with amazement, love, and happiness.

"I don't dance, Legs," I tell her with a smile.

"Nice try, buddy," she laughs.

"This song makes my ears bleed."

She laughs again and that sound is still the best thing I've ever heard. Well, almost.

A loud, happy screech can be heard above the music and I laugh as I look down at our daughter, her pudgy legs dangling down out of a pink carrier against my wife's chest and secured over her shoulders.

"See? It makes *her* ears bleed, too," I inform Shelby.

"Cameron Rylan James, tell your father to stop being such

a sissy and dance," Shelby says to our daughter's head. "You can say no to me, but you can't say no to this adorable face."

Grabbing Shelby's hip and tugging the two of them close, I grab Cameron's little hand and hold it out to the side, moving my feet and dancing all three of us to the music.

"Is it too soon to buy Cameron her own pony? What about a car? Something big and safe, like a dump truck. I should also stock up on a few shotguns and a couple extra padlocks. I don't like the way that Southerland kid keeps looking at her," I tell Shelby, looking down at Cameron and making a goofy face until she makes that loud, happy screeching sound again.

"Everett Southerland is six and he's a sweetheart. Our daughter is seven months old. I'm pretty sure she doesn't need a pony, a dump truck, or a father with an arsenal to scare off boys just yet," she reminds me as we continue dancing.

"A father always needs an arsenal, Shelby. Always."

She laughs and shakes her head at me.

"You doing okay?" she asks softly.

I lean down and kiss the top of my daughter's head, her soft silky hair the same strawberry blond as her mother's, before coming back up to kiss Shelby. The entire room erupts in a chorus of *eeeeeew*'s and I quickly pull back with a laugh, looking around the room before my eyes come back to Shelby's.

I still don't know if I'll ever be fully healed, I'll always miss my friend, and I'll never be able to completely erase the bad memories, but now I have two people in my life who make it all go away. I was given a second chance and I will do everything I can to make sure I don't take it for granted or piss it away.

"I'm doing okay," I reassure her, squeezing my hand around her hip. "Better than okay."

Prologue

Dear Everett:

If you're reading this, I'm dead.

Sorry, that's probably not the best way to start off a letter to my best friend, after my sudden and horribly tragic death. You'll surely never, ever be able to move on, because I was such an amazing person, but there it is. You know I've never been one to mince words. And while we're on that subject, you're an asshole.

It's been four years since we've seen you. FOUR. I get it, believe me, I do. The first time I met you, when we were ten years old, you told me you wanted to be a doctor. For sixteen years I listened to you talk about how you wanted to do something with your life you could be proud of. We're all proud of you, Everett. Proud that you accomplished what you set out to do, proud that you took charge of your life and made something of yourself. But you can't stay away forever.

I don't know what happened between you and Cameron the night you left, but I know she hasn't been the same since. Neither one of us has. The Three Musketeers has been missing one of its members for four years, and if you aren't here already, it's time for you to come home.

Yes, I'm guilting you into coming home because I'm dead.

Finished.

Gone.

Never coming back from the Great Beyond.

Do you feel guilty yet? You should. Because Cameron misses you, even though she won't admit it. I've tried my best to make her happy without you here. She puts up a good front about not giving a shit that you've been gone for so long, but I know she's lying. She needs you now, more than ever. She needs you to get that stick out of your ass, suck up the reasons you've stayed away from us, and come home.

I'm not going to be there to make her laugh, wipe away her tears, or cheer her on when she does something amazing. I am officially passing the baton over to you. It's your turn now. You've traveled around the world, you've saved lives, you've become a goddamn hero to strangers. Now it's time to be a hero back here at home, where you belong. It hasn't been the same without you. *We* haven't been the same without you, and now that I'm gone, you can make it up to me by GETTING YOUR ASS BACK WHERE YOU BELONG.

And just so you know, I read your box of wishes. You know the ones we swore we'd never, ever read until we were all old and gray. Dude, I'm dead, so you can't be pissed at me for that. But I am *so* pissed at you from beyond the grave for never telling me about that shit. I mean, I knew, of course

I knew. I'm not blind or stupid. But all these years when I thought you were just being an idiot and refusing to admit how you felt, or figured you must have changed your mind and moved on, you were actually admitting everything to those fucking stars! I'm your best friend and you didn't even tell me. Is that why you stayed away for four years? If it is, you're an even bigger asshole than I thought. It's time to stop wishing on those fucking stars every year and make your dreams come true by actually doing something about it.

Brace yourself, because I'm going to say a few things now that will make me sound like a pussy. Just remember, I'm doing this for *you* and I'm still a manly man.

I know what it's like to look at a woman and, suddenly, everything makes sense.

I know how it feels to love someone so completely that you have no idea how you survived before her.

I've had that love returned tenfold, and even though I know I don't deserve it, I've done everything I could to make sure I don't fuck it up. You know, aside from the whole dying thing, but what can you do?

Don't fuck this up, man. Cameron has been hurt enough. She's going to be hurting even more after I'm gone and I need you to pick up the pieces and put them back together. I need you to give her everything I won't be able to anymore.

I'm sorry I won't be there to see Cameron kick your ass for staying away for so long. Be careful, she's developed a mean right hook over the years. But go easy on her, man. She's going to pretend to be okay, pretend like everything is fine and she's fine and her whole damn life is fine... you know how she is. Always more concerned about everyone else than she is about herself. But she needs you now, more than ever.

I'm sorry I didn't tell you I was sick the last time we

talked on the phone, but what would have been the point? It's not like you could have done anything about it, aside from sitting here and watching me die. I don't want you to remember me like this. It's bad enough Cameron has to have this picture of me in her head for the rest of her life—I won't do that to you, too. I want you to remember me as the devastatingly handsome, perfect specimen of man that I was. I want you to remember the good times, the laughter, growing up together at the camp, and me being full of life instead of confined to this fucking bed with barely enough energy to write this damn letter. Don't you dare feel guilty about not being able to save me. I know you're an amazing doctor, but sometimes, cancer wins.

Come home, Everett. Come home and finally do something about those wishes.

You can't save me, but you can come home and save our girl.

Aiden

Chapter 1

Everett

How do you know when you've reached your breaking point?

Watching children die right in front of their parents' eyes?

Telling someone that they're sick, but you don't have the resources to help them?

Seeing countless people get infections from unclean water and live in horrible conditions, and the only thing you can do is hand them pills and wait for them to get sick again?

Trying your hardest to travel to every third world country you could possibly think of to avoid going home, only to find out your best friend since you were ten years old died of pancreatic cancer?

And because you didn't even know he was sick, you weren't there to help. Never got a chance to apologize for being such a shitty friend. Never got a chance to say goodbye.

How much is too much?

I take another swig of vodka and let my head thump back against the wall, wondering how much more I can take. I've been trying to numb the pain with booze since I came back to the States. It works for a little while. The blur of vodka when it pumps through my veins makes me forget about everything for a few minutes.

A few minutes of peace.

A few minutes of not hearing the cries of babies or the pleas of mothers begging me to save their children.

A few minutes of not seeing Aiden's face in my head, smirking at me and calling me an asshole.

A few minutes of not thinking about her.

One-hundred-and-eighty seconds when I can close my eyes and feel nothing.

With my ass on the floor and my legs sprawled out in front of me, I close my eyes and let the quiet oblivion take over, but it's gone too soon. It never lasts long enough. Not anymore. Not after that letter he wrote.

That fucking letter.

I open my eyes and my body breaks out into a cold sweat when I see it crumbled up and tossed a few feet away from me. The letter I've been rereading for the last three months, ever since it showed up in my mailbox in Cambodia, exactly two weeks after Aiden died.

My eyes stay glued to the ball of paper, Aiden's shaky and uneven handwriting peeking out of the crushed page. I bring the vodka back up to my lips and try to drink away the pain and misery swirling around inside of me. It doesn't even burn anymore when it goes down, and I can almost fool myself into believing the water bottle I poured it in really contains just water. I don't know why I bother trying to hide it at this point. My brother, Jason, has seen all the empty vodka bottles I've hidden under my bed and out in the garage behind shelves and boxes. In the trunk of my car yesterday, he found an entire box of empty liter bottles, which I'd meant to take out to the garbage dump and get rid of, but never got around to it. Probably because I was too drunk to drive there.

I laugh when I think about the intervention he had with me yesterday morning. He went in my trunk to borrow my jack for a flat tire he needed to change before he left for work, and saw that damn box of bottles. He made me promise to stop drinking. He made me promise to get help. Of course I agreed. He's my baby brother. I live here with him in our grandparents' old house until I can get back on my feet. A house my grandmother left to me when she moved away, the place Jason was forced to stay in and take care of while I was always gone. And he's still here, taking care of the house and taking care of me instead of moving out and getting his own life. He puts up with my sorry ass day in and day out, and he deserves so much more than having a drunk for a brother who can't get his shit together.

And I kept my promise. For almost twenty-four hours, I didn't touch the one last bottle of Tito's I had stashed on the top shelf of my closet. I gritted my teeth through the pain of withdrawal, and I threw up every ounce of water I tried to get in my system, but I did it. I pushed through it for Jason. I sucked it up for my little brother, who'd survived the same shitty childhood I had, but never got to escape like I did. I dealt with the shakes and the headaches and the puking and the fever so I wouldn't have to see that same tired, disappointed look in his eyes when he got home from another day of work while I just sat my useless ass on his couch.

"You weren't supposed to die!" I scream at the letter, still lying a few feet away, taunting me to crawl over to it and read the words inside again. "Why in the hell didn't you tell me sooner?!"

The water bottle of vodka crinkles in my hand when I squeeze my fingers around it and angrily bring it up to my mouth, chugging it until it's almost gone.

Aiden's voice is buzzing in my ear like an annoying housefly you can't swat away. It just keeps coming back and coming back, pushing me over the edge until I want to cover my ears and make it stop. The alcohol isn't working. His voice just won't go away.

You're an asshole.

I hope you feel guilty.

Come home.

Come home.

Come home.

I *am* an asshole. I *do* feel guilty. And I'm home. I got on the next flight out of Cambodia as soon as that damn letter arrived, not even bothering to call home, just wanting to get back here before it was too late. I acted without thinking and of course I was too late. Two weeks too late to say good-bye, too late for the funeral, too late to make amends, too late to do anything but pick up a bottle and try to forget all the mistakes I'd made. It's been exactly three months and two weeks to the day my best friend died in his sleep when his body just couldn't fight anymore. Three months and two weeks to the day that he stopping existing.

I've spent every waking moment since I got home trying to forget about the pain Aiden's death caused, and then a few hours ago a box of photos fell from the top shelf of my closet when I was looking for something. It came crashing to the floor, spilling memories of Aiden all around my feet. Aiden laughing at me during a game of basketball when we were ten, Aiden smiling at the camera with his arm wrapped around one of his many dates when we were in high school, Aiden smirking as he holds up his college diploma. Every memory of him seeped into my brain and squeezed the life out of my heart until that fucking letter I'd shoved into the back of my dresser drawer started taunting me to read it again. I could almost feel Aiden standing next to me, telling me I deserve to be miserable for the shit I've pulled. I was trying to do better and he just shows up in my brain, provoking me and pushing me to fuck it all up, make me forget about the promise I made to my brother until nothing else mattered but taking a drink so I could make it all go away. I came home, just like Aiden wanted, and all I want to do is leave.

"Do you really want me to take care of our girl now, Aiden?!" I shout toward the ceiling. "I bet she'd be really happy to see me show up at the camp like this."

I laugh at my words, wondering if it's the booze or my fucked-up head that's made me start talking to myself like a crazy person.

"You weren't supposed to die. You were always supposed to be here," I mutter, my throat clogging with tears when I look over at his letter again.

I took everything for granted, and I have no one to blame but myself. I walked away from my two best friends and never looked back because I was a coward. I always thought in the back of my mind that one day I'd be able to get over my shit, get over how I felt about Cameron, come back home and they'd both be waiting for me, ready to forgive me for being an idiot. But now that's never going to happen.

Aiden is never going to be there with a smirk on his face and a sarcastic comment at the ready. Cameron is never going to forgive me. For not being there while Aiden was sick, for not doing everything I could to try and save him, and for not going to her right when I got home.

I should have gone to her. We should have been able to mourn Aiden together, but I couldn't deal with my own pain, let alone hers. I *still* can't deal with my own pain.

No one understands what it's like to come back home after you've been on the other side of the world, experiencing horrors no one back here sees or even realizes is happening. People here live in their happy little worlds, going about their happy little lives, and they forget there are men, women, and children without basic necessities, like clean water, so they, too, can have those happy lives.

Jason doesn't understand, even though he tries to.

No one understands what it's like to be back here. What it's like to have nothing to do with your free time but think and feel guilty about the people you couldn't save in another country, or the person you should have saved right here at home. To feel like you're constantly living in a nightmare where every thought and every memory is a film reel of all the ways you fucked up.

I'm so tired of feeling this pain. I just want relief. I just want to feel nothing at all. My eyelids grow heavy and my vision starts to blur as darkness and the sweet bliss of numbness covers my body like a warm blanket.

"Goddammit, Everett! Son of a bitch..."

I hear my brother's voice, and even though it sounds muffled and far away in my drunken brain, I can still hear the anger in it. I don't even realize I've slumped over onto my side until I feel Jason's arms come under me and slide me back upright against the wall.

"Open your eyes. Open your fucking eyes!" Jason shouts close to my face.

The darkness surrounding me disappears when I blink my eyes open as his palm smacks against my cheek.

Sadness, worry, anguish, and fear.

That's what I see written all over my brother's face as he looks at me and shakes his head. I want to apologize to him that he found me like this, but what's the point? He's found me in similar situations many times since I got home, and my apologies aren't worth shit at this point.

I want to tell him that I don't want this crutch of alcohol. I don't want to need it, feeling like it's the only way I can survive the pain. The pain in my gut, the pain in my head, and the pain in my heart. Without drinking, it all comes back until I want to claw at my skin and scream until my throat is hoarse. I open my mouth, but the words won't come.

He sits down next to me and kicks his legs out in front of him, mirroring my own.

"What was it this time? Flashback? Bad dream?" Jason asks quietly, listing off all the excuses I've given him over the last few months when he's smelled the alcohol on my breath or found me passed out on the couch.

I lean forward to grab the letter from Aiden, but the room spins and I have to quickly lean back against the wall before I puke. Instead, I lift my arm and point to it.

He looks away from me to the crumpled-up ball of paper, letting out a big sigh before reaching over to grab it. I watch silently as he uncrinkles it and smooths it out against his thigh. I stare at his face, blinking a few times to keep it in focus, as he reads through the letter.

"Jesus Christ," he finally whispers. "Where did this come from?"

I clear my throat and look away from him to stare at the opposite wall in our grandparents' living room before answering him.

"It came when I was in Cambodia. Two weeks after he died."

Jason doesn't say anything for a few minutes, and I take

the time to look around the room. I always loved this house growing up. An old farmhouse on the outskirts of Charleston, it was filled with happy memories and good times, the complete opposite of the home we shared with our mother in New Jersey. I looked forward to spending every summer here with our grandmother. She baked us cookies, she fed us home-cooked meals, and she paid attention to us. She loved us and she cared for us and she did everything she could to make us happy.

This house that was once full of dreams now feels like hell. I can't stand these four walls that surround me, caging me in, not letting me get away from the memories and the pain.

"I'm sorry, Everett. This letter is... shit. I don't even know what to say about this thing. Why didn't you tell me? Is this why you've been drinking yourself into a coma since you got home?" Jason asks.

"It is what it is," I shrug, ignoring the drinking comment. "He's right. I'm an asshole, but there's nothing I can do about that now."

My brother scoffs, pushing himself up from the floor to stand over me. It hurts my head to look up at him. The overhead light is shining in my eyes and stabbing into my skull, and I curse when I have to shield my eyes to see his face.

"I know I'll never understand everything going on in that head of yours. I know I'll never be able to sympathize with all the shit you saw over there. And I know the sadness I feel about Aiden being gone is nothing compared to what you feel," Jason tells me. "But enough is enough. You were doing something you loved over there and you didn't know he was sick. Even if you had, you couldn't have done anything about it. He had the best medical team money could buy, flown in from all over the world. What he had, even your fancy medical skills couldn't have fixed. You're still alive and you need to start fucking acting like it. I'm sorry that letter hurt you, but I'm not sorry Aiden wrote it. He's right. You need to get your head out of your ass."

I can feel anger start to replace my buzz, and I clench my hands into fists in my lap. I don't want to hear this bullshit coming out of his mouth. I know I deserve it, but I don't want to hear it.

"What the fuck happened to the promise you made me yesterday?" he asks, snatching the water bottle out of my hand and hurling it across the room.

It smacks against our grandmother's oak curio cabinet filled with her good china and drops to the floor, the last few sips of vodka leaking out onto the hardwood floor.

"It hurts," I whisper, looking down at my balled fists, unable to look him in the eyes anymore.

"Of course it hurts, you dumbass! It's called alcohol withdrawal for a reason. It's not supposed to feel good, but I guess you don't even want to try," he fires back.

Jason squats down next to me and grabs my chin, forcing me to look at him.

"I'm sorry Aiden's gone. I'm sorry you're hurting and you feel guilty for not being able to save him. But *screw you* for not even trying. I was too young to remember losing Dad, but watching Mom fade away and drink herself to death was bad enough. You can go fuck yourself if you think you're going to leave me behind, too. If you won't do it for me, do it for Cameron. She lost Aiden, too, you know. What do you think will happen if she loses you as well?"

With that, he gets up and walks away. The angry stomp of his construction boots banging against the hardwood floor makes me drop my head into my hands to stop the damn thing from feeling like it's going to explode.

I want to go back to the people that need me, but my employer won't let me.

I want to stop hearing Aiden's voice in my head, but he won't let me.

I want to drown myself in booze, but my brother won't let me.

No one will just fucking let me be.

My brother has no idea what he's talking about. Cameron will be fine without me, just like she's been for the last four years. She doesn't need me. She's never needed me.

Everyone needs to just fucking Let. Me. Be.

About the Author

Tara Sivec is a *USA Today* best-selling author, wife, mother, chauffeur, maid, short-order cook, babysitter, and sarcasm expert. She lives in Ohio with her husband and two children and looks forward to the day when they all three of them become adults and move out.

After working in the brokerage business for fourteen years, Tara decided to pick up a pen and write instead of shoving it in her eye out of boredom. Her novel *Seduction and Snacks* won first place in the Indie Romance Convention Reader's Choice Awards 2013 for Best Indie First Book, and she was voted as Best Author in the Indie Romance Convention Reader's Choice Awards for 2014.

In her spare time, Tara loves to dream about all of the baking she'll do and naps she'll take when she ever gets spare time.

You can learn more at:

TaraSivec.com
Twitter @TaraSivec
Instagram @authorTaraSivec
Facebook.com/TaraSivec.authorpage

Fall in love with these charming small-town romances!

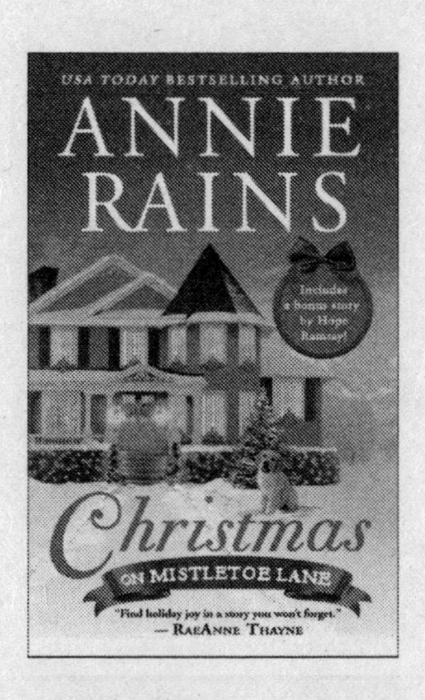

CHRISTMAS ON MISTLETOE LANE
By Annie Rains

Kaitlyn Russo thought she'd have a fresh start in Sweetwater Springs. Only one little problem: The B&B she inherited isn't entirely hers—and the ex-Marine who owns the other half isn't going anywhere.

THE CORNER OF HOLLY AND IVY
By Debbie Mason

With her dreams of being a wedding dress designer suddenly over, Arianna Bell isn't expecting a holly jolly Christmas. She thinks a run for town mayor might cheer her spirits—until she learns her opponent is her gorgeous high school sweetheart.

Discover exclusive content and more on forever-romance.com.

CHRISTMAS WISHES AND MISTLETOE KISSES
By Jenny Hale

Single mother Abbey Fuller doesn't regret putting her dreams on hold to raise her son. Now that Max is older, she jumps at the chance to work on a small design job. But when she arrives at the Sinclair mansion, she feels out of her element—and her gorgeous but brooding boss Nicholas Sinclair is not exactly in the holiday spirit.

THE AMISH MIDWIFE'S SECRET
By Rachel J. Good

When *Englischer* Kyle Miller is offered a medical practice in his hometown, he knows he must face the painful past he left behind. Except he's not prepared for Leah Stoltzfus, the pretty Amish midwife who refuses to compromise her traditions with his modern medicine...

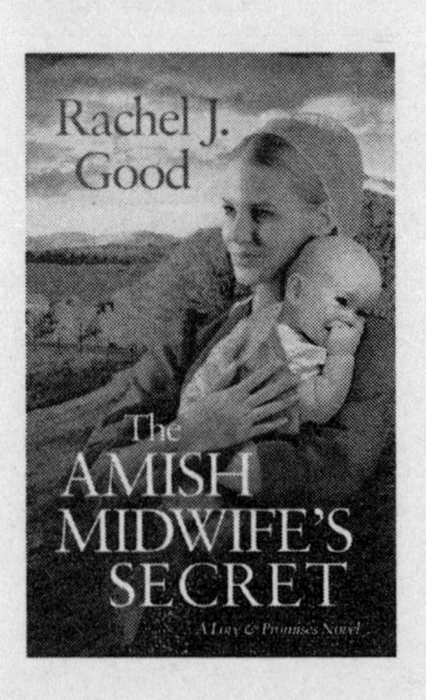

Find more great reads on Instagram with @ForeverRomanceBooks.

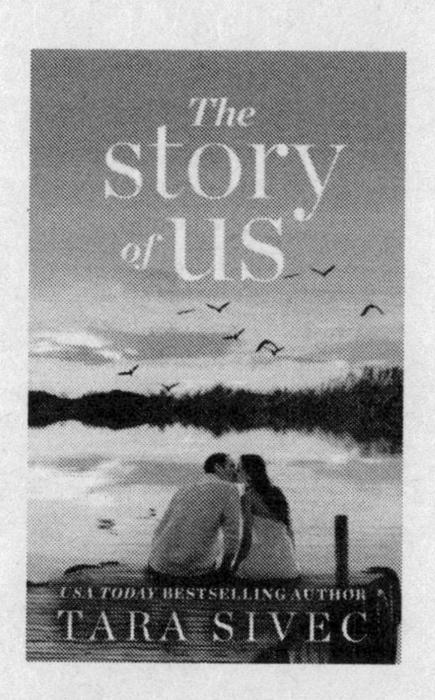

THE STORY OF US
By Tara Sivec

1,843 days. That's how long I survived in that hellhole. And I owe it all to the memory of the one woman who loved me more than I ever deserved to be loved. Now I'll do anything to get back to her…I may not be the man I used to be, but I will do whatever it takes to remind her of the story of us.

THE COTTAGE ON ROSE LANE
By Hope Ramsay

Jenna Fossey just received an unexpected inheritance that will change her life. Eager to meet relatives she never knew existed, she heads to the charming little town of Magnolia Harbor. But long-buried family secrets soon lead to even more questions, and the only person who can help her find the answers is her sexy-as-sin sailing instructor.

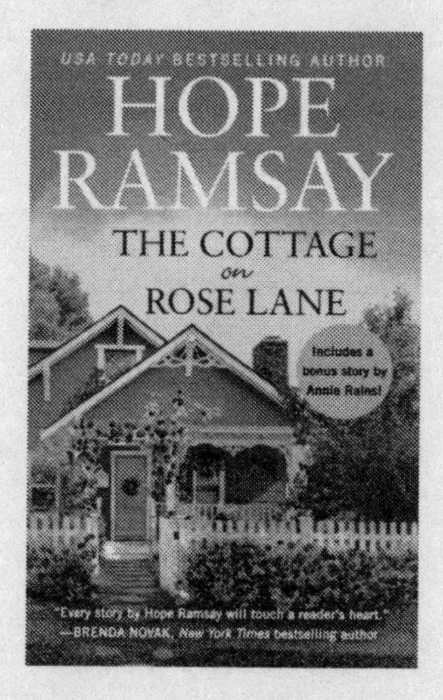

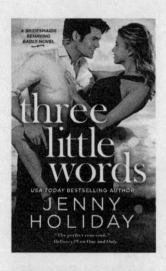